D0207279

Berkley Titles by Sharon C. Cooper

BUSINESS NOT AS USUAL

IN IT TO WIN IT

Praise for
BUSINESS NOT AS USUAL

"In her first romantic comedy, Cooper strikes the perfect balance of romance and comedic moments. . . . [The main characters'] chemistry, compatibility, and obvious love for one another made my inner romantic sigh. Well done!"

—*USA Today* bestselling author Delaney Diamond

"Fresh, funny, and with all the feels I expect in a rom-com. Fabulous read for when you're ready to lose yourself in tropetastic fun."   —Vanessa Riley, bestselling author of *Island Queen*

"Reading a book by Sharon C. Cooper is like sitting under a warm blanket with your favorite beverage as your wildest imagination plays out on the big screen! *Business Not As Usual* is a testament to Cooper's storytelling talents. She breathes life into her characters; gives you side-splitting, laugh-out-loud moments; handles tough topics with clever precision; and tells a story beautifully."

—Deborah Fletcher Mello, author of *Rescued by the Colton Cowboy*

"Cooper (the Reunited series) effortlessly blends the worlds of two characters from wildly different socioeconomic backgrounds in this hilarious, bighearted rom-com. . . . The supporting cast is a hoot—especially Dreamy's grandfather—and every obstacle Cooper throws at the central couple only serves to showcase their compatibility and strength. This sexy, feel-good love story will leave readers breathless."   —*Publishers Weekly* (starred review)

"This sexy rom-com is exactly what you need as the seasons change."   —Book Riot

"Dreamy continually blossoms throughout the novel, and her unshakeable drive makes each success even more gratifying for the reader cheering her along. A sweet and sincere love story that hits the jackpot of rom-coms."
                                                    —*Kirkus Reviews*

"*Business Not As Usual* is easy to slide into, like a hot toddy, a box of good chocolate, or a fuzzy sweater. It's warm, friendly, and tender—a fantastic romance novel, and a totally satisfying one."
                                                    —All About Romance

"Karter had no plans to fall for Dreamy, either—after all, he comes from a family of rich socialites, which means he has certain expectations to live up to. Still, chemistry like theirs is too rare to simply be ignored."
                                                    —PopSugar

"Dreamy Daniels, the heroine of Sharon C. Cooper's latest contemporary romance, *Business Not As Usual*, truly lives up to her name and will charm the pants off readers (and off her love interest, too)."
                                                    —BookPage

"Hilarious and heartwarming, it's what I would call a literary rom-com. I was laughing throughout the story and at the same time rooting for the main characters to succeed in their personal endeavors and find a way to make their relationship work."
                                                    —Brown Book Series

Cooper, Sharon C.,author.
In it to win it

2022
33305255265708
ca   12/15/22

In It
to
Win It

SHARON C. COOPER

BERKLEY ROMANCE
NEW YORK

BERKLEY ROMANCE
Published by Berkley
An imprint of Penguin Random House LLC
penguinrandomhouse.com

Copyright © 2022 by Sharon C. Cooper
Penguin Random House supports copyright. Copyright fuels creativity,
encourages diverse voices, promotes free speech, and creates a vibrant culture.
Thank you for buying an authorized edition of this book and for complying with
copyright laws by not reproducing, scanning, or distributing any part of it in any
form without permission. You are supporting writers and allowing Penguin
Random House to continue to publish books for every reader.

BERKLEY is a registered trademark and Berkley Romance with B colophon
is a trademark of Penguin Random House LLC.

Library of Congress Cataloging-in-Publication Data

Names: Cooper, Sharon C., author.
Title: In it to win it / Sharon C. Cooper.
Description: First edition. | New York : Berkley Romance, 2022.
Identifiers: LCCN 2022022247 (print) | LCCN 2022022248 (ebook) |
ISBN 9780593335277 (trade paperback) | ISBN 9780593335284 (ebook)
Subjects: LCGFT: Romance fiction.
Classification: LCC PS3603.O582985 I52 2022 (print) | LCC PS3603.O582985 (ebook) |
DDC 813/.6—dc23/eng/20220510
LC record available at https://lccn.loc.gov/2022022247
LC ebook record available at https://lccn.loc.gov/2022022248

First Edition: December 2022

Printed in the United States of America
1st Printing

Book design by George Towne

This is a work of fiction. Names, characters, places, and incidents either are the product of
the author's imagination or are used fictitiously, and any resemblance to actual persons,
living or dead, business establishments, events, or locales is entirely coincidental.

In It to Win It

Chapter One

WITH A DEATH GRIP ON HER CELL PHONE, MORGAN REDFORD sprinted down the quiet hallway as fast as her four-inch Louboutins could carry her. She rushed past the large copy machine and the small conference room before sliding to a stop when she reached her best friend's office.

"Oh, my God, Izzy!" Morgan panted and stumbled into the tuna-can-size space. "I'm so glad you're here. I need your help!"

Isabella bolted from her seat and rounded her desk. "What? What happened?" She gripped Morgan's shoulders. "Are you hurt? Is it one of the kids?"

Morgan waved her off, shaking her head as she eased out of her friend's grip. Still huffing and puffing, she leaned forward and placed her hands on her knees, swiping a few microbraids out of her face in the process.

"Morgan, so help me . . . You're scaring me. If you don't tell me what happened, I'm going—"

"Give me a second. Running through the halls in these shoes and these tight-ass pants," she wheezed, "takes a lot out of a woman." She finally stood upright. "Okay, I have a TikTok emergency. I need you to help me with one of the dances, and I need you to do it now. Otherwise, there's going to be hell to pay."

Isabella's stormy gaze bore into her like two serrated knives, ready to twist and turn into her gut.

Morgan frowned. "*What*? What did I do?"

"Are you freaking serious right now?" Isabella stomped past Morgan and slammed the office door. "Your ass scared me to death! If you *ever* barge in here like that again, you really are going to need help because I'm going to wrap my hands around your scrawny little neck and—"

"All right, all right, geez," Morgan said, eying her friend.

Tall, with olive skin and long, orange-ginger hair that was pulled into a messy ponytail on top of her head, Isabella Jeter, her best friend since kindergarten, was a knockout even on her bummiest days, like today. Instead of her usual work attire—a nice blouse and dress pants—she sported an old, fitted T-shirt and worn, gray sweats that made her look grungy from the neck down, but that didn't detract from her perfectly made-up face, and she still wore her signature red lipstick.

She was dressed down since she planned to finish painting the small, upstairs multipurpose room.

Isabella continued glowering.

"Calm down. There's no need for threats of violence," Morgan told her.

Isabella threw up her hands. "I can *not* believe you," she snapped, and marched back to her desk.

Morgan stood speechless as her friend and business partner dropped down into her leather desk chair.

"Why are you mad at me? This is important." Morgan set her phone down and leaned on the desk. "Last week, the kids challenged me to a TikTok dance, and I totally forgot about it. I'm not prepared and, Izzy, if I don't make a good showing, I'm never going to hear the end of it."

Isabella continued glowering. "Why am I mad? 'Cause you scared me to death. I thought something was really wrong. Mo, I love you like a sister, but everything I love about you also drives me nuts. You're acting so flippant about the meeting you have in a couple of hours, and instead, you're worried about your damn dance moves. Where are your priorities?"

"Iz, my priorities are on point. Why are you trippin'?"

Isabella pounded her fist on a stack of file folders. "Because this meeting is important, Morgan. Open Arms needs that building, and you know that," she said. "Instead of strategizing a plan, you're out there perfecting your Cardi B shuffle or whatever! You don't have time to be clowning around."

Six months ago, she and Isabella had founded the nonprofit Open Arms with the lofty mission of helping young adults between the ages of eighteen and twenty-two who'd aged out of foster care. Morgan could never claim to relate to their struggles. With a father who was an A-list actor, she'd been fortunate to grow up with more than enough, but her heart went out to every one of those kids.

When kids arrived at Open Arms, they came clutching a black trash bag that contained all their possessions and the hope that she and Isabella could help them with everything from securing housing and getting scholarships to finding full-time employment.

Unfortunately, the demand for assistance was greater than what Open Arms could fulfill. But Morgan was hopeful that within a year, their foundation could accommodate at least a hundred clients. Right now they could comfortably only take in twenty. Which was why obtaining the forty-thousand-square-foot Hollywood mixed-use building was so important to her and

Isabella. That prime piece of real estate was in the perfect location. That was the good news. The bad news—they were competing with several other investors who also wanted the property.

"Are you even ready to meet with Mr. Kellner?" Isabella asked.

Jeffrey Kellner was the eccentric billionaire owner of the property, as well as an old family friend of Morgan's father. She hoped that relationship would give her an advantage. Normally, she was the epitome of confidence, but she'd be lying if she said that she wasn't a little nervous about the process. Especially when the price tag of the building was 18.9 million dollars. That alone was intimidating as hell.

She folded her arms across her chest. "I'm as ready as I'll ever be. Besides, what's there to get ready for? It's just an informational meeting. I've done all I can do at this point. I submitted my offer and it's still on the table."

Buying commercial property was new for Morgan, and according to her brother Karter, a venture capitalist, the process Kellner was putting her through was a bit unusual. Karter planned to attend the meeting with her to find out what else she needed to do to get her offer accepted, and that's what Morgan told Isabella.

"All right, I guess I'm going to have to trust that you have everything under control," Isabella said, tapping her fingers on her desk.

"I do. Now, can you help me figure out how to load a TikTok dance? I need to learn the steps in the next fifteen minutes."

Isabella looked at her with raised eyebrows. "And you're planning to dance in that?" She pointed at Morgan's black Dolce & Gabbana pantsuit.

Morgan stared down at the outfit that molded to her body like a second skin. The fitted jacket with peak lapels and classy eyelet detailing on the sides screamed sophistication and style. She looked professional and like she meant business.

"I don't have time to change into workout clothes. So I'm going to have to dance in this."

"I think that's a bad idea. You're not going to be able to move, and what happened to the red suit you were planning to wear? The color looked amazing against your dark skin."

"It's hanging up in my office."

"Girrrl, I think that red suit is one of your flyest designs to date. It's gorgeous. I know you said that you're done with fashion design, but—"

"Stop right there," Morgan interrupted and held up both hands. "Last night I suffered through one of my mother's soul-destroying speeches. She went on and on about what a talented designer I am and how I needed to finish my degree. I'm in no mood to hear another lecture this morning. And to answer your question, I opted for this suit because it looks more professional than the red one."

The red suit was sexy and chic and attracted male attention whenever she wore it. That wasn't what she was going for today. She wanted Mr. Kellner to see her as a badass boss-lady ready to handle business.

Morgan picked up her cell phone from the desk. "Okay, enough about my outfits. Show me how this TikTok stuff works."

"You can't even run down the hall without practically passing out. How are you planning to hang with these kids who are half your age? They do these dances probably more than they brush their teeth."

"First of all, they are not half my age. I'm only twelve years older than most of them, but if that's a crack at me turning thirty in a few months, remember, you're older than me. Now, can we get started?"

The words were barely out of her mouth when someone knocked on the office door.

"Come in," Isabella called out, and the door slid open.

"Miss Izzy, have you seen . . . Oh, Miss Morgan, you're the person we're looking for," Melody, one of their clients, said with a smile. Two other girls peeked into the room. "Are you ready?" Melody asked.

"She's ready," Isabella said, humor lacing her words.

Morgan whirled around to see her friend grinning mischievously.

"I can't wait to see you ladies dance." Isabella shot out of her seat and moved a guest chair and rolling file container out of the way. "Feel free to do your thing right here in my office."

"I'm going to kill you," Morgan mumbled under her breath as Izzy reclaimed her seat.

The girls spilled into the room, and Melody set her cell phone up on the desk so that everyone could see the screen.

"We picked an easy dance that we all can follow," she said to Morgan. "It's only five minutes, and we can do a little walk-through if you want before we go for it."

Never one to back down from a challenge, Morgan fell in line next to Melody, Bia, and Dionne. As promised, they went slowly through the dance moves the first go-round. Clearly they knew Morgan wasn't prepared.

"Miss Morgan, you have to squat a little lower," Bia said and showed her by bending her legs deeper and slightly opening them. Her butt almost touched the floor.

"If Morgan tries that, you're going to have to help her back up," Isabella said on a laugh.

Morgan discreetly gave her friend the finger while lifting her left arm toward the sky the way Bia was doing and then added a little shimmy. The song was definitely more suggestive than Morgan thought it would be, but she was here for it.

"Now rock to the left. *One . . . two . . . three* and to the right," Dionne coached. "*One . . . two . . . three . . .*"

They practiced for another few minutes, and Morgan could see why TikTok dances were all the rage. It was fun, and if she did them often enough, they would make a great workout.

"Okay, I think we all have it. Let's get started," Melody announced.

She turned up the volume and "Whatta Man" by Salt-N-Pepa blasted through the office.

Morgan let her inner vixen loose as she got into the groove, gyrating her hips and throwing in a couple of vogue moves for good measure. She might've missed a few steps, but considering this was her first attempt at a TikTok dance, she thought she was doing great.

"*Heeyyy,*" she said, totally feeling herself as they did a swagg bounce with a little hop while swinging their arms.

"Okay, get ready to drop it like it's hot, ladies," Bia said in a singsong voice.

Morgan was right there with them until a loud ripping sound overrode the music. Everyone froze.

"Oh, shit," Morgan murmured and popped up. Her hands flew to the back of her pants, where she could feel air that she hadn't felt moments ago, and the girls burst out laughing. The dance was all but forgotten as they literally fell to the floor in hysterics.

Morgan's mortified gaze flew to Isabella, who was no better. She hung over the arm of her chair cackling hysterically. She tried saying something to Morgan, but each time she got a word out, she'd break down laughing again.

"Urgh," Morgan shrieked and hurried toward the door, her hands covering her backside.

Thank goodness I brought that red suit.

Chapter Two

"WHICH DO YOU THINK KIRA WOULD LIKE BEST? THE BLACK hairy spider, even though it's missing a leg, or a ring-necked snake with a yellow band around its neck?"

Drake Faulkner pulled his gaze from the blueprint that was spread across his desk and glanced at the doorway of his home office. Tall and lanky, his fourteen-year-old brother, Aiden, stood there holding up the two rubbery items, looking back and forth between them.

What made his question even more ridiculous was that he was serious.

Drake shook his head and huffed out a breath. "Neither," he said dryly and placed his palms facedown on top of the blueprint.

He gave his brother a hard look, taking in his hair, a loosely curly high-top fade that needed to be tightened up at the barbershop soon. They both had the same deep brown skin tone, brows that looked as if they were professionally arched, and dark eyes that were almost black.

But that's where the similarities stopped.

Drake had always been neat and cared about his appearance. That wasn't always the case with Aiden. Although today, dressed in a white graphic T-shirt and jeans—that for once weren't hanging low on his narrow hips—his little brother actually looked presentable.

"You're an idiot. Now move out the way. I need to talk to Drake," Addison, Aiden's twin sister, said, and shoved past him to enter the office. "Drake, can you take me to the store before you drop us off at school? I need another sketchbook and I want to get some eyeliner."

Drake stared at the two people he loved more than life itself. They were growing up too fast.

Addy might be a teenager, but mentally she was going on twenty, and she seemed to get prettier every day. She shared the same skin coloring as he and Aiden, but her baby face gave her a sweetness that made pubescent boys fall all over themselves to talk to her. Her dark wavy hair, which she usually wore hanging past her shoulders, was up in a loose ponytail with long tendrils framing her face.

Seemed like it was just yesterday that they were rambunctious toddlers getting into everything and leading Drake to the decision to never have children of his own.

He had been eighteen and heading to UCLA on a full academic scholarship when all three of their worlds exploded into fiery devastation. Aiden and Addison had been two years old when he became their legal guardian.

Drake would never forget that day. He had arrived home from playing basketball in the neighborhood to find two detectives on the front stoop. Cops at the door was never a good sign. Little did he know that they would blindside him with news about his parents—they had died in a plane crash.

For the first few days, he operated in a haze, his every action on autopilot. Even now he wondered how he'd survived those years.

But he did.

Drake shook thoughts of the past from his mind and stood to his full six feet, two inch height. He folded his arms across his chest. As a real estate developer, most of his days were spent in meetings, and it seemed the mornings that he had to meet with someone, the twins found a way to make him run behind schedule.

"Aiden, don't even think about taking spiders, snakes, or any other insect, reptile, or rodent to school with you. You're in high school now. Act like it."

"What? You guys don't know Kira like I do. She's going to think it's funny. Come on, you can't tell me this isn't funny," he said, holding up the fake reptile that looked a little too real for Drake's comfort.

Addison jammed her hands onto her hips. "Like I said, you're an idiot, and Kira's going to think so too."

"Okay, no name calling," Drake said weakly.

"But Drake, we've been in high school for a few weeks and already he's trying to embarrass me by doing stupid stuff," Addison complained.

Drake was in agreement with his sister. He couldn't figure Aiden out. The kid was a book smart, straight-A student, but on most days, his social skills could use a little work.

"Something is wrong with you," Addison said to her twin. "Common sense should tell you that no girl is going to want any of the crap that you think is cool. You need to start using that big brain of yours," she said pointing to her head.

"And you." Drake leveled his sister with a *hear me and hear me good* glare, "I told you, no makeup until you're sixteen, and even then, I might change my mind."

Addison huffed out a breath. "Draaaaake." She dragged out

his name. "I'm in high school. All of the girls wear at least eye-liner."

"All of them except for you," he said with finality.

No way would he allow her to start wearing makeup. It was bad enough that her style of dress was changing from girl next door to girl trying to get attention with tight sweaters and snug-fitting jeans.

Aiden stepped farther into the office and dropped down in one of the chairs in front of Drake's desk. "I thought high school was going to be cool, but so far, it's not working for me. I need more than Mrs. Duncan's algebra class to stimulate my mind."

Unease clawed through Drake. He braced himself for what-ever else Aiden was going to say. The twins were good kids, but they were in that dangerous in-between stage—no longer little kids but not quite adults.

He already hated this age.

"I'm thinking I need a pet," Aiden continued. Drake released the breath he hadn't realized he'd been holding. "Not just any pet, but a snake, and before you say no, I promise to not let it out of my room. I'm thinking that a California kingsnake would work for me. It doesn't get super big, and it won't eat us out of house and home. I'll even share my food with it and make sure to cover any vet bills. And don't worry, that species is real chill, just like me.

"Basically," Aiden added, "you won't even know it's here. Oh, and if a rattlesnake happens to get into the house, my kingsnake will handle it. They devour rattlesnakes. Hence the name *king-snake*. That alone should make you say yes, and—"

"No," Drake said and glanced back down at the blueprint he'd been reviewing before being interrupted. He wondered how his brother could keep a straight face with some of the nonsense that came out of his mouth.

"You didn't let me finish," Aiden said, with an air of excitement still in his tone. "His name will be—"

"If he gets a snake, I'mma need to find another place to live," Addison said with her arms folded. She tapped her foot, her black patent leather flats silent against the thick carpet.

Drake rubbed the back of his neck. "You know what? I'm thinking *I* should move out and let you guys have the house."

"But you'll miss us too much," Addison said, concern in her eyes as if she thought he'd ever be able to leave them behind.

They were his whole world. Sure, he gave them a hard time and threatened to run away whenever they got under his skin, but they knew how important they were to him.

"You're right. I would miss you two, but right now, I'm seriously thinking about leaving. That is, leaving you guys here to figure out how you're getting to school. Because if you're not in the garage in ten minutes, you'll be walking."

"No way am I walking to school." Addison hurried out of the room.

"Now, about that snake," Aiden continued. "It would make a perfect pet. What do you think of the name Mr. Slither?"

"Get out!" Drake yelled, pointing to the door and trying not to laugh.

Aiden was funny sometimes without even trying to be. He was also relentless when it came to something he wanted. Drake had no doubt that the pet snake topic would come up again, and again, and yet again.

"Ten minutes and I'm leaving," he said.

"*Fine.* I'll be ready." As Aiden walked out of the office, Drake heard him mumble, "Kira's going to love my snake."

Drake glanced up at the ceiling. "Why me? What did I do to deserve two teenagers at the same time?"

His cell phone rang, and he couldn't help but chuckle wondering if the universe was calling to answer his question.

A smirk covered his mouth when he glanced at the screen and saw that it was his business partner and best friend.

Nope. He wouldn't get any answers from Matteo Badami. That is unless Drake wanted to know about money or women—Matt's two favorite topics.

"What's up, man?" Drake answered on speaker as he shoved a few files into his laptop bag, then started rerolling the blueprint.

"What do you mean, what's up? I was expecting a call from you after your blind date last night. What did you think of Sophia? She's hot, isn't she?"

Drake put in his earbuds and took the phone off speaker, never knowing when Aiden or Addison would walk in. "She's very nice-looking," he said, which was an understatement. Sophia was a very beautiful woman with an incredible, curvy body, but that's where the attraction stopped.

She talked too much about things he couldn't care less about.

Drake was all for a woman who could hold an engaging conversation, discuss the latest news or sports stats, or share why she loved her job. He had quickly learned that Sophia couldn't do any of those. He didn't give a damn about which superstar was dating which or how much money they made. Though he wasn't much of a world-news watcher, he would've even tolerated conversation about politics rather than Hollywood royalty. And when it came to her job as a personal shopper for one of her mother's friends, Drake learned more than he ever cared to know about fabrics, hemlines, and designer clothing.

There wouldn't be a second date.

Drake was done with trust-fund princesses. Unfortunately, the women he'd been meeting or had been introduced to lately were wealthy because they rode on the coattails of their family's fortune. They weren't self-made millionaires like him, and they had no clue how to survive without their mommy and daddy's money.

"That's it? She's nice-looking? Hell, man, I knew that before I set you up. What about her other qualities? Funny, smart, resourceful?"

"Sorry. I must have missed those attributes," Drake said sarcastically.

Matt sighed dramatically. "Man, she's perfect. If you keep shooting down everyone I introduce you to, I'm going to stop and—"

"Dude, I asked you to stop five women ago. Yet, you either put me on the spot or, like this latest one, set me up on blind dates. I don't need your help. I can find a woman on my own."

"Yet you haven't. You're not going to be able to use Aiden and Addy as an excuse much longer, Drake. They are old enough to take care of themselves, and they're at the age now where they probably want a little space from your overprotective ass."

Drake closed his eyes and pinched the bridge of his nose. Matt was right. The twins were getting more independent by the day, and Addy was already telling him that he needed to get a life.

But Drake wasn't so sure that dating was the answer for him right now. His real estate development business was booming. Did he really have time for a serious relationship?

Drake opened his eyes and grabbed his laptop bag and the blueprint before heading to the door. "Listen, man. I appreciate your concern about my love life, but I got this. I don't need—"

"It's Morgan, isn't it?"

Drake's gut twisted and he pulled up short, stopping in the middle of the room at the mention of his ex—his college sweetheart. Morgan Redford. The only woman he'd ever loved, or thought he had, and the only woman to ever rip out his heart, metaphorically, and throw his love back in his face.

"She still got you all up in your feelings, doesn't she? You don't even have to answer. I already know, but man, come on.

That was like a hundred years ago when you guys dated. She was cool and all, but not cool enough for you to give up on women."

Drake frowned. "I haven't given up on women. I just have more important things going on right now. As for Morgan, I haven't seen her in like ten or eleven years. I think it's safe to say that I'm over her."

"Just because you haven't seen her doesn't mean that you're over her. Considering the way things ended between you two, you'll never get over her until you have closure. And the way she cut out on you, it's safe to say—"

"I'm done discussing my personal life, Matt. Do you want to meet at the office and drive to the meeting together? Or should I meet you at Jeffrey's?"

"At the office. I'll be there in twenty minutes and we can ride together. What do you think Kellner is up to?"

"I have no idea, but I heard there were numerous offers on the building," Drake said and glanced back at his desk to make sure he had everything.

"I'm not surprised. A property of that size, in that Hollywood location, is prime real estate, but you're his mini-me. You guys are practically the same person minus the fifty-year age difference. Besides, you're the son he never had. There's no way he won't accept your offer."

"Yeah, we'll see." Drake moved to the door and shut off the office light. "The old man is up to something, and I have a feeling I'm not going to like whatever it is."

Chapter Three

MORGAN FOLLOWED HER BROTHER KARTER INTO THE IMPRES-sive glass skyscraper, and they blended in with other professionally dressed people who were coming and going. Anxiousness crawled through her body as they strolled across the spacious lobby. She wasn't necessarily nervous, but not knowing what to expect in the meeting had her a little on edge, and she couldn't wait until it was over.

"Karter Redford, what's up, dude?" A man about his height, wearing a high-end jogging suit and sporting spiked blond hair and a huge grin, gave him a hearty handshake. "Where the hell have you been hiding?"

Karter greeted him just as enthusiastically, then introduced the man to Morgan as a graduate school friend before they fell into an animated conversation.

Morgan moved a few steps away to give them a little privacy. Based on the bits and pieces of the conversation she heard, it sounded like the blond was just as successful as Karter. But while her brother was in business mode and decked out in a charcoal-gray, three-piece Tom Ford suit, his friend clearly wasn't on his way to a meeting. He looked as if he was about to hit the gym.

Morgan's thoughts returned to the meeting she was about to attend. She inhaled deeply before slowly releasing a breath. Everything was going to be fine, and she was expecting a good outcome. At least that's what she was telling herself. If nothing else, she was dressed like she meant business.

Her red suit, with the short, fitted jacket and skirt that had a flirty hemline and stopped just above her knees, had ultimately been a good choice. The black suit might have made her appear professional, but the red suit had her feeling powerful and in control. It definitely gave her a boost of confidence.

But what had she been thinking, dancing with the kids before this meeting? Not one of her best decisions, even if it had been fun. At least until her wardrobe malfunction.

God, how embarrassing.

Morgan had given the girls a good laugh, but all the while she had been changing clothes, Isabella had been front and center saying, *I told you so.* She'd been right. Morgan should've been mentally preparing for this meeting instead of dancing around with the kids as if she had nothing better to do.

Now, even as she tried to remain optimistic, she just wanted to get this meeting over with.

"Relax," Karter murmured, cutting into her thoughts. "I can feel the tension bouncing off you. It's just a meeting."

Morgan fell in step with him, and they headed to a bank of elevators. "Yeah, just a meeting, you say. I wish it was a closing and Mr. Kellner was getting ready to slide the keys to the building over to me. Instead, I feel like I'm walking into the unknown, and he's going to say or do something that's going to have me running for the exit."

Her brother's dark brows furrowed. "Dramatic much? Geesh . . ."

Morgan laughed when he gave a mock shiver, and she swatted his arm.

The two of them had always been close. Karter understood her. He never judged her, even during the start of her entrepreneurial phase. He might've thought she was nuts when she had decided to start a professional cuddling business many years ago, but he'd supported her. And he hadn't even batted an eye when she told him about her hangover aide business, nor the pet hotel idea.

He always supported and encouraged her to do whatever made her happy. Unlike their oldest brother, Randy, who called her a spoiled brat every chance he got.

But look at me now.

She was on to bigger and better things . . . grown-up things, like having a career she loved where she got to help their clients find their way in a tough world.

"But seriously, you'll be fine," Karter said. "And I'm not sure if I told you, but you look nice." He tugged on the lapel of her suit jacket. "Is this one of your designs?"

"It is and thanks."

"You know this is why Mom keeps wanting you to get serious about fashion design. You have a gift, Morgan."

"I know, but like I told you and the rest of the family, it's not my passion. Yes, I'm good at it," she said, knowing she was better than good—at least that's what Vera Wang had told her a few months ago—but it still didn't change how she felt. "It's just not what I want to do with my life. I love what we've accomplished so far with Open Arms, and I'm pumped about our future plans. I doubt if designing clothes for Mom's friends will ever give me the satisfaction I get from my nonprofit."

Their socialite mother never missed an opportunity to tell Morgan how disappointed she was by her career choice. Apparently, what she was doing for those who'd aged out of foster care wasn't glamorous enough for her mother to brag about to her snooty friends. It didn't help that Morgan had dropped out of college and never gone back. Though that decision had more to do with her trying to figure out what to do with her life rather than giving up on designing clothes.

But now she had purpose.

Before Morgan could say more to her brother, the elevator arrived. Several businesspeople exited, and she and Karter, along with a handful of other people, strolled into the mirrored elevator. Within seconds, they arrived on the top floor.

When the steel doors slid open, they stepped into a large space that was a severe contrast to the all-glass building. No, this reception area would've been better suited for a nightclub with its dim lighting and dark furnishings. Yet it was an inviting space that embodied a warmth that seemed to wrap around Morgan like a cozy fur coat.

"Hmm, nice," she mumbled as they moved farther into the office suite.

The dark hardwood floors gleamed under the limited lighting and paired well with the deep tan walls. She recognized the furnishings as part of the Cantoni collection, and it was nice to see it up close instead of in a magazine.

Morgan had always been drawn to anything visually creative, whether fashion, home decor, or even landscapes. This space didn't disappoint. In fact, it delighted her artistic senses.

She followed Karter past the sitting area to the long reception desk. An older, impeccably dressed woman with wire-rimmed glasses perched on her nose stood and smiled at them.

"Good morning. May I help you?"

"We're here to meet with Mr. Kellner," Karter said as Morgan continued glancing around. People in business attire bustled about, moving in and out of offices, while others gathered in small groups in the hallways.

She knew Mr. Kellner made most of his money in real estate, but she'd read somewhere that he owned several businesses, like Karter.

"May I have your names?" the receptionist, Sarah, asked.

"Morgan Redford, and this is Karter Redford," Morgan hurried to say. This was her deal. She needed to make sure that she stepped up and took charge. Otherwise, Karter would. Not that he was trying to make her look bad, but it was his nature to lead. A quality she loved and appreciated about him.

"Okay, you'll be in conference room C," Sarah said as she glanced down at the electronic tablet in her hands before looking back up. "That's down the hall to your right, and it'll be the fourth door on the right."

"Okay, thank you," Morgan said. She and Karter followed Sarah's directions, but then she stopped and turned back to the woman. "Excuse me, sorry, but where is the ladies' room?"

"Actually, it's in the opposite direction." She pointed down another hallway. "It's all the way at the end. The last door on your left."

"Great, thank you."

After agreeing to meet her brother in the conference room, Morgan pulled her cell phone from the side pocket of her oversized handbag and checked the time. She had at least fifteen minutes before the meeting was scheduled to start. As she crossed the sitting area and walked down the hall, a tingling at the back of her neck had her steps slowing. She glanced around, wondering what caused the impromptu sensation. At first, she didn't see anything or anyone that seemed out of place, until her gaze landed on two men standing near the elevator.

Morgan did a double take.

The guys were in deep conversation about twenty feet away, and there was something familiar about the taller one. The one with broad shoulders and skin the color of rich mocha . . . but what?

Then realization dawned on her. The man's head was turned slightly, giving her a better view of his profile, but . . .

No way.

It can't be him, she thought as she turned fully. Part of her wanted to move closer. All she would have to do was put one foot in front of the other, but it was as if she was cemented to the floor. She couldn't take that step. Besides, it might not even be him. At least that's what she thought until the man laughed, and her heart stuttered.

Oh, my goodness.

Drake Faulkner?

Chapter Four

MORGAN HADN'T SEEN DRAKE IN YEARS. WERE HER EYES PLAY-ing tricks on her? Sure, she thought about him more often than she cared to admit, but had her imagination conjured him up?

Unable to help herself, she allowed her gaze to travel the length of him. Back in college, he'd always looked good, usually opting for a button-down shirt and jeans, sometimes khakis. To-day, though, he was wearing the hell out of a slim-fit Armani suit with notched lapels and a two-button jacket. The expensive gar-ment hung impeccably over his wide shoulders that tapered down to a narrow waist.

Back then, Morgan thought he was perfect, in more ways than one, but it was safe to say he'd added to that quality in heaps. If his attire and the way he was carrying himself were any indi-cation, he was as successful as he'd planned to be.

Even at a young age, Drake had been the type of man who always had a plan and excelled at everything. There had been no doubt in her mind that he would one day be successful. That was part of why Morgan knew years ago that she couldn't be what he wanted or needed in his life. She wasn't the right woman for him.

He laughed again.

God, his hearty laughter swept over her like a gentle breeze taking her back to a sweet, simpler time in life when her only concern was what she would wear to the next football game.

Her heart did a happy dance at the memory, and her attention went back up to the profile of his face. His dark skin and those chiseled features had him looking like African royalty, and those lips . . .

Good Lord.

Those thick, juicy lips had once loved on her so thoroughly, it was as if Morgan could still feel them on her body.

Yup, that's definitely him.

As if sensing someone staring, he slowly turned his head in her direction, and the earth stopped spinning and everything faded away, except for the two of them.

After a few heartbeats, surprise radiated in his eyes and his mouth dropped open as he watched her watch him. Morgan felt like a deer caught in headlights as his gaze traveled down her body and slowly back up again.

But then, after recognition settled in, his expression turned blank. The temperature in the hallway dropped thirty degrees, and an involuntary shiver scurried down her back.

One look and she knew . . .

He hates me.

Morgan quickly turned on her heel and without a backward glance, she took off down the hallway.

Drake Faulkner.

What was he doing there? Did he have an office in the building? She'd loosely kept up with his career and knew he was in real estate, but she didn't know much more than that.

Wait. Did he work for Mr. Kellner?

Or . . . could he be there for the meeting too?

God, she hoped not.

Morgan didn't even want to think about them competing for the same property.

No. The universe wouldn't be that cruel and make them rivals. Besides, there were plenty of people milling about the office suite. He could be there for any number of reasons.

Stop. Just stop thinking about him, Morgan chastised herself as she rushed into the restroom to handle her business.

Maybe she could get to the conference room without running into him. Then again, she had told herself that if she ever saw him again, she would apologize for the way she'd ghosted him.

Maybe before she headed back to . . .

No. Morgan shook the thought free before it could fully form. She didn't have time to be thinking about Drake. Besides, what had happened between them was a long time ago. She needed to be focusing on her current goal—convincing Mr. Kellner to sell the Hollywood property to her.

Nothing else should be occupying her mind, especially thoughts of her college sweetheart. Once Kellner heard about her plans for the space and how it would benefit those aging out of foster care, he'd want to do whatever he could to help.

But Morgan couldn't shut off the thoughts of Drake.

She missed him. Everything from his handsome face and brilliant mind to his confident nature and his gentle spirit. At least that's how he had been in college. Back then, he'd carried himself like someone twice his age.

Was he still the same?

Was he as driven as he used to be?

Drake had been everything she wasn't—mature, focused, and determined to succeed at all costs.

He also had kids.

Kids, as in plural. Granted, they were his brother and sister, but still . . .

Morgan might love children, but she knew her strengths and weaknesses. What the kids needed and what Drake had wanted at the time, she hadn't been able to give. She hadn't been the type of woman he deserved in his life, so she'd taken herself out of the equation. If only she had been mature enough to share her concerns with him. Instead, she'd run.

Not only had she run, but she'd dropped out of college and left the country without a backward glance.

Morgan growled under her breath at the memory.

What a wimp.

If there was a way to turn back time and make better decisions, she would do it in a heartbeat. Too bad life didn't work that way.

Morgan released a long, drawn-out sigh and stepped out of the bathroom stall. As she washed her hands, she glanced in the mirror and turned her head side to side to check herself out.

Not bad. I just need to freshen up.

As she touched up her lipstick and readjusted some of the braids on top of her head, her mind was still reeling. Based on the frigidness she'd seen in Drake's eyes, he hadn't forgiven her for the way she'd left. Hell, had she been him, she wouldn't forgive her either.

Dammit. Just stop thinking and let it go.

Drake was a part of her past that she'd screwed up and there was nothing she could do about it.

"I am a mature adult now. I need to start acting like one," she said with authority to her reflection.

A toilet flushed, and Morgan startled. She'd thought she was the only one in the bathroom.

Seconds later, the stall door on the end opened and an older woman with perfectly coiffed gray hair and pretty green eyes stepped out.

She smiled at Morgan as she made her way to one of the sinks. "The skirt is a little short. Other than that, you look mature to me," she said, flashing a set of perfectly straight teeth as she washed and dried her hands. "Oh, but you might want to get rid of that toilet paper trailing behind you."

Morgan glanced down and gasped. Sure enough, there was at least three feet of toilet paper snagged on the bottom of her heel.

Oh crap.

Laughter followed the woman out the door while Morgan hurried and got rid of the paper.

"How embarrassing," she murmured, but was glad for the heads-up.

Now it was time to go and claim her property.

Feeling confident and in charge again, she stood straighter, pulled her shoulders back, and gave herself one last once-over in the mirror.

I've got this.

With that last thought and her smile firmly in place, she marched to the door, swung it open with flair, and pulled up short.

Her heart slammed against her chest.

Her smile fell.

And her mouth went dry.

There before her, leaning against the wall with his arms folded and his legs crossed at the ankle, was the only man she had ever loved.

Drake Faulkner.

"Hello, Angel. It's been a long time."

Chapter Five

ANGEL.

Funny how the nickname he had given her the first time they'd met at UCLA naturally rolled off his tongue.

Drake would never forget that day. He'd been rounding a corner in a hallway, and Morgan had plowed into him like a Mack Truck going a hundred miles an hour down the highway. The impact sent both their books flying across the shiny travertine floor. Wild curly hair, large doe-like eyes, lips made for kissing, and the face of an angel greeted him. The nickname was born.

That was a long time ago, and the woman standing in front of him was *definitely* not the same girl from back then.

Even though she was close enough for him to reach out and touch, Drake couldn't believe he was face-to-face with Morgan Redford. He hadn't seen her since junior year of college, which would've been her sophomore year. She was more beautiful than he remembered, and his body reacted immediately.

Wound tighter than a coil spring, he had to force himself to breathe . . . and not stare at her.

I can't believe she's here . . . in front of me . . . looking like God's gift to men.

He'd felt like some type of pervert, waiting for her outside of the ladies' room, but he had to see her. He had to make sure it was really her.

What he hadn't planned, though, was what he'd say when she finally walked out. Now that they were standing face-to-face, he was at a loss.

How many times had he practiced what he'd say when they saw each other again? In some of those scenarios, he imagined himself making eye contact, glaring, then walking away without a word. Other times, he saw himself demanding that she tell him why she'd run. Then there were other times when he imagined not doing anything but looking at her, taking in her beauty and pretending she hadn't left him. They would just pick up where they'd left off.

But now . . .

"Hi, Drake," she said, moving closer to him but still maintaining a safe distance.

He couldn't speak.

He could barely think.

He couldn't get his mind to catch up with what was actually happening here.

It's really her.

He hadn't been hallucinating. How was it possible that after a decade, he'd suddenly run into the woman who'd been so hard to forget? A woman who he never thought he would see again. A woman who, the last time he'd seen, had barely looked of legal age, but now . . .

This woman . . . this grown-ass woman was absolutely stunning.

Her usual untamed, curly hair was now in long microbraids. He had loved the hairstyle she'd had in college since it accentuated her carefree, *I love life* attitude. This new look signaled a more buttoned-up, professional woman.

Back then, there was a cuteness about Morgan. Like girl-next-door cute. She rarely wore makeup. She hadn't needed it. Her clothes were usually made by some well-known designer or were some outfit that she had created herself.

Gone was the girl that he had fallen in love with, and in her place was a woman who was dressed like a badass boss.

Bold.

Self-confident.

Poised.

Her makeup was flawless. Her body—slammin'.

Morgan might've still been slim, but she had filled out in all the important places, giving her curves that any man would appreciate. And those legs. Her skirt was short enough to show off shapely legs and a hint of toned thighs. The outfit molded over her body as if it had been tailored specifically for her. Then again, knowing Morgan and the wealth that she came from, it probably had been.

On that thought, Drake's gaze returned to her face, and all the anger, hurt, disappointment, and dammit, even longing he'd felt when she'd ghosted him came rushing back.

He thought he had put that time in his life behind him. He thought he had shed the anger he'd harbored all those years ago. He thought he had moved on emotionally.

Apparently not.

She had just up and left him. No note. No phone call. Nothing. The only woman he'd ever loved, she had reeled him in, made him fall in love with her, then ripped out his heart by disappearing.

She had ruined him for any other woman, and he didn't think he could ever forgive her.

But despite how things had ended between them, his body was still in tune to her presence. His heart rate was elevated. His pulse was pounding loudly in his ears, and the desire to hold her in his arms and kiss her senseless was as powerful as it had been when they'd dated in college. She'd always had an effect on him, and the years hadn't changed that.

Drake's frustration threatened to overpower him. He had fallen for her hard and wanted more than anything to know why she'd left him. Why she had vanished from his life without a word. It hadn't mattered that he was raising two toddlers at the time; he'd been determined to have it all—keeping his family together, getting through college, and one day marrying the woman of his dreams—Morgan.

Two out of three wasn't bad.

"What are you doing here?" he asked.

His tone was gruffer than he'd intended as he pushed off the wall. He started to move closer to her but stopped short to combat a sudden urge to cup her face between his hands and re-acquaint himself with her luscious mouth.

Growling internally, he shoved his hands into his pants pockets.

"I'm here for a meeting," she said, her eyes searching his as if looking for something. *What?* He wasn't sure, but he diverted his gaze and glanced down at his leather oxfords before returning his attention to her.

"It's nice seeing you," she said quietly, her voice as gentle as a feathery touch against his ears. "It's been a long time."

He nodded, unable to stop staring at her lovely face. "Yeah, it has been a while. I haven't seen you since the day before you disappeared on me." The words sounded as bitter as they felt leaving his mouth. "Imagine my surprise when your best friend told me that you didn't just drop out of school without telling me. You left the country."

She huffed out a long breath. "Drake, I owe you an apology, and I want to explain why I—"

"Save it," he bit out, anger bubbling just below the surface. She winced and he knew his tone surprised her, but he couldn't help himself. "You've had years to apologize and explain yourself, but you never did. What makes you think I want to hear anything you have to say now? What's been done is done. I've moved on, and I'm sure you have too."

Matteo hurried their way and Drake glanced at the Cartier watch on his wrist. *Nine o'clock.* Damn, the meeting had probably started.

"They're waiting for you two," Matteo said, a wicked gleam in his eyes. "What's up, Morgan? It's been a long time." Being the ladies' man he was, he leaned in and gave her a friendly hug before pulling back.

Morgan gave a tentative smile as she studied Matteo, and Drake could tell she didn't remember him, but was trying to place his face.

"This is my best friend, Matteo. He attended UCLA with us and is now the CFO of my real estate development company." Drake saw the moment Morgan recognized Matt.

"Oh, yes. I thought you looked familiar," she said.

Her smile was devoid of any warmth, which was unusual. Maybe he'd been too harsh, but he wouldn't apologize. He wanted her to feel a little of what he'd felt back then. She needed to know that she had hurt him.

"Nice to see you again." Morgan's perfectly arched brows dipped into a frown as her gaze bounced from Matteo to Drake and back to Matteo again. "Wait, did you say that they're waiting for *us*?"

Drake realized what that meant. They were heading into the

same meeting. How was it possible that he hadn't seen this woman in years, and here she was competing for the same property he wanted? The property he intended to own in the very near future.

Morgan pointed a thumb over her shoulder. "You were invited to Mr. Kellner's meeting?" she asked, concern radiating in her pretty brown eyes as she shook her head. "You're not going for—"

"Yes, and I'm positive that Jeffrey will be selling the property to me," he said, an edge to his tone.

This meeting was just . . . hell, Drake wasn't sure what was up with the meeting, but no way would he allow Jeffrey to sell that property to someone else. It might've been prime real estate, but it meant so much more to Drake than that. It was a part of his legacy, and he might need to reiterate that to Jeffrey.

"Shall we?" Drake extended his arm for her to go before him down the hall. "We wouldn't want to keep the others waiting."

She gave a small smile and turned from him. "No, we wouldn't."

Drake started to follow her, but his friend jerked on his arm and held him back. "We'll be there in a second," Matteo called out to her.

She gave a slight wave, and Drake watched her walk away. Her flirty skirt hem swished back and forth, and he didn't miss the way her hips rocked left . . . then right . . . then left . . .

"Don't. Even. *Think*. About. It!" Matteo bit out. "We're on a mission. That woman screwed you up years ago, and it took months for you to get your shit back together. Don't fall for her pretty face and sexy ass again, man. *Don't* do it. You . . . no, *we* can't afford for you to start thinking with the wrong head right now. We have too much to lose and everything to gain."

Drake shook out of his friend's hold and frowned at him. "I have no intention of revisiting the past," he ground out, and buttoned his suit jacket as they moved down the hallway. "No way am I letting *anyone* get in the way of our plans."

Not even the beautiful Morgan Redford.

Chapter Six

MORGAN WAS DETERMINED NOT TO LOOK AT DRAKE EVEN though she could feel his gaze burning a hole through her. He might've been sitting across the table and one chair over, but the way her body was tingling, it was as if he were sitting right next to her.

Don't look at him. Do not look at him.

How was she supposed to focus when all she could do in that moment was remember how good they'd been together? How much fun they used to have, and even the shenanigans they pulled to keep college life interesting.

God, she missed those days. More than that, she missed him.

This is not good. This is so not good.

After so many years without even a glimpse of him, being in his presence was a little overwhelming. But Morgan needed to pay attention before she missed what Isaac and Mr. Kellner were saying.

"You can't be serious!" Drake barked out, startling Morgan, and her gaze bounced to him.

Darn it! She had missed something important, if the way he was glaring at Jeffrey Kellner was any indication.

At the head of the table, Kellner leaned heavily on a beautifully carved walking stick and stood next to Isaac, his assistant, who was glowering at Drake.

The fifteen people sitting at the conference table were those who had submitted an offer on the property. Their guests, including Karter, occupied chairs along the wall. Interest in this property was off the charts.

"What do you mean you're not accepting any of our offers? Come on, Jeffrey. What are you up to? Why have us all meet here if you have no intention of selling the property?"

Everyone talked at once, tossing out questions and expressing their displeasure at being called there on false pretenses. Others complained that Kellner's team was wasting their time.

They had a right to be angry if that was the case, but Morgan didn't believe it was. His time was just as precious as all of theirs. Besides, who the heck made people—investors willing to pay an obscene amount of money for a property—jump through pointless hoops?

"Quit being such a hothead and let me finish," Kellner snapped at Drake, who glowered right back at the older man and his assistant.

It was apparent they were very familiar with one another, but what was their relationship?

"Now, as I was saying before I was rudely interrupted . . . I didn't say I wasn't selling the property," the old man explained, his gray-eyed gaze slowly meeting everyone who was sitting at the table.

At eighty years old and maybe an inch over six feet tall, he wasn't as muscular and broad as he'd been in his prime, but his presence still commanded attention. His head full of hair was all gray now, but his sienna-brown face only held a few wrinkles.

Except for the slight bend in his posture, he could easily pass for a man in his mid-sixties.

"I said that there is more to the process than just submitting a monetary offer."

Morgan listened as Jeffrey gave them a little history regarding the property, mainly about how he came to own the building. It was where he had first seen his beloved wife, Rebecca, who died a few years ago. The two had been in their late fifties when they met and then married a few months later, and she was the love of his life.

Morgan understood why the property was sentimental to him, and why he really didn't want to sell it for financial gain. It was one of the last commercial buildings he owned, and he was finally ready to let it go.

He should just sell it to me.

Like with Kellner, the property meant something to her. Not only would it provide housing for the kids the nonprofit served, it would be her very first major investment in real estate, something Morgan had been looking forward to for a long time.

"I don't always do what's expected," Kellner continued, "and I've decided I want the sale of this property to mean something . . . to accomplish something more meaningful than just making me money."

"What does that even mean?" a guy at the far end of the table asked. He reminded her of her old econ professor, down to the wire-rim glasses he was wearing.

Morgan's gaze drifted back to Drake before she could stop herself, and just as she'd assumed earlier, he was watching her. Heat rushed to her face, and she quickly diverted her eyes, but not before her pulse amped up and need soared through her body.

Don't let him distract you, girl. Focus.

"I wish I could sell to all of you, but I can't," Mr. Kellner was saying when Morgan tuned back in. "And I'm sure right now you're calling me all types of fool in your mind, but I hope by the time this process is over, you'll understand my thinking. I also hope that when it's all said and done, you'll get much more out of this than just a building and land." He shifted slightly and glanced at his assistant. "I'm going to step out. Isaac will explain the next steps. Enjoy the rest of your day."

The old man shuffled out of the room, paying no attention to the gaping faces he left behind.

"Mr. Kellner knows that his way of choosing to sell this property is a bit unorthodox," Isaac said. "If at any point in this presentation you decide that you're no longer interested, you're welcome to leave. Otherwise, feel free to ask questions at any time.

"There's a three-step process in becoming the owner of this Hollywood property. You've already completed step one—submitting an offer. The second step is writing a two-page letter, single spaced, explaining what you plan to do with the property once you own it, and why Mr. Kellner should sell it to you."

Okay, this was weird even to Morgan. This might be her first time purchasing a commercial building, but she was pretty sure this wasn't how the process usually went.

"After that, will one of our offers be accepted?" the woman sitting next to Morgan asked.

"No. Ten of you will be invited to another meeting explaining the last step in the process of purchasing this property."

"This is bullshit," a large man sitting at the other end of the table grumbled. He looked as if he could be a defensive tackle for the Los Angeles Chargers. "I will be running all of this by my lawyers, because I'm pretty sure Kellner is breaking some laws. Who adds these types of stipulations to the sale of commercial real estate? He probably already knows who he wants to sell the property to." The man looked at Drake pointedly.

Interesting.

Now more than ever, Morgan wanted to know what Drake's relationship with Kellner was.

"Mr. Ford, I assure you that Mr. Kellner has run his plans by his legal team. But if you'll feel better checking in with your attorney, by all means, go for it. Just know that if we don't have your letter by tomorrow morning, nine a.m. to be exact, your offer will be taken off the table. Are there any more questions or concerns?"

Morgan raised her hand.

"Yes, Miss Redford."

"When will we be notified whether or not we're moving on to the next round of the process?"

"That's a good question. Mr. Kellner will read through the entries, and I'll contact you personally." He lifted his hands and glanced around the table. "That goes for everyone who makes the cut. You'll hear from me by Friday evening. Everyone else will hear from their real estate agent letting you know that your offer wasn't accepted."

More grumbles spread around the room. Some of the bidders held side conversations with the people who were sitting in the seats against the wall.

"What happens when we move on to the next level?" Drake asked, apparently confident that he'd be one of the chosen ones.

"Mr. Faulkner, assuming you move to the next level," Isaac said, a challenge in his gaze, "next steps will be given to you on Friday, if your letter is one of the chosen ten."

Drake said nothing else, but it was clear he wasn't happy with Isaac's brusque tone.

"So that I don't take up any more of everyone's time, feel free to stick around after the meeting or contact me later if you have additional questions. Thanks for coming."

Morgan was slow to leave the conference room since she

didn't want to run into Drake. However, as there was a chance that they'd see each other again, maybe she should say something to him. The last thing she wanted was another awkward moment whenever they came face-to-face.

"Do you have any questions, Miss Redford?" Isaac asked as he gathered the few items that he had brought in with him.

"No, but I have to say, I'm a little surprised by this whole process. Wouldn't it be easier to just pick one of the offers and be done with it?"

Isaac chuckled. "It would be, but my boss never takes the easy route. If you do plan on submitting a letter, I think you'll be pleasantly surprised by the next step in the process."

"Can you give me a hint?" Morgan asked, flashing her sweetest smile.

The left corner of his mouth lifted into a crooked grin. "It's tempting, but if I want to keep my job, I'd better keep my mouth shut."

"In that case, I guess I should get to work on that letter."

They walked out together, but parted ways when they reached the reception area. A few of the people from the meeting were still standing around talking, including Drake, who was in deep conversation with Matteo.

"Ready?" Karter asked when he approached Morgan in the hallway.

"Yeah, but . . ." She glanced at Drake, whose back was to her.

What if she went over there and tried to apologize and he ignored her or cursed her out? She was pretty sure he would never disrespect her like that, but she could totally see him walking away in the middle of her pouring out her heart and asking for forgiveness.

But at least I'd have tried.

"Friend of yours?" Karter asked. "The guy couldn't take his eyes off of you during the meeting."

Of course her brother had noticed. Not much got past him.

"Yeah, we were friends . . . once. We attended college to-gether," Morgan explained, then nibbled on her bottom lip.

She and Drake had dated a while, but she'd never introduced him to her family. Not that she hadn't wanted to; it just hadn't happened.

"I'm assuming you were more than friends. If you need to talk to him, I can wait for you downstairs. I need to make some calls anyway."

Morgan glanced at Drake again. "Yeah, let me speak to him. It shouldn't take long."

"Okay. I'll meet you out front."

Morgan nodded. When Drake's laughter carried across the room, she figured it would be a good time to head over.

Well, here goes nothing.

Chapter Seven

"I HOPE JEFFREY ISN'T GOING TO MAKE A HABIT OF THESE meetings," Matteo said only loud enough for Drake to hear. "Because if he does, we're screwed."

Drake frowned. "What are you talking about? I'm not giving up on that Hollywood property. Whatever obstacles he tosses our way, we're going to rise to the occasion."

"I'm not talking about the property situation, even though I think he's finally lost his mind. I'm talking about the beautiful Ms. Redford. I'm surprised you heard anything they said in there since you barely took your eyes off of her, and I'm sure I'm not the only one who noticed you staring."

"I don't know what you're talking about," Drake lied. "I have one thing on my mind—write a letter that gets us to the next level of whatever foolishness Jeffrey is pulling."

He glanced around. He told himself that he wasn't looking for Morgan, but that's exactly who he was looking for. Relief flooded his body when he didn't spot her anywhere.

Matteo gave an appreciative head nod to a beautiful woman

who passed them on her way down the hallway. "Damn, this place is loaded with gorgeous women. But like I was saying, I hope this is the last meeting. If you honestly expect me to believe that you only had the property on your mind in there, then you're not only lying to me, you're also lying to yourself."

"Let's just drop it. I need to get to the office for an eleven o'clock meeting. Will you be able to meet with the Reagan Group by yourself this afternoon? I want to work on the letter for Jeffrey and send it to him before the day is over."

"Yeah, no problem, but what's up with the guy? I don't get why he has you all jumping through hoops like this."

"I'm not sure, but I'm planning to call him tonight," Drake said. He thought about stopping by Jeffrey's office before they left, but thought better of it. The man was likely already pissed at him for the way Drake behaved in the meeting. No need to make things worse.

"If you have everything you need, we can head out," Matteo said.

Drake patted his pockets, making sure he hadn't left his phone in the conference room. "Wait, let me make . . . What the heck?" he said when he found something else in his pocket and pulled it out.

A rubbery toy spider. The same one that Aiden had been playing with earlier.

"I'm going to kill that brother of mine," he mumbled, holding up the creepy crawler.

Matteo burst out laughing. "I see my godson is up to his usual tricks. I thought he would've grown out of it by now."

"Apparently he—"

"Drake?"

Drake spun around at the sound of Morgan's voice, and the spider flew out of his hand.

"Argh!" she screamed. The ear-piercing shriek ripped

through Drake as he watched her stumble backward when the toy landed on her nose. "Oh, my God! Get it off! Get it off!"

She wasn't afraid of much, but he recalled her being terrified of spiders. Apparently, even those that were fake.

"Morgan, it's just . . . look out!" Drake lunged toward her, trying to grab her arm before she tumbled over a table in the sitting area.

She was too busy swatting at the spider that now clung to one of her braids, she wasn't paying attention to anything around her. At least not until her heel caught and she stumbled on a rug.

She was going down.

Aw, hell.

Too late.

She screamed again as her leg bumped the table and she lost her balance. Horrified eyes, mouth hanging open, and her arms flailing would've made for a comical sight if he wasn't afraid she'd hurt herself. It was like watching a video in slow motion, and just when he thought he could reach her hand, she crashed to the floor with a thunk.

Her legs were up in the air and her skirt had ridden up, revealing red lace between her shapely thighs. Drake wasn't trying to look, but he couldn't help it.

What a sight.

He stood there for a split second, getting his fill, until he realized other folks had moved closer to see what had happened. He used his body to block their view, and he tried smoothing down her skirt as she struggled to sit up.

That's when Drake spotted the hairy spider on the floor next to her. He quickly snatched it up and shoved it into his jacket pocket, not wanting her to freak out again.

"Are you all right?" he asked when she finally got her bearings.

His heart slammed against his chest when pretty, brown,

teary eyes met his. God, he hoped she didn't start crying. He'd never been good at handling a woman's tears, though Addison had given him tons of practice.

"Morgan, you okay?" he asked again, but all she did was glare at him. "Let me help you up." He extended his hand.

"I don't need your help, you stupid jerk!" she seethed.

The tears were gone, but there was nothing scarier than an angry black woman looking as if she wanted to rip his head off.

"You hate me so much that you would throw a spider at me?"

"Of course not!" he ground out between clenched teeth, shocked that she would think he'd stoop that low. "You know I would *never* do anything like that to you. Hurting people is your MO. Not mine."

Morgan flinched at the barb that hit home. He wasn't trying to be mean, but she should know him better than to think he'd try to scare her to death, especially with something as tacky as a fake spider.

"Then what were you trying to do?" she asked and leaned a little closer to him as he shielded her from prying eyes.

"I wasn't trying to do anything. You caught me off guard when you touched my back. When I turned, the damn thing flew from my hands." Sitting on his haunches next to her, he sighed and rubbed the back of his neck. "My idiot brother, who I'm going to kill, somehow snuck it into my jacket pocket. I'm sorry. I know how you feel about spiders. You gotta know I would never torture you with one."

She sighed. "Aiden?"

Drake nodded, a little surprised that she remembered his brother's name.

She lowered her gaze, probably feeling embarrassed because there were still a few people in the reception area.

"Sorry to interrupt . . ." Matteo came partially into view then stepped back again.

Morgan's gaze shot up, and she scooted closer to Drake.

He glanced over his shoulder at his friend, who was biting his lip to keep from laughing. Maybe Drake would have a good laugh later, but at the moment, the situation wasn't funny.

"I'll meet you downstairs in a second," he said.

Matteo gave him a nod, and Drake turned back to Morgan.

"Now, are you going to let me help you up? Or are you planning to spend the rest of the day sitting here?" He was trying to lighten the moment, and it seemed to be working since she wasn't glaring at him anymore.

She finally placed her hand in his, and Drake gritted his teeth as an electrical charge swept through him and nipped at every cell in his body. His gaze shot to hers and, judging by her surprised expression, she felt it too. The connection they once shared. It was as if they were the only two people in the room. Her eyes reflected the intense emotions and memories warring within him.

He had forgotten what it was like to touch her, to have her small hand in his. Her skin was as soft as he remembered. Her delicate scent of flowers and vanilla brought back fond memories of them snuggled together, and everything about her permeated his senses.

As if that wasn't enough torture, his eyes dropped to her lips. Full lips that he remembered being soft, pillowy, and perfect for kissing. And the overwhelming need to do just that engulfed him like a fiery inferno.

Drake growled under his breath at the way his body tightened with need. What was wrong with him? The woman had almost killed herself, and he was standing there thinking of all the ways he wanted to kiss her.

Once Morgan was steady on her feet, he quickly released her hand as if he'd been burned. He needed a distraction. He grabbed her large purse from the floor and handed it to her.

"I really am sorry about this," he said, trying not to look into her eyes, but failing. "Are you sure you're all right?"

"I'm fine," she said on a sigh and brushed the back of her skirt with her hands. "I'm just embarrassed and feeling like a total dweeb."

"If you want, I can act as a human shield and try to sneak you past prying eyes."

"Thanks, but I think it's a little too late for that. With the way my legs were up in the air, I'm pretty sure I'll be a meme before the day is over. Unfortunately, the words attached to it will probably read something like: *Wave your legs in the air. Wave 'em like you just don't care.*"

On that, he threw his head back and roared with laughter. So did she. Hearing her melodious giggle was like stepping back in time. At least she still had her sense of humor.

He'd missed her.

He still hated how she'd walked out of his life years ago, but he would be lying if he said that he wasn't happy to see her.

The thought caught him off guard. She was his competition.

Never underestimate the competition.

Morgan was also his past, and he needed to remember that. He needed to forget about her and keep his distance at all cost, because if he didn't, Drake was sure things wouldn't end well for him.

Chapter Eight

MORGAN PROPPED HER ELBOWS ON HER DESK AND HELD HER head between her hands. "Izzy, I made a complete fool of myself. I have never been so embarrassed in all of my life."

Hearing her friend hiccup between giggles, Morgan glanced up and frowned. Isabella was laughing so hard, her olive skin was blotchy from the tears rolling down her cheeks.

"Dang, girl, it ain't that funny," Morgan griped, but if she hadn't still been traumatized by the experience, she'd probably think it was hilarious.

Isabella laughed even harder, if that was possible, and Morgan tried not to join her. Had it been someone else who had showed their ass, literally, maybe it would've been funny to her too. But as it was, she was the one who had humiliated herself in a public place full of professionals.

"I'm sorry, sis, but it really is funny, and that's just based on your recap. I probably would've hurt myself laughing had I been there. But of course, I would've made sure you were okay first."

Morgan pursed her lips. "Of course."

"Now I wish I'd gone with you. I could've used a good laugh this morning, and the thought of your bird legs in the air with your skirt around your waist? *Girrrl*," she sputtered another laugh.

"Okay, that's enough. You're lucky my feelings aren't easily hurt. Otherwise, you could really be giving me a complex right about now."

Wiping at her tears, Isabella strolled around the desk and gave Morgan a hug. "I'm sorry. I don't mean to embarrass you. Between splitting your pants this morning, and now the spider incident, you've had enough of that for one day."

Morgan knew she wasn't sorry at all. She could hear the humor in her friend's voice, and that made her chuckle.

"Don't try to placate me," she said, playfully shoving Isabella away. "I know you live for my screwups."

Isabella grinned and backed away. "You know I do, and come on, you know this shit is funny."

Morgan laughed. "Girl, go somewhere. I can do without your type of sympathy. Besides, I have work to do," she said, thinking about the letter she needed to write.

Isabella reclaimed her seat. "One thing, though, I hope you at least had on cute underwear because I have a feeling the red bottoms on your shoes weren't the only thing the people in that room were privy to," she said on a laugh.

Morgan groaned. "I'm never going to live this down."

She closed her eyes. Thankfully, not only did she have on cute underwear, but she was also glad that she stayed well-groomed down there. Drake's shocked expression when she hit the floor probably had more to do with her red lace showing than the fact that she had almost broken her neck.

"I'll never be able to face him or anyone else in that building again. It was horrible. I'm talking like farting in front of dignitaries horrible. People there are probably still laughing."

"Maybe, but I'm sure they're relieved you didn't hurt your-self. We're living in the days of people suing anybody and every-body. The last thing they want is a lawsuit on their hands."

The receptionist had been very kind, stopping Morgan before she left to make sure that she was all right. The woman had even assured her that she hadn't see anyone videotaping her.

That thought made Morgan feel even worse. Despite her fa-ther's notoriety, she was rarely a part of any entertainment news, but the media would've been all over something like what had happened at Kellner's office. Just like the time she'd gotten drunk at a party with some of her trust-fund friends, and a photo of them had ended up on TMZ. Her parents had been livid, espe-cially her mother, who was all about appearances.

Morgan shook free of the memory and returned her thoughts to her current situation. More specifically, Drake.

There was so much distance and time lost between them, but there had been a moment, after he had helped her off the floor, that something passed between them. Something intense, pas-sionate, and . . . familiar.

But that was insane. Sure, she was still attracted to him. Hell, any woman with a heartbeat would be attracted to the man, but the sensation that swirled through her when he touched her hand was something she hadn't felt in a long time. Not since . . . him.

"What aren't you telling me?" Isabella said, snapping Morgan out of her thoughts and looking at her through narrowed eyes.

Morgan wanted nothing more than to forget that she'd run into Drake, but she couldn't. His intense dark eyes that used to hold so much love and compassion when he looked at her kept seeping into her mind. Other than that moment they'd shared after the spider fiasco, his eyes had held distrust and hurt.

"Remember, I know you. I was there when you walked away. You cried that whole day and cried even more at the airport be-fore you left for Europe."

"I wasn't crying over him. I was just nervous about leaving the country by myself."

Isabella shook her head. "Save it for someone who doesn't know you. Even if you're not still in love with Drake, there was a time when you were, and you two never talked about what happened."

"I tried," Morgan said weakly.

"You tried what?"

"Today . . . at the meeting. I tried to apologize and explain why I left the way I did, but he wouldn't let me. I was barely able to get a word out before he cut me off, telling me that he didn't want to hear it. He said it was too late."

"Well, maybe you'll get a chance to try again. I'm pretty sure you both need closure. Because if he's been anything like you . . ."

"Wait. What do you mean like me?"

"I mean if he hasn't settled down and has been comparing every woman to you, it's past time you two talked."

Morgan's heart squeezed at the thought of him being with someone else. She hadn't noticed a ring on his finger, and yes, she'd looked, but that didn't mean he wasn't married or in a relationship.

"He was the last serious relationship you had, and you didn't get a proper breakup. You just left."

Morgan didn't bother arguing because that was exactly what she'd done, and to this day, she regretted the decision. The years that she was away, she'd thought about what she'd do if she ever ran into Drake again. What she'd imagined wasn't nearly as intense and heartbreaking as the reality. Seeing the hurt in his eyes, even though they'd parted ways years ago, had almost been her undoing.

"Drake was it for you. I think that's why now you only go out with guys who you know you'll never get serious with."

"I still have feelings for Drake," she blurted, surprising herself by saying what she was feeling.

Morgan eased her gaze to Isabella, not surprised to see her friend's mouth hanging open.

Isabella closed her mouth, opened it, then closed it again, looking like a guppy.

Morgan groaned. "I know it sounds ridiculous but seeing him again stirred up all of the old feelings. Not to mention that the man looked absolutely delicious," she said, picturing his soulful eyes, juicy lips, and a body that she was sure was worshipped by women young and old.

"It actually doesn't sound ridiculous at all. You guys were once crazy about each other. On top of that, I remember how *fiiine* that brotha was back in college. I can only imagine how good he looks now."

"He hates me, Iz. When we first ran into each other, you should've seen the way he glowered, looking at me like I was a dumpster-dive reject. Or like I was something stinky the dog dropped off on the neighbors' lawn. Or like I was a mud-drenched cat that had just dirtied up his white carpet. Or like I was—"

"Stop! I get it already! He wasn't happy to see you. Just tell me what happened? What did you guys say to each other at first sight?"

"It was one of the most awkward moments of my life, second to the spider incident. At first, I couldn't believe it was him. I heard his voice and figured it couldn't be him, but then I turned." Morgan shook her head as the moment flashed through her mind. "I thought my eyes were playing tricks on me. He was there with a guy he used to hang out with—Matteo, I think, was his name."

"Wait." Isabella leaned forward with wide eyes. "You're not talking about Matteo Badami, are you? They used to hang out all the time. He was there?" she asked, her voice raising at least three octaves.

Morgan nodded. "Yeah, he and Drake work together. You remember him?"

Isabella sat back and fanned herself. "Girl, Matteo is *un bellissimo uomo*," she said.

Morgan quirked an eyebrow. "I assume that's something good?"

"Definitely. It means a handsome man. My Italian isn't all that good. Otherwise, I would've said, the man was hot as hell. If he looked half as good as he did back in the day, I'm going to that next meeting with you."

"Well, before we can even think about another meeting, we need to draft a kick-ass letter of why we want the property." She wanted that building so bad, she was prepared to do almost anything, but even if her bid was accepted, it would still take months to a year to get the building set up for the nonprofit.

If Morgan could, she would use her own money to provide temporary housing for the teens who were on their waiting list. But when she and Isabella founded Open Arms, they'd agreed that the nonprofit would stand on its own. That meant Morgan couldn't just throw her own money at situations that popped up.

But she wanted to. She never felt guilty about her family's wealth, but she always wanted to do something in a big way to help those less fortunate. Not only was their nonprofit giving her that chance, but she finally felt like an adult. Like she was contributing to society and not just living the good life.

Isabella hadn't grown up with money, and after getting her bachelor's degree in social work, she'd paid off her student loans and vowed to put her degree to work. Not only was she doing that, but she was also back in school getting her MBA.

For the next few minutes, they brainstormed what they were going to include in the letter. Once they had a decent list, Isabella typed while Morgan dictated. Not wanting the letter to be too long, they revised it until they got it down to two pages.

Isabella read it aloud, and Morgan couldn't stop the grin from spreading across her face.

"*Damn*, we're good. We might as well go ahead and hire an architect, because that property is going to be ours!"

So what if Drake was competing? Morgan had no doubt that she would win the bid.

Chapter Nine

"EARTH TO DRAKE. COME IN DRAKE."

Drake blinked several times as Harris, one of his employees, snapped his fingers in front of his face. He hadn't realized he'd zoned out on the architect.

"Boss, you all right?"

Drake hated how distracted he'd been since leaving the Hollywood property meeting hours ago. Between dealing with Jeffrey not returning his calls, and reliving the run-in with Morgan, he'd been useless all afternoon.

Unfortunately, Morgan was the one dominating his thoughts the most. Guilt gnawed at him, twisting inside his gut like a double-edged sword. Part of him wanted to seek her out and make sure she was okay after the whole debacle at the office. The other part, though, knew he needed to keep his distance. Drake was defenseless when it came to her. Always had been. She was the only person who could get under his skin and lodge into his heart before he even realized it happened.

And he hated it.

"I'm fine. I just have a lot on my mind."

"Oh, all right. Well, what I was saying is, if we move that door to the west side of the office suite, it'll offer a better flow. But if you really want to—"

"No, if you think it would work better over here," Drake said, pointing down at the blueprint that was spread across a workbench, "then let's go with that. I trust your judgment."

"Now, that was a little too easy," Harris cracked. "Are you sure you're okay? You're not going to give me a list of reasons why you want it where we originally planned for it to be? You know, like you usually do."

"Quit being a smart-ass before I change my mind. Anything else on the drawing that we need to revisit?"

Harris shook his head as he glanced at his notepad. "Nah, I think that's it."

They were doing a major remodel to an office building that Drake's company had recently purchased, and the plans needed to be approved by the city before they moved forward.

"By the way, I heard that the proposal for the Lincoln project is a no-go. How'd that happen?"

Drake rubbed the back of his neck as tension seeped into his muscles. Just once he wanted a project to go off without a hitch, but that was impossible. When it came to construction, one hundred percent of the time they ran into a snag with inspectors, or an issue with contractors, or some major disaster that blew up the budget. He knew it was the nature of the job, but still . . .

"Glad you asked because I'm going to pull you in on that project. I'll fill you in on it next week. Right now I want to make sure we're all set with the plans for this building."

He and Harris walked through parts of the five-story building again, double-checking the changes they were thinking of making to the design. Drake loved this part of his job—planning and creating something new. The best part was watching the spaces transform into his vision.

If he could, he'd give up his office and hang out in the field, but being the boss meant sitting behind his desk and being on the telephone for most of his day.

Forty-five minutes later, Drake was back at his desk going through emails. His cell phone vibrated and he picked it up, glad to see that Jeffrey was calling him back. He owed the old man an apology, and he also wanted to talk to him about the added stipulations regarding the offer he had submitted.

"Hey, Jeffrey, thanks for calling me back."

"What I should be doing is going upside your head with a bat," the old man said, and that brought a smile to Drake's lips.

How many times had Jeffrey threatened to do just that over the years? He often said that Drake was an impatient hothead. Drake was glad he had grown out of that stage. Mostly.

"In my defense, you and Isaac caught me off guard. Why didn't you tell me what you were planning?"

"I don't have to tell you everything. I keep you informed with the things I want you to know. It's always been like that, and this time is no different."

Drake sighed. "I'm sorry for the way I acted this morning. I was way out of line."

"Yes, you were, but I understand, and I forgive you. I know what that property means to you," his mentor said, his voice softening.

Drake threw up his hands and rocked back in his seat. "Then why didn't you just sell it to me, instead of making me jump through unnecessary hoops? You know why I want that building."

Not only would the property look good in his financial portfolio, but his main reason for wanting it was because it was a part of his family's legacy. The Hollywood property was the first building Drake's father had ever designed. As an architect, he had designed numerous structures, but nothing like the Hollywood property that was for sale.

"I know, but son, who's to say others don't have just as good a reason to buy the building?"

"But if you had sold it to me before putting it on the market, it wouldn't have mattered why others want the building because it would be mine."

Frustration grew inside of Drake, but he was determined to keep his cool. Then he thought about Morgan. What were her intentions for the property?

Considering he hadn't given her an opportunity to say her peace before the meeting, he also had no idea why she had approached him afterward.

For a person who claimed to not want anything to do with her, he couldn't help wondering what she'd been going to say. He might never know, and for some reason, that bothered him. Yeah, he was still hurt by the way she'd treated him years ago, but he was also curious about the person she had become.

"Trust me. Anything that's meant to be will be," Jeffrey said, and if Drake didn't know any better, he'd have thought the old man was talking about Morgan. "I have no doubt that all will work out just fine. If that property is meant to be yours, it will be."

Drake huffed out a breath and pinched the bridge of his nose. He loved his mentor like a father, but there were times when the old man worked his last nerve.

"So after the letters, what's next in this process?" he asked.

"You'll find out if your letter is chosen. I suggest you get off the phone and start working on it."

"Come on, Jeffrey. Just tell me."

Silence filled the phone line, and Drake pulled the device from his ear and glanced at the screen, which was black.

Well, damn. The old man had hung up on him.

Drake sat the phone on the desk and figured now was as good a time as any to start pouring his heart out in a letter. He just hoped it would be enough to move on to the next stage.

Chapter Ten

"WHY ARE YOU IN SUCH A GOOD MOOD?" ADDISON ASKED Drake as he strolled alongside her, pushing a shopping cart. They were doing their bimonthly trip to the grocery store as a family, though he had no idea where Aiden had run off to.

"I'm always in a good mood," he said, and laughed when his sister gave him an *are you serious* look.

He had to admit that this Saturday morning did seem brighter than usual. It probably had everything to do with the fact that he had heard from Jeffrey's assistant, Isaac, the day before. His company, Faulkner Development Group, had moved to the next level. With the passionate letter he had written about his father and what it would mean to own a building that he helped design, Drake had no doubt that he would be one of the ones that were chosen.

What came next was still a mystery, though. According to Isaac, next steps would be explained during yet another meeting, taking place Monday morning. Drake wondered why Jeffrey came up with the whole idea of turning a simple building purchase into some type of X Games event.

"Am I the only one getting tired of grocery shopping as a family?" Drake asked as he grabbed a jumbo-size peanut butter from the shelf and placed it in the cart. "I'm thinking we should make some changes."

"Nooo," Addison protested. "This is our bonding time. It's the only day that we all intentionally hang out together."

Out of the three of them, she was the most family-oriented, wanting them to do as much as possible as a trio. That was how the whole group grocery trips came to be.

When the kids were younger, Drake had set up the grocery run as a way for them all to do something together. The older they got, the more mundane the experience became. As far as he was concerned, they did plenty together. It would be so much easier to do the food shopping himself or hire one of those delivery services to handle the task.

"I vote we keep up the tradition until Aiden and I go off to college. Then you and your future wife can decide what you want to do about the groceries."

Drake glanced at Addison to see if she was being facetious, but she was serious as she grabbed barbecue sauce and placed it into the cart. She and Matteo were double-teaming him about dating. At least Addison's intentions came from a good place. She was concerned that he would be all alone when she and Aiden left for college. He wasn't a hundred percent sure why Matteo was trying to marry him off, though.

Until recently, dating had been the last thing on Drake's mind. Now he wavered back and forth. Just when he thought he was ready to put himself out there, he'd have a bad date that made him think twice about settling down. Like his outing with Sophia the other night.

He shivered internally at the thought of getting together with her or anyone like her ever again.

But after running into Morgan, Drake was reminded of the life plan that he had created while in college. He had accomplished everything except for marriage and having kids of his own.

Granted, over the years his desire to have kids waned, but deep down, he still wanted to find that special woman to share his life with. There'd been a time when he'd thought that would be Morgan. When things didn't work out between them, he'd put the idea out of his mind.

Maybe now it was time to revisit that goal.

"Wait up."

Drake glanced over his shoulder and spotted Aiden hurrying toward them. His arms were full as he precariously juggled items to keep them from falling. When he reached the cart, he dropped everything in, clearly not caring that he could break or smash something.

Aiden blew out a breath and leaned on the cart. "Man, that was close. I almost dropped this stuff twice." He glanced down at his treasures. "We should be able to leave soon since I got all of the important stuff."

Donuts, cookies, chips, ground beef, bratwursts, and hamburger and hotdog buns. Before Drake could tell him what to put back, his brother left them again.

"God, I hate when he does this," Addison grumbled, and took out the items she knew that Drake wouldn't approve of.

At least one of them knew the routine.

"I'll be back," she said holding up the donuts and chips. "I'm going to return this stuff."

That was code for: *I'm putting these back and getting the items I want.*

Drake glanced down at his phone, which held the grocery list, and grabbed relish before leaving the aisle. He had barely made it down the next one when Addison returned with a different, larger pack of cookies, plus cheese, yogurt, and a few other items that were on the list.

"Thanks, sweetheart."

"Maybe instead of the three of us doing the shopping in the future, it can be just the two of us," Addison said. "I'm sure Aiden won't care. Besides, then we can do this in half the time because I won't have to return all of the junk he picks up."

"Good point and not a bad idea," Drake said. Addison held on to the end of the cart, guiding it a little as they turned the corner to head to another aisle.

"Drake, can we . . ."

They had barely taken two steps when he noticed a woman stepping on the lower shelf in order to reach something on the very top one.

Definitely an accident waiting to happen, he mused. No sooner had the thought crossed his mind than a couple of boxes of breadcrumbs tumbled to the floor.

It looked as if the store was rearranging shelves and had stopped before they finished, leaving many of the bottom ones almost empty. Breadcrumbs, cornstarch, flour, and sugar were mostly up top, and unfortunately, people had to reach up high to get what they wanted.

The pint-size woman stepped down with a container of cornstarch, and before she could pick the items up off the floor, more boxes and containers fell, and the domino effect was in full force.

Drake had never seen anything like it.

"Whoa!" Addison gasped, and her hands went to her mouth.

"Oh no!" The woman covered her head with her arms and shrieked, "No, no, no, this can't be happening!"

Drake pulled up short. *No way.*

He knew that voice.

He'd heard the sweet, lyrical sound enough in his dreams over the last week to know who it belonged to.

Morgan?

His heart kicked against his chest, but before Drake could totally process that the petite woman trying to gather boxes from the floor was Morgan, he spotted a bag of flour right above her teetering on the edge of the top shelf.

"Look out!" he yelled and lunged forward, snatching the bag midair. It split open and fell, sending the white powdery substance falling like snow.

There was nothing he could do about it, and his momentum threw him off balance at the same time that Morgan decided to stand up.

Sonofa . . .

Unable to stop, Drake slid his arm around Morgan, turning slightly to keep from falling on top of her. Instead, they both crashed to the floor, covered in flour.

"Oomph," he said when she landed on top of him, knocking the air out of him.

Her pretty brown eyes were wide with shock and her mouth hung open until she realized it was him.

"Are you kidding me? What is wrong with you? Did you really just tackle me to the ground right now? Urgh!"

"Seriously?" he ground between clinched teeth. "I try and keep your cute little ass from getting pounded by breadcrumbs and flour and you think I'm tackling you?"

She shoved against him. "Just let me up." She shifted on top of him. Their precarious position had him feeling every inch of her lithe body, and the familiarity was doing wicked things to his peace of mind. But with the way she was moving, she was getting a little too close to his . . .

Shit.

Drake sucked in a breath and groaned when she made contact with his dick. Considering the way she froze, it was safe to say she felt his semi-erection pressing into her.

"Oops," she whispered, and amusement radiated in her eyes. Her plump lips that he used to feast on twitched. To her credit, she didn't burst out laughing, but he sensed she wanted to.

Drake closed his eyes and groaned when she started trying to get up again.

"Just. Stop. Moving," he said between gritted teeth.

This time she did laugh, and he growled in frustration, only making her laugh harder.

With a little effort, he lifted her off himself and moved her to the side so that he could sit up. Flour was everywhere, including on his clothes.

That's also when he saw the small crowd of people who had gathered to gawk at them.

Oh, this just keeps getting better.

Drake made eye contact with his sister, who was giggling behind her hand while her shoulders shook. Others weren't trying to hide their amusement and were outright laughing.

He guessed they did look pretty ridiculous lying in flour on the floor and surrounded by various containers. The only person not laughing was the elderly woman with shocking white hair and a disapproving scowl on her face.

Morgan hurried to her feet, while it took him a little longer as he slipped on the flour.

"What a mess," Morgan said as she dusted off her dress and assessed the damage she'd made. "We really have to stop meeting like this," she cracked.

Drake just stared at her.

One of the things he used to love about her was her carefree attitude and ability to bounce back from any situation. But right now that carefree attitude was pissing him off, and he wanted to strangle her. Minutes ago, he'd gone out of his way to help her, leaving him embarrassed and on the floor in a grocery store aisle covered in flour. Yet her entitled ass couldn't even bother to say thank you or ask if he was okay.

Irritation and disappointment warred inside of him. This situation was college all over again. Clearly, she still lacked the ability to see that certain circumstances weren't just about her. Years ago, she'd left him without saying goodbye, not caring what her leaving would do to him. He'd been crushed while she galivanted around the world. Though this instance wasn't nearly as emotional as back then, her careless attitude and lack of awareness about the incident only made him angrier.

Drake's attention was brought back to their present situation when their small audience dispersed.

Morgan stared down at the mess on the floor and shook her head. "I can't believe this."

"Are you hurt?" Addison asked her. "Because if you are, I'll be your witness that this stuff fell on you. I recorded most of it on my cell phone. Maybe we should find the manager and—"

"Oh, no. I'm fine. Just embarrassed."

Drake moved over to Addison. "Erase it. Now," he said, his voice making it clear that he was serious.

Addison smacked her lips. "Fine. Geez." She turned her attention back to Morgan. "I'm glad you're not hurt."

"*Hurt?*" Drake scoffed. "You should be asking *me* if I'm hurt, considering she had me flat on my back."

His sister slammed her hands on her narrow hips. "Drake, you're bigger than her. You could've crushed her."

He threw up his arms. "Did you not see that she was on top of me?"

"Oh, I saw it, and so did half the people in the store," Addison said on a giggle. "Good thing Aiden wasn't here. You would never live this down."

"Yeah, good thing," Drake grumbled.

The store manager and another employee came over to make sure everyone was okay. Once it was determined that they were, the staff hurried to clean up the mess.

Drake had stepped to the side and was dusting himself off while listening as Addison and Morgan chatted as if they'd known each other for years. The twins had been so young when he and Morgan had dated. There was no way his sister remembered her . . . or did she? By their conversation, it didn't seem like it.

Drake studied Morgan, and all the old feelings came back in a rush. Good and bad ones. She was so gentle, kind, and compassionate. Like no other woman he'd ever met. In college, they hadn't been at a place in their lives to be thinking about marriage. Drake had been in love with her. He had thought the feeling was mutual; at least that's what she'd told him. Apparently, she hadn't loved him enough.

"By the way, I'm Morgan," Drake heard her say when he tuned back in to their conversation, and Morgan stuck out her hand to his sister, who shook it.

"I'm Addison. It's nice to meet you. Oh, and this is my brother, Drake."

"We've met," Drake said gruffly.

"Yeah, I know your brother very well. So well, in fact, I'm hoping that he and I can talk for a minute."

"We have nothing to discuss," Drake bit out, and Addison gasped.

"What's wrong with you? Why are you being so rude?" his sister snapped. "Especially when I want to know where she got her dress from."

Drake's brow lifted at her outburst, and then he almost smiled at her admission. Addison loved fashion and had recently mentioned that when she grew up, she wanted to be either a buyer, a stylist, or a fashion designer.

Actually, now that he thought about it, that had been Morgan's plan too.

"Don't mind him. He doesn't usually act like this. He's a really . . . Wait. How do you guys know each other?"

"Well, we . . ." Morgan started, and Drake wasn't sure what she saw on his face, but she quickly diverted her gaze. "We met in college."

"Oh," Addison said, looking back and forth between them when suddenly her eyes grew large. "*Ohhh*, I see. You guys must've *reeeally* known each other. Tell me more."

"There's nothing to tell. We dated. Then we didn't. Case closed."

Drake knew he was being an ass, but he couldn't seem to help himself. Why should he be nice to Morgan when she treated him like shit on the bottom of her overpriced shoes?

Nope. She doesn't deserve kindness.

Chapter Eleven

MORGAN WANTED TO THROAT PUNCH DRAKE.

Why was he being such a jerk? She should be the angry one. Yes, she made a mess in the middle of the aisle, but it wasn't like she'd asked for his help—he just butted into her business.

His funky attitude was getting old, and she wanted to pop him upside his big, stubborn head.

But more than anything, she wanted them to talk and clear the air. Yet, how could she do that if he refused to hear her out?

And the twins? Well, Addison. Morgan couldn't believe how big she was, and it was mind-blowing how much she resembled Drake. The age difference made him come across more like her father than her older brother. Then again, he pretty much had played both roles.

"Morgan, what are you even doing here?" Drake asked with annoyance in his tone.

"I was grocery shopping until you slammed into me," she said, putting a box of breadcrumbs in her cart. "What are *you* doing here?" she asked with the same amount of indignation in her tone. "I've lived in the area for months and haven't seen you here before."

"Well, this is our store," he countered.

She frowned. "You own this place?"

Addison laughed. "No. We've just been coming here for years. Now, even if my socially challenged brother doesn't want to talk to you, can you tell me where you got your dress? I need one for our homecoming dance at school. Maybe wherever you got your outfit from, they'll have something appropriate for me."

Homecoming dance?

Morgan did a mental calculation trying to determine how old the twins were now. If they were in high school, then they were at least fourteen or fifteen.

Where had the time gone? When she and Drake were dating, the twins were toddlers, getting into everything. She had only seen them a few times, but one had stuck in her mind.

One particular date night, he had received a call from the sitter, telling him she was sick and needed to go home. Drake hadn't had time to drop Morgan off back at her dorm, so she went home with him. Aiden and Addison were only a few years old, and the cutest little kids she'd ever seen.

But Morgan hadn't stuck around long, needing to get back so that she could study. At least that was the excuse she'd given Drake when he suggested she stay the night. That was the start of her understanding the type of responsibility he was dealing with.

"I made this dress," Morgan said, her heart swelling with pride at the shock on Addison's face.

Even Drake's expression softened as his gaze roamed the length of her, taking in the short emerald-green dress that had a slit and ruffles going up the left side of her body. The long bell sleeves were Morgan's favorite part of the outfit.

She was glad that she had taken care in deciding what to

wear. She was heading to brunch with a couple of friends but stopped at the grocery store to prepare for cooking lessons with her former nanny, Nana, later that day. Nana had insisted on coming over after Morgan had burned the food she'd cooked the night before, and had even emailed her a grocery list. "You really made that outfit? Do you sew for a living?" Addison asked, reeling off one question after another. Her excitement was rubbing off on Morgan.

She could admit to enjoying the attention and the admiration she received when people saw some of her designs and liked them. But not enough to return to school and finish her degree.

She had always loved all things fashion. Everything from fabric to the cut of an outfit. When she was Addison's age, she'd been practically obsessed with drawing and shopping. She would see an outfit on a hanger and try to decide how she could make it better or different. Shopping was still her jam, but she didn't sketch as much as she used to.

"Yes, I make quite a few of my clothes, but I don't sew for a living." The part of Morgan that wanted everyone to know she was doing something worthwhile professionally wanted to tell Addison that she had a more important, fulfilling job. Maybe then Drake would take her seriously if he knew she was actually doing something with her life.

"Do you make clothes for other people? Can you make me a dress for my homecoming dance? I'll pay you," Addison said, hope brimming in her eyes.

Oh boy. Morgan wouldn't mind making her a dress, but big brother Drake looked like he had eaten something bitter.

He cleared his throat. "I don't think that'll—"

"I'm talking to her, Drake," Addison said with authority, and Morgan struggled to keep from laughing. She didn't know Drake's little sister, but already she liked her. Clearly, she had a mind of her own and wasn't afraid to put her brother in his place.

That alone had Morgan ready to say yes to whatever Addison asked.

"I'd be happy to." Morgan looked at Drake, daring him to object. He didn't, but the angry glare he sent Morgan could've burned her to the ground. "Do you have a cell phone?" she asked Addison. "I'll give you my number."

Addison bounced up and down with excitement as she handed over her bejeweled phone. "Thank you so much. Can you make anything? Do you have ideas? Or should I come up with some?"

As Morgan typed in her number, she said, "I have some ideas and can let you look through my portfolio." That wasn't something she did often. In fact, her soon-to-be sister-in-law, Dreamy, was the only person she'd let look through it lately. Mainly because Dreamy had wanted to get some ideas before she had Morgan design her wedding gown. That had been a few months ago.

Dreamy and Karter's wedding was coming up quick, and in a couple of weeks, everyone would see the most beautiful dress Morgan had ever created. She was excited because it had turned out even better than she'd imagined. The only problem with that, though, was Morgan's mother. Kalena Redford would no doubt start hounding her again about a career in fashion.

"Here you go." Morgan handed Addison's phone back. "I texted myself so that I could have your number too. Call me when you want to get started."

"I will," Addison squealed and hugged Morgan before pulling away. "Now I'm going to go find my knuckleheaded brother and let you and this brother talk." She turned to Drake, and though her voice was low, Morgan still heard her say, *Be nice to her. Or else.*"

After his sister left them alone, Drake moved closer, unapologetically invading her personal space as he towered over her. He seemed even taller today since she was wearing flats, but not intimidating to the point of making her uncomfortable.

And were his shoulders broader?

It seemed each time she was in his presence, she noticed something else about him. Like his heady cologne, a mix of sandalwood and vanilla, which surrounded her like a warm blanket on a cold winter's night.

This man. This tall, gorgeous, stubborn human being still made her body come alive. The visceral effect he had on her without even saying a word or touching her was mind-blowing, even after all these years.

"We have nothing to discuss," Drake said, his voice low and sharp. "But I've already told you that."

"I think we do, and it's time we cleared the air. That way when we run into each other again it won't be so awkward."

"We won't be—"

Morgan stopped his words with a lift of her hand. "Have you forgotten that I agreed to make your sister a dress?"

He cursed under his breath and rubbed the back of his neck. "Tell her you changed your mind."

Morgan leaned back and frowned. "There's no way I'm telling her that. Did you see how excited she was? Besides, do you really want to be dragged around from one department store to another to find an outfit that she'd be satisfied with?"

Drake huffed out a breath. "Fine, we can talk, but not here."

They agreed to meet later that evening at a bar that they both were familiar with.

"That'll work. I'll see you later." He turned and walked away without a backward glance.

As Morgan pushed her cart down the aisle, she wished she'd asked Drake if he had heard from Kellner's office. She had gotten the call that her letter was accepted and she was moving on to the next stage. Was he?

I can ask him later, she thought as a smile spread across her face. Not only would she get to see him again, she would also get to explain her reasons for walking away all those years ago.

Her smile slipped and dread seeped into her body. He already hated her. What if she couldn't get him to understand that she'd had to leave, that she'd had to step back and figure out her future? Would he hate her even more?

A groan bubbled inside of her. Of course he wouldn't understand. Dealing with his stubborn ass, she was probably going to make the situation worse.

I need to get my story straight, because he's not going to make this easy.

Chapter Twelve

"WHAT ARE YOU DOING? I THOUGHT YOU HAD A DATE," AIDEN said as he stood in the doorway of Drake's closet, a can of soda in his hand. His attention went to the two suits that Drake was inspecting.

"It's not a date, and I'm trying to decide which one of these I'm wearing tonight."

He had narrowed his choices down to a black suit with faint gray pinstripes and a gray shirt or a dark gray suit with a burgundy shirt. He'd planned to leave out the tie, wanting to look as casual as possible.

"Good thing it's not a date, because those suits look like something you would wear to a meeting or maybe even a funeral. Uncle Matt said you're hooking up with an old girlfriend. She's going to think you're an old dude if you show up in one of those." Aiden leaned against the doorjamb. His legs were crossed at the ankles as he took a swig of his drink. "If you're trying to get back with your girl, those aren't going to work."

"First of all, I'm not trying to get back with her—or anyone else, for that matter. Secondly, I don't look old in my suits. I look hip . . . cool . . . phat," he said, unsure what the latest terms were to describe that he still had it going on.

Aiden shook his head. "Just stop. You sound so ancient right now. And if you're not trying to get back with this lady, why are you going out with her?"

Why indeed.

Drake had been asking himself the same question ever since they'd left the grocery store. He should've stuck with his original plan where she was concerned—stay the heck away from her. But he'd be lying if he said he wasn't interested in learning what happened to make her leave him back in college. It wasn't the fact that she had dumped him that had him still pissed. No, his anger and disappointment stemmed from the way she'd done it.

Who leaves the country without telling her boyfriend that she's going?

No phone call.

No letter.

Hell, not even a postcard.

Yeah, Drake wanted to know why. He just had to make sure he was prepared for the answer, but he was fairly sure she couldn't say anything that would be forgivable. Her rejection had crushed him at a vulnerable stage in his life. He'd been juggling raising the twins, attending college full time, and working a part-time job. All the while trying to give Morgan as much of his attention as he could. Somehow through all of that, he had managed to fall in love with her.

Still, she hadn't thought enough of him to tell him to his face that they were over.

Sure, they had been young, and it probably hadn't been a good idea to get so serious with her, but Drake hadn't been able to help it. There had been something about Morgan from day one that drew him to her like a moth to a flame, and based on his reaction to seeing her again, that hadn't changed. Since the meeting, he hadn't been able to stop thinking about her, wondering what she was up to these days, and curious about whether she was seeing anyone.

"Hold up. Is your date the hottie from the grocery store?" They all had spotted Morgan leaving, and Addison had told Aiden about their encounter with her.

"Don't call her a hottie. She's a grown woman. Show some respect," Drake chastised, even if he agreed. Morgan somehow managed to get more beautiful each time he saw her.

"Dang, bro, grown women can be hot. Even I know that. If it is that lady, she was *hot*, and you need to see an eye doctor if you didn't notice."

"Man, be quiet. I noticed, and yes, she's the one I'm meeting tonight," Drake mumbled and went back to looking at the garments in his hands. "And her name is Morgan."

Aiden huffed out an exasperated breath and stomped into the walk-in closet that was larger than some average-size bedrooms.

When Drake had built the home a few years ago, he'd wanted a master closet that could accommodate clothing for two people. He might not have been actively looking for a partner, but he figured one day he might. His home was built for a family. A family that included a wife for him.

"You're going to have to step up your game if you're going to be hanging with Morgan. I could tell from a distance that she had it going on, and she can probably get any dude she wants." He set his drink on top of the center island in the closet, despite Drake's scowl. "Where are you taking her?"

"We're meeting at a bar in Hollywood." Drake couldn't believe he was seriously thinking of taking advice from his knuckleheaded brother. The kid still played with rubber snakes, but he had to admit, Aiden knew the latest styles and might be able to help.

He bypassed the suits and slowed at the row of sports jackets, giving them a once-over, before moving to the trousers. "Have you been to this place before? Is it a dressy bar or more like a sports bar?"

Drake narrowed his eyes at his brother. "What do you know about bars? Please tell me you haven't—"

"Dude." Aiden turned to him, his brows in a deep *V.* "I don't have to go to a bar to know that some are dumps while others are nice. And come on, I binge-watched that old show you used to talk about all the time . . . *Cheers.* I've seen the inside of a bar."

Aiden shook his head and sighed loudly while Drake stifled a laugh. His brother acted like a punk kid sometimes. While other times, he acted and sounded older than his fourteen years.

And that *old* show that he was referring to was a classic. Their parents watched it all the time, and after they died, Drake found himself watching the reruns.

A smile kicked up the corner of his lips as he remembered how he used to call Matteo *Sam,* especially while they were in college. His friend had a steady flow of women vying for his attention the way the *Cheers* character had.

"The bar is nice. It's a large sports bar," Drake finally said, and hung up the suits that he'd been holding. Now that he thought about it, he would stand out—and not in a good way—if he strolled into the place on a Saturday night wearing a suit. He hadn't been there in a while, but he couldn't imagine that it had changed that much.

"Okay, the Lakers are playing tonight. It'll probably be a lot of people there slamming back beers and stuff," Aiden said, though it sounded like he was talking to himself. "You should wear some jeans . . . or maybe khakis and a Henley. Oh, and boots. Women like men in boots, especially Timberlands." He pointed at his feet. "Which is why I wear mine a lot."

Drake folded his arms across his chest and leaned a hip

against the center island. "And what do you think you know about women?" he asked as Aiden proceeded to lay out an outfit for him, including the Timberland boots that he and Addison had bought Drake for Christmas the year before. The same pair Drake had worn once or twice, and only because they complained that he never liked the gifts they bought him.

"Clearly, I know more than you do since I know how to dress for a date. Besides, I was right when I said that Kira was going to love my snake."

"Your ass better be talking about that stupid toy," Drake said, though he was sure that's what Aiden was talking about. Well, he was pretty sure.

"Of course that's what I'm talking about. What else would I be referring to?" his brother asked seriously, but Drake didn't miss the mischief in his dark eyes.

"I thought I told you not to take that thing to school."

"I didn't. We met at a smoothie place this morning. I showed it to her then, and for the record, when I set it on the table, she fell out laughing. I'm talking she was *rolling*, man! I knew she was going to think it was cool. She even asked if she could keep it. Which means, I'm going to need another snake, but a real one this time."

Unbelievable.

Drake had practically given Morgan a heart attack with the spider fiasco. Granted, he hadn't meant to scare her, but he'd handled the situation all wrong. Clearly, his kid brother had more game than he did.

"Wait a minute. I told you and Addison that you guys are too young to date. Hooking up at a smoothie place sounds like a date."

Aiden lifted his arm and glanced at his smartwatch. "Oh, would you look at the time. Shouldn't you be going?" he asked as he hurried out of the closet. Before Drake could say anything else, Aiden had fled the room.

He was right about one thing. Drake needed to hurry up if he didn't want to be late for his date.

Wait. Not a date. This is just two people getting together to talk. Nothing else. At least that's what he told himself.

AN HOUR LATER, DRAKE SAT AT THE BAR NURSING A BEER, wondering if Morgan would show up. She was twenty minutes late, which wasn't unusual, because the old Morgan couldn't be on time if her life depended on it.

Apparently, some things hadn't changed.

The problem was, it wasn't until a moment ago that he realized that they hadn't exchanged contact information. Drake couldn't call her even if he wanted to. Well, unless he called Addison, who actually had Morgan's telephone number, but no way was he calling his sister for this. Because who went on a date with someone without getting their contact information?

Drake sat up straighter when he realized the route his thoughts had gone.

This is not a date.

This was two people getting together to clear the air. That's all. Nothing more. He'd keep telling himself that until it sunk in.

He brought the beer bottle up to his mouth and took a long drag on it. He'd give her until he was done with his drink. After that, he was out of there. He might never know what went wrong between them, but at this point, would that be so bad? It wasn't like he could reach back into the past and change anything.

Maybe some things really are better left unsaid.

Cheers went up around the bar when LeBron James made another three-pointer, his sixth one in a row, with only two minutes left in the game. It seemed more people had entered the building and were standing closer to the bar as the minutes of the game ticked by.

Perhaps meeting there hadn't been a good idea. Everyone talked at once and the noise level on top of the televisions blaring was almost deafening. If Morgan showed up, maybe he'd suggest they go somewhere else. Or hell, they could talk in his truck.

Drake brought his beer bottle to his mouth but stopped inches before it touched his lips when the hair on the back of his neck stood at attention. He didn't have to look behind him to know what had caused the stimulating sensation. He already knew.

Morgan was there.

He set the beer bottle down with a thunk and slowly swiveled around on the bar stool. At first, he didn't see her as he scanned the area near the entrance, but then the top of her head came into view, and then the rest of her.

Drake's mouth went dry.

He still remembered her as that girl in college with her natural beauty on full display as she roamed around campus in baggy clothes and not a care in the world. It was hard to reconcile that this was the same woman. This version of Morgan was all grown up and classy while managing to look sexy as hell.

She hadn't spotted him yet, and that gave him the opportunity to soak in all of her sexiness. Again, her braids were piled high on her head the way they'd been the other day, but instead of being nice and neat, she had them in a loose ponytail, giving her a carefree vibe.

The skintight, beige button-down shirt that was tucked into a pair of matching riding pants molded over her upper body and emphasized her more-than-a-handful perky breasts. His gaze traveled down her hourglass figure, admiring the way her pants hugged her firm thighs and shapely legs. The high-heeled, camel-colored, knee-high suede boots and the large matching bag added to the outfit, making her ooze sophistication while also looking trendy.

Gorgeous.

The woman is frickin' gorgeous.

When she finally spotted him and the right corner of her lips lifted into a seductive grin, Drake's heart kicked against his rib cage and his breath stalled. It was as if someone was squeezing his windpipe and stopping blood flow to his brain. Instead, all of it traveled south.

This was such a bad idea.

He shouldn't have ever agreed to meet her. All the old feelings for her were back, and there was no way he could spend time with her and not want more.

Shit. I'm screwed.

That's how it had been back in college. He wouldn't say it was love at first sight, but pretty damn close. Morgan had effortlessly snagged his attention and he'd been a goner from that point on.

Well . . . until she left him.

Chapter Thirteen

MORGAN'S SMILE DROPPED AND HER STEPS FALTERED WHEN
Drake's appreciative gaze suddenly turned sour. First a flat tire,
now she had to deal with his jacked-up attitude.

Well, she was ready for him. She would tell him what she
wanted him to know, then move on with her life. And no way
would she allow him to ruin her evening.

"Sorry I'm late," she greeted.

"Some things never change," Drake mumbled, barely sparing
her a glance as he brought his beer bottle to his lips.

"Not that you care, but when I went to get into my car, I realized I had a flat tire. I had to call for a car to pick me up."

That made him look at her. "Are you okay?"

Hmm . . . so maybe he didn't despise her as much as he was
acting like he did. Her heart leaped at the thought, and she didn't
miss the concern in his eyes. But just as fast, his detached expression was back.

She'd seen it. A flicker of her old Drake. Well, not hers, but
the man she used to know. The man she used to love. Sitting

next to her was a virtual stranger. There was so much she didn't know about his life now, and if she was honest with herself, she wanted to know everything.

Did she have that right? He woulda, coulda, shoulda still been hers, but she had foolishly walked away. No, she hadn't walked. She'd run.

"I'm fine, but the last thing I wanted was to be late. I appreciate you taking the time to meet with me."

"Sorry to hear about your car," Drake said, and returned his attention to the television.

Instead of responding, Morgan lifted her hand to signal the bartender. A moment later, he was putting a cocktail napkin down in front of her.

"Hey, beautiful. What can I get you?"

"Can I get a dirty martini? Two olives."

"Coming right up."

"Oh, and put it on his tab," she said pointing at Drake with her thumb.

The bartender smirked and glanced at Drake, who rolled his eyes but gave an imperceptible nod. If he was still the man he used to be, he would've bought her drink anyway. However, Morgan wasn't sure which Drake she was dealing with. Her loving, compassionate, protective college sweetheart, or the guy who'd barely cracked a smile since she ran into him the other day.

Morgan had spent most of the day mentally preparing for this moment, but now that she was there with him, she wasn't sure where to start. And considering how noisy it was, meeting in a sports bar might not have been a good idea. There was only a minute left in the game that the Lakers were leading. Maybe everyone would leave after they won.

The bartender set her martini in front of her.

"Thanks."

"My pleasure," he said, his eyes lingering on the spot above the swell of her breasts just a little longer than she deemed appropriate. She was used to men ogling her, but it was interesting that he'd done it in front of Drake. Then again, it wasn't like he could tell they were together.

Morgan glanced toward the back of the building where tables and no televisions were located. When she spotted an empty one, she nudged Drake's arm to get his attention.

"Would you mind if we grabbed a table? It's a little too loud over here." Besides the tables, in the back there were a couple of pool tables and dart boards. They were being used, but still, there weren't as many people in that area.

"Sure. Lead the way."

He dropped a few bills on the bar, grabbed his beer bottle, and stood.

Morgan smiled when she noticed they were wearing the same colors. Back in college, they'd never been the type of couple to match outfits, but they'd often end up dressing similarly as if they'd planned it. Tonight, Drake was dressed casually while also looking *GQ* in a white button-down, khakis, and a pair of Timberland boots that were the same camel color as the boots she was wearing. The man was extremely handsome in a suit, but she definitely liked this dressed-down version of him as well.

As she walked in front of him, Morgan could feel Drake's eyes burning her backside, causing her to put a little extra hip action into every step. Which wasn't easy considering she had to maneuver through pockets of people.

"Man, you're crazy. You don't stand a chance," a college-aged guy said as Morgan tried to move around him.

She gasped and lifted her glass away from her body when he and the other man started roughhousing and bumped into her. Alcohol spilled over her hand and down her wrist.

"Hey!" Drake barked and stiff-armed one of them when they

bumped into her again, this time practically knocking her over. "Watch what the hell you're doing."

The guy, whose eyes were bloodshot red, blinked several times, and staggered from side to side, trying to get his balance. The man was so drunk, a slight breeze could've knocked him over.

He looked at her and Drake as if seeing them for the first time.

"Oh, hey, my . . . my bad," he slurred and narrowed his eyes, clearly trying to focus in on them.

Drake cursed under his breath and placed his hand at the small of Morgan's back, sending a sweet thrill up her spine. He was so big and intimidating, and she secretly loved how protective he was and how secure in his hold she felt.

"Just move out the way," he said to the guy but guided Morgan around him. He didn't drop his hand until they were at the table.

"I guess this bar wasn't a good idea." Morgan slid into the booth. "Normally, it's not this crowded in here."

"So, what did you want to talk about?" Drake said.

Well, all-righty, then. No small talk.

"Are you planning to be an asshole all night?" she asked.

"Yes," he said with a straight face.

Morgan tried not to laugh but a grin slipped through anyway. Drake just glowered. If he was trying to be a hard-ass, it was working. *Kinda.* But each time she looked at him, including now, she didn't see an asshole. She only saw the man she had fallen in love with so many years ago. The one who was ambitious, never rude or disrespectful, and always treated her like she was a gift from God.

Morgan had fallen hard for him, mainly because he was such a gentle and kind sweetheart of a man. But she had to admit that she found Asshole Drake just as alluring.

"I don't have all day. Talk."

Morgan sighed. "You're not going to make this easy, are you?"

"Nope. You didn't make it easy for me when you left. Why should I make it easy for you now?"

Damn. A dagger straight to the heart.

"Drake, I get that you're still angry, and I don't blame you." Morgan covered his hand with hers and was glad he didn't pull away. "I get it, and I understand why you hate me."

His thick, dark eyebrows scrunched together. "I never said I hated you. I just despise the way you treated me and the way you left. For years, I've struggled to understand why you did that."

"Okay, sorry for the delay," the server interrupted. The young woman pushed a lock of long auburn hair behind her ear, then tugged down the cropped T-shirt that was paired with skin-tight black leggings. "What can I get you two?" she asked cheerfully.

Morgan might've been a little hungry when she first walked in but diving into the conversation with Drake had ruined her appetite. "Just a glass of water for me," she said, and drank more of her martini.

Drake tucked the menu back into the holder on the table. "Can I get an order of buffalo wings, potato skins, and mozzarella sticks?" He held up his bottle. "And another beer."

Well, clearly his appetite was fine.

Once the server confirmed the order, she stepped away from the table and Drake said, "Why'd you leave? Why not just talk to me?" He sounded exasperated, with a twinge of hurt in his tone.

"I couldn't," she said weakly. "At the time, I just felt too inadequate to be with you. It was hard enough to admit it to myself. There was no way I could admit it to you." After a beat, when he didn't respond, Morgan continued. "I never meant to hurt you, and I'm so sorry."

"I don't want an apology, Angel!" he snapped, then huffed out a breath and looked away. After a slight hesitation, he said, "I mean, Morgan. I just want . . . I want to understand. We talked about everything, or so I thought. I—"

"I wasn't ready for what you were ready for, Drake. You had your life all mapped out and knew what you wanted. I didn't." When he started to speak, she held up her hands. "Please, let me finish." Because if he didn't, she might not be able to tell him all that she wanted to say, what he needed to hear.

He nodded for her to continue.

"I . . . no, *we* were so young back then, but I had never met someone as smart, driven, and in control as you. And being with you made me realize how much I was lacking, how much growing up I still needed to do. I barely had declared a major, but you, you had your shit together.

"A weaker man wouldn't have been able to attend school, raise two toddlers, and work part time. I felt like such a slacker. Then when you started talking about all of your big plans for the future, and you had included me in them, I panicked."

Thinking back, her excuses sounded weak, but at the time, her panic was very real. In college, she might've been considered an adult, but Morgan hadn't been prepared for the real world. At least when it came to loving someone and thinking about a future with them.

Isabella had been right. After Drake, Morgan had dated occasionally, but had never got serious with anyone. The relationships never felt right, or permanent. She never got butterflies bouncing around in her gut when a guy entered a room or when she was on a date with them, not like how it was with Drake. Nor did anyone make her feel as cherished as he had.

When she'd finally realized what the two of them had, years had passed, and she knew there was no going back to him.

Morgan released a shaky breath. "So much has . . ." she

started, but stopped when the server returned with her water and Drake's food, which smelled enticing.

"Can I get either of you anything else?"

Drake glanced at Morgan, and she shook her head.

"No. We're good. Thanks," he said.

Silence fell between them as Drake started eating. He pushed the order of potato skins across the table to her, and Morgan smiled.

He remembered. She loved anything that consisted of potatoes, but especially potato skins with cheese, bacon pieces, and sour cream.

She nibbled on one and almost moaned at how good it was. Before she knew it, she had eaten three of them. Maybe she was hungrier than she'd thought, or it could be that her subconscious was tired of talking about the past and this was a way to shut her up.

"I was so in love with you," Drake admitted quietly after a long hesitation, then shook his head. "I was devastated. God, I was lost. After my parents' death . . . I didn't have anyone. Sure, people tried to help where they could, but ultimately, it was just me and the twins. Being with you . . ." He wiped his mouth with a napkin and glanced away as if searching for the right words.

Morgan's heart broke. When she had made her decision to leave, she hadn't thought about the hell he'd already been through. She knew he'd be mad, but she hadn't considered the emotional damage her leaving would bring to him.

"Attending college and dating you gave me some normalcy. For a little while each day, I was able to forget about my responsibilities at home and just be a college student who was dating the prettiest girl at school."

Damn. Just crush me, why don't you, Morgan thought.

Memories of all that he'd gone through just before starting

college flooded her mind. Drake had been offered a full scholarship before his parents' death, but it was contingent on him starting school that fall, weeks after his parents died. He explained to the school about his situation and suddenly being the guardian of twins, then begged them to let him start a year later. Not only had the school agreed, but someone in the financial aid office had found funding to help him with housing.

His type-A personality had come in handy back then. He was organized and knew more about finances then most people his age. To make sure he and his siblings had enough to live on, in addition to the financial aid he had received, he sold the house he'd grown up in and they moved into a smaller place. By being careful with the money, they were able to live off of the profit from the house sale and their parents' life insurance.

Morgan watched him as he stared down at the table, and she rubbed her chest as if that would help ease the ache in her heart. For a person who considered herself empathetic, even back then, how had she not considered how her leaving would affect him?

"It wasn't so much that you left," Drake said, cutting into her thoughts, "but it was the fact that you didn't think enough of me to say goodbye."

Tears pricked the back of Morgan's eyes. He had once told her that his biggest regret in losing his parents was that he felt he never had a chance to say goodbye to them. With their death, they'd been ripped out of his life.

"I couldn't," Morgan choked out, trying to keep her tears at bay. "I loved you, and I knew if I tried talking to you before I left, I wouldn't leave."

"Would that have been so bad? Would it have been a bad thing if I'd talked you out of leaving me?"

"Yeah, it would've. Drake, I didn't want to leave town. Nor did I want to leave you, but I had to. I needed to find myself, figure out what I wanted out of life. My world was so wrapped up in you, and our relationship developed so quickly, totally catching me off guard.

"Back then, I didn't know myself. I didn't know what I wanted. Unlike you, who knew exactly where you were going in life."

Drake shook his head. "I wanted you by my side. Those early years with raising the twins was the scariest time in my life. I didn't know if I could do it. I wanted . . . no, I needed you by my side in some capacity. I wasn't planning to ask you to marry me right then. I definitely didn't mean to scare you away. When I shared my goals with you, I just wanted you to know that I saw you in my future."

"At the time, leaving seemed like the best option," she said, pushing the rest of the potatoes away and wrapping her hands around the water glass.

"I thought you were happy with me. I thought everything was fine between us. I—"

"Drake, you were the best thing that ever happened to me. If I'm honest, my decision had nothing to do with you. It was all me." She patted her chest, struggling to get him to understand. "Yes, I loved you. I have never loved another man the way that I loved you, but I had to take care of me. I had to get my shit together in order to be the best version of myself that I could be."

Morgan took a breath while swiping at a rogue tear. Frustration charged through her body because she wished she hadn't put them in this position. Had she been a stronger . . . better person, she would've known how to talk to him then.

"Besides, you might not have asked me to marry you at the time, but the way you were talking, you were heading that way. I wanted to be with you more than anything, but I had to think about the twins' needs too."

"I know, but—"

"I'm not mommy material, Drake," she said, needing to put

all of that out there so he could understand her frame of mind back then. "I was so overwhelmed when we were together, and I wasn't sure if I had a place in all of your lives."

At the time, she hadn't been sure what she wanted out of life, which was also why she'd left.

"Drake, I still don't have that maternal gene that most women have. I knew—"

"Do you really believe that?" he asked, his eyebrows scrunched together as he nailed her with a hard look. "Who told you that you don't have a maternal gene?"

"Nobody had to tell me." She didn't bother explaining that she was like her mother in that regard. Kalena Redford loved her children, but she wasn't the most affectionate person, and there always seemed to be a disconnect whenever she and Morgan talked.

Drake shocked her when he reached out and covered her hand with his. "I don't know why you believe that about yourself, but—"

Suddenly, loud arguing pierced the air, and Morgan screamed when a burly man landed on their table.

What the hell . . .

Chapter Fourteen

MORGAN COULDN'T BELIEVE HER EYES WHEN SEVERAL OTHER men near them started fighting. One minute she and Drake were in a serious conversation, and the next food was flying everywhere. She screamed when a glass shattered, sending shards sailing toward her face.

She quickly turned her head, but still, small slivers caught her in the side of the neck. It didn't hurt much but stung just enough to be irritating.

Drake hustled out of the booth. "You okay?" he yelled over the whoops and hollers. He shoved the guy out of the way, but two other men fighting slammed into him.

Morgan screamed again when they rolled onto her side of the table. She scrambled into a standing position on the red pleather booth seat and looped her purse over her head and across her body. Moving close to the wall still didn't seem as if it was giving the fighters enough space.

When the small group of brawlers moved a short distance

from them, Drake quickly laid down some cash to settle up and stretched out his hand to her. "Come on. Let's get out of here!"

He grabbed her fingers, but Morgan couldn't hold on when the fighting got too close. The men slammed into the table again, then bumped into Drake, knocking him off balance.

Morgan gasped and her hands went to her mouth, but he caught himself before his face connected with the floor.

"Oh, so you want some of this?" the burly man, who was clearly drunk, said to Drake, and shoved him again, then swung.

"Motherfu . . ." Drake ducked, then slammed his right fist into the man's jaw and sent him to the floor.

"Drake! Look out!" Morgan shouted when another guy came up behind him, wrapping his arm around him and putting him in a choke hold. Drake was holding his own, but the first guy had gotten to his feet and zoned in on him.

"Oh, no you don't." Morgan climbed onto the table, then jumped on his back. She tightened her arm around his neck, holding on while pounding his head and shoulder. Her body swung back and forth as he tried shaking her off, but Morgan held on.

She felt like she was riding a bucking bronco, and now that she was on him, she wasn't sure how she'd get off. The guy, in his drunken state, turned in circles, making her just as dizzy as he probably was. When he finally stopped going around and around, he staggered left and then right, then dropped to his knees.

"Arghh!" she screamed when she almost flew over his head, but something or someone grabbed the back of her shirt.

"Dammit, Angel. Quit screwing around, and let's get out of here!" she heard Drake bark.

Apparently, she didn't move fast enough. Drake untangled her from the beast she'd been riding and lifted her into a fireman's carry as if she weighed nothing. His arms were like vise grips around her legs while she hung on upside down, clinging to the back of his shirt.

"Put me down. I can walk."

Fists were flying as well as glass, chairs, and even a small table, which barely missed them. While others were screaming, yelling, and joining the chaos, Drake kept moving. He skirted around people and pushed others out of the way.

It wasn't until Morgan felt a cool breeze over her heated skin that she released the breath she hadn't realized she'd been holding. They were outside, but Drake didn't stop walking until they were a good distance from the building.

"Oh, my goodness," Morgan breathed, readjusting herself since his shoulder was cutting into her stomach.

Drake carefully lowered her, and Morgan groaned as she slowly slid down him, feeling his rock-hard body against her sex-starved one. It was as if they were fused together; the feel of him awakened everything within her, reminding her of just how long it had been since she'd been with a man.

Way, way, way too long.

Even when her feet were on the ground, Drake didn't release her. Instead, he held her close, and Morgan stared up into his handsome face.

"Are you okay?" he finally asked, his voice thick and sexy instead of breathy, the way it should have been considering that he'd just been fighting and had pulled them from a bar brawl.

Morgan nodded, but stopped when her neck stung, and she remembered the glass flying.

She lifted her head and turned it slightly, wanting him to see her neck. "Do you see any glass in my skin?"

His brows furrowed and that concern she'd seen earlier was back. "You were hit by glass?" he asked, pulling his cell phone from his pants pocket and turning on the flashlight. He gently gripped her chin and turned her head slightly to get a better look. "Does your neck hurt?"

"It's nothing serious. I think a sliver or two might've gotten me. It doesn't really hurt, but this area does sting a little." She pointed to the spot on the side of her neck, and a shiver passed through her when he got closer.

Too close for comfort, and he was wreaking havoc on her self-control. Drake's fresh, clean scent was subtle, but still potent enough to stir something inside of her that hadn't been awakened in years.

Morgan shivered again when his fingers brushed over the spot in question.

"Damn, did that hurt?" he asked, still bent slightly, examining the area despite the limited lighting.

Her shudder had nothing to do with the skin irritation and everything to do with his gentle touch. Especially when his large hand slid slowly behind her neck, and he cradled the back of her head.

Drake's face was so close. All Morgan would have to do was turn slightly and press a kiss on his tempting lips. An hour ago, he was glaring at her, but now his tenderness made it hard for her to think straight, and she was all twisted up inside. Her body yearned to be wrapped up in his strong arms again.

An involuntary whimper slipped through, and his attention moved from her neck to her face. His gaze volleyed between her lips and her eyes and back to her lips again, and Morgan's need for him bloomed, sending a tingling sensation scurrying through her body.

Yeah, it had definitely been too long since she'd been with a man, and this was no ordinary man. He was the only one she had ever given her heart to. The only one she'd ever trusted completely.

The urge to kiss him grew stronger. She wanted to relive a less complicated time in her life where she'd been carefree and crazy in love. What if she happened to lift up on her tiptoes ever so slightly and cover his mouth with hers?

Should she?

Her family had often complained about her impulsiveness, but this was different.

Wasn't it?

Better to ask for forgiveness than permission.

Before she lost her nerve, Morgan fisted the front of Drake's shirt and pulled him closer, covering his lips with hers. Heat charged through her body upon impact, and she held on to him tighter as their tongues got reacquainted.

The moment seemed so unreal, but the feel of his mouth on hers and the touch of his hands sliding up the side of her body was real . . . very real. As his strong arms went around her, holding her against his hardness, Morgan moaned and melted into him.

She'd never imagined that she'd one day share a kiss with Drake again. It was like a dream come true, and oh, what a kiss it was. The fire spreading through her scorched every cell in her body and sent heated lust pumping through her veins. It was as if she had suddenly awakened from a deep sleep. Everything seemed clearer, brighter, and more exciting being so close to him. Just like old times.

She might've started the kiss, but Drake had absolutely taken over. Morgan moaned into his mouth as their tongues tangled. Her pulse beat wildly with each lap of his tongue, and she couldn't seem to get enough of him. His kiss was demanding, yet tender and thorough, filling a need within her that she hadn't realized existed.

Another moan pierced the air, and this time Morgan wasn't sure if it came from her or Drake as he tightened his hold around her waist. Memories of them together like this came rushing back, and more than ever, she questioned how she could have ever walked away from this man. His kissing abilities alone should've stopped her, but she'd had a one-track mind, and not even that could keep her from doing what she felt she had to do.

Leaving Drake was unquestionably one of the biggest regrets of her life.

Police sirens could be heard in the near distance, and Morgan groaned against his lips, not wanting the kiss to come to an end. She wasn't sure if she'd ever get a chance to do it again and wanted it to last forever. But when he eased his mouth from hers, she loosened her hold on the front of his shirt.

Neither of them spoke. Morgan knew what was racing through her mind—*let's go back to my place and finish where we left off.* But she couldn't tell what Drake was thinking. He no longer looked at her as if he wanted to pummel her. In fact, the desire radiating in his eyes matched what she was feeling.

Could they be on the same page?

Drake cupped her cheek and Morgan leaned into his touch while he continued to stare into her eyes. The moment was almost hypnotic as the pad of his thumb brushed up and down her jaw.

"About that kiss," he started, but stopped abruptly.

"Yes," Morgan said, hope bubbling inside of her, though she wasn't sure what she wanted him to say. An hour rehashing their past didn't mean they were even close to being friends. But a girl could hope for more. That kiss and the magnetic force that still vibrated between them spoke volumes. They might not be able to pick up where they'd left off years ago, but they could start over, build from the here and now.

"That kiss . . . was amazing," he finally said.

Yes! Yes! Yes! Her inner voice cheered. Morgan wanted him to be just as affected by it as she was, and it seemed they were indeed on the same page.

"But we can't let it happen again. This," he waved his hand back and forth between them, "is too complicated."

Her excitement incinerated into a heap of ash.

We are definitely not on the same page.

What the hell? Could he not read her face? Not sense the burning desire pumping through her body? Yeah, she understood that a short talk in the bar didn't make everything right between them, but . . . damn. That kiss was *hot*!

Instead of shaking some sense into him, she said, "Okay," but cursed him out inside her head.

Drake put a little distance between them as if he could hear her internal monologue, and he rubbed the back of his neck. "Since your car is out of commission, I can give you a ride home."

"I'd appreciate that. Thanks."

Too bad I won't be riding anything else tonight.

Chapter Fifteen

AS DRAKE FOLLOWED MORGAN'S INSTRUCTIONS TO HER place, he replayed the last hour in his mind. He hadn't missed the disappointment in her eyes when he'd said the kiss shouldn't have happened. What he neglected to say was that while it shouldn't have happened, he was glad it had.

She tasted as sweet as he remembered, and he wanted nothing more than to take her home and show her how much he had missed her.

But he couldn't. He wouldn't.

He was glad that she'd explained why she left. He even understood her reasoning, but they were different people now. They couldn't just pick up where they left off all those years ago. Even if he was curious about where she'd been and what she was currently doing.

As for what just happened at the bar, that had turned into something straight out of a movie, and Drake couldn't believe his ass got caught up in it. He almost laughed out loud at how crazy the evening had played out. The last time he had thrown a punch might've been high school, or maybe even middle school. Grown men fighting like hoodlums was just something he couldn't wrap his brain around. Yet, it was still funny.

His laughter started as a chuckle, but as he thought about the shock of finding Morgan riding a guy's back like she was on a bronco, he burst into a full-on belly laugh.

"What's so funny?" she asked.

Drake split his attention between her and the road. Each time he looked at her, yearning stirred inside of him. Being with her felt surreal, and he wasn't quite sure what to make of this reunion of sorts.

"Drake?" Morgan prompted.

"Oh, sorry. I was just thinking about how you attacked the guy at the bar. What were you thinking, jumping on his back? You looked like a rag doll being tossed about in a tornado."

A grin stretched across her sexy mouth. "Yeah, that was wild, but I had to do something. I didn't want him to hurt you. So I was trying to help."

He smirked at that. She thought her petite self was mightier than she actually was. "You're the one who could've gotten hurt."

"Well, I guess I didn't think that far ahead. I just reacted."

"I see you're still a little spitfire, getting into stuff and struggling to get out of it."

"He started it," she said in mock indignation. "He was about to pound you into the ground, and I couldn't let that happen. And you're welcome, by the way."

Drake sputtered a laugh. "Oh, thanks for the help, but I actually think you're exaggerating. I had everything under control."

She scoffed. "*Sure* you did."

Bantering with her brought back fond memories. Their personalities and how they handled situations were so different, but Drake had always thought they balanced each other well. While he tended to be more on the serious side, Morgan was somewhat of a good-time girl. She loved life and everyone loved her. At least that's how he remembered her, and if tonight was any indication, that was still the case. The way she'd jumped into the fight without a second thought was so like her.

"Stop!" Morgan yelled and grabbed his forearm.

Drake slammed on the brake. "What the . . ." His gaze shot to the rearview mirror, glad to see that no one was close behind him.

"Oops, sorry. I should've said slow down." She looked at him sheepishly. "I didn't want you to drive past this street up ahead."

"Seriously? You almost gave me a heart attack because of some street? I thought you said you lived—"

"No, it's not where I live, but it's where my favorite diner is located."

"Morgan—"

"Don't say no," she said in a rush. "Since we didn't get a chance to really catch up at the bar, I'm thinking we can talk over dessert at the Little All-Nite Diner that I hang out at sometimes." Morgan pointed ahead. "Turn right at the next corner. Hopefully you're not in a hurry to get home."

"Would it matter, since you already have me taking you to the restaurant?"

She flashed him a huge smile, her pearly whites gleaming in the dark interior of his truck. Her pretty eyes shimmered with mischief, and Drake's heart kicked against his chest. This gorgeous, vibrant woman had his body wound tighter than an antique clock.

How was that possible after so many years?

It didn't make sense.

He had been so angry with her for so long and, all of a sudden, she falls back into his life and the anger is replaced with . . . with, hell, he wasn't quite sure. Curiosity? Fascination? Attraction?

Morgan used to intrigue him, but that was then—before she took off and left him behind.

Why was he still enthralled by her? He should be running in the opposite direction like his ass was on fire. Yet, he followed her instructions to the diner.

After a few more minutes and several right and left turns, they ended up in an unfamiliar neighborhood that wasn't too far from his house. He pulled into one of the parking spots on the side of a building that looked as if it was straight out of a seventies sitcom. What surprised him more was the name of the restaurant—Little All-Nite Diner. He'd thought that was just a description that she was using, not the actual name.

"How'd you find this place?" Drake asked while he unfastened his seat belt and checked out his surroundings. The building looked like a large, old trolly car wrapped in silver with mostly glass in front. It was well lit and practically provided light for the whole block.

"A friend of mine owns it," Morgan said, grabbing her purse off the floor. "I stop by when I want a slice of pecan pie or when I'm bored at home. It's a cool place to just chill."

She reached for the door handle, but Drake stopped her. "Sit tight," he said and walked around to the passenger side to help her out of the truck.

"One more thing," Morgan said as they headed to the door. "If a guy named Lester is working tonight, can you pretend to be my boyfriend?"

Drake pulled up short and gaped at her. "What are we, twelve? No, I'm not going to pretend to be your boyfriend. Who is this guy anyway? Your real boyfriend?"

"He's not my boyfriend. Just a guy who can't take *I'm not interested* for an answer. And he might not even be working tonight. Then this back and forth we have going here will be for nothing. So will you do it?"

"No."

She stomped her foot. "Come on, Drake. You don't even really have to do anything. Just stand there and look big, bad, and angry. You know, like you did the other day at Kellner's office." She snapped her finger and nodded. "Yeah, just like that. Keep that look."

"You know what?" Drake said, and his lips twitched while he tried not to laugh. "I can already tell this is a bad idea. Let's go. I'm taking you home." Morgan grabbed the back of his jacket when he started to walk away.

"It's still early, and I'm not ready to go home." She jumped in front of him, and her sweet, intoxicating scent reached his nose. "What else do you have to do tonight? Probably nothing."

She folded her arms and the move brought attention to her skintight shirt that was low-cut and barely contained her perky breasts. His dick twitched at the thought, and he almost groaned when beige lace peeked above where the shirt buttons started.

Drake knew the treasures that were hidden behind the garment, and the memories of her breasts in the palms of his hands slammed into him. She had a body that would make a grown man weep.

Apparently, his eyes stayed on her breasts a little too long, because when he glanced up, Morgan smirked at him as if knowing what he was thinking.

Shit.

If a little lace and perky breasts could make him want to strip her out of her clothes and get her naked, he was in trouble. It was bad enough he had enjoyed the last hour with her, but lusting after his ex? Not good. Not good at all.

Hanging out with her any longer was a bad idea. A *really* bad idea, and if he had any common sense, he'd drop her off at her place and never look back.

"What are you afraid of?" Morgan taunted, humor in her

tone as she moved closer. Her small hand slid up his torso to his chest, and he didn't dare move as heat spread through his body like a wildfire. "I promise to be on my best behavior, and I won't freak out if you throw another spider at me. And I promise I won't kiss you again," she said. "So what do you say. Oh, and I won't come to your rescue and beat up any more guys for you tonight."

Drake couldn't stop himself from chuckling. He didn't know how she could say any of that with a straight face. He missed her nonsense, and grudgingly admitted he wanted to catch up more, but his inner voice was saying *Run!* Yet he didn't want to leave. Besides, leaving now would be a punk move. She would assume that he was scared that he would catch feelings for her.

I'm staying. I'm not a punk.

"One hour," he bit out. "That's it, and I'm *not* pretending to be your boyfriend." He opened the door to the restaurant, but Morgan was still standing in the same spot, a Cheshire Cat grin on her face. "You coming or what?"

She laughed and strutted past him into the building like she owned the place, and he followed her inside. "Superstition" by Stevie Wonder was playing through the red jukebox in a nearby corner, and Drake felt like he'd been tossed back in time.

The place truly did look like a seventies throwback, with red and white vinyl seats in the booths, black-and-white checkered floors, and old black-and-white photos covering practically every inch of the baby-blue walls. There was a long counter with at least ten silver bar stools in front of it, and several employees working behind it.

It was almost ten at night and the place was full of young and old patrons hanging out and chatting loudly. Servers with large round trays flitted about, and one almost bumped into Drake.

"Seat yourself, love, and I'll be right with . . ." the server started, but stopped. She was dressed in a pale pink shirt and matching short skirt, and she smiled when she saw Morgan. "Oh, what's up, MoMo? You know the routine."

"Hey, Val. Let me get two of my usual and two black coffees," Morgan said and strolled over to the only empty booth.

Drake sat across from her and slipped out of his jacket. "Is it always this crowded this time of night?"

"Yeah, usually. It's a fun place, isn't it?"

Drake could see the appeal. "Yeah, it seems all right. So, what's your usual?"

"This time of night? Pecan pie with a scoop of vanilla ice cream. You're going to love it."

He probably would since he'd never met a pie he didn't like.

"Is he here?" Drake asked. "Your admirer?"

He studied a few guys, especially those behind the long counter serving people and even some sitting on the bar stools. He had no intention of pretending to be Morgan's man, but he'd be lying if he said that he didn't resent the fact that some dude was interested in her.

Hell, probably every guy Morgan met wanted to get to know her better. She was *that* woman. The type of woman to leave an impression even with a simple hello. And any guy given the opportunity to have some type of conversation with her undoubtedly considered themselves blessed by God. They'd probably fall in love within five minutes of talking with her. She made everyone feel special. At least that's how it had been back in the day.

Morgan slowly looked around the large space, and then nodded toward someone behind Drake. "There he is. He's on his way over."

Drake glanced over his shoulder. All he saw was a man with salt-and-pepper hair and a slight beer belly, wearing bright red suspenders. They were holding up black-and-white checkered pants that looked too tight to be comfortable. He was also shuf-fling toward them. The guy was average height, walked slightly bent over, and looked old enough to be their grandfather.

Drake's brows dipped and he turned back to Morgan. "*Him?*" He pointed his thumb over his shoulder. "*That's* the guy who's been hitting on you?"

Morgan burst out laughing and couldn't seem to stop, even when tears pooled in her eyes. "I wish you could see your face right now," she managed to get out.

"Seriously? You had me thinking—"

"Wow, you sure do know how to brighten up a place," the old man said when he reached their table. He sat next to Morgan, who was still laughing, and wrapped his arm around her shoul-ders before kissing her cheek. "How's my little lovebug?" There was a Southern twang in the man's words, and the guy didn't just *look* old enough to be their grandfather. He *was* old enough.

Drake leaned back in his seat and shook his head.

She got me.

Apparently, Morgan wanted to get a rise out of him, and it had worked. Drake had told her that he wouldn't pretend to be her man, but that wasn't totally true. He didn't consider himself the jealous type but if the guy had been tall, with broad shoul-ders, and good-looking, the green-eyed monster no doubt would've made an appearance. Drake would've not only pretended to be her boyfriend, but he would've also made it believable by cov-ering her mouth with his and kissing her senseless.

What did that say about him? He claimed to be over Morgan, but was he really?

Chapter Sixteen

"DRAKE, I'D LIKE FOR YOU TO MEET LESTER DANIELS, ALSO known as Slick Lester, but to me, he's Gramps," Morgan said, giving their visitor an adoring smile.

At first, Drake was confused because he remembered her telling him that her grandparents were deceased. But then she explained that Slick Lester was her soon-to-be-sister-in-law's grandfather. Morgan had adopted him as her own.

"Her real name is Dreamy?" Drake asked, making sure he had heard Morgan correctly when she mentioned the sister-in-law's name.

Morgan's mouth spread into a wide smile. "Yeah, and her name fits her personality perfectly. She's the most positive person I've ever met, and she makes a friend wherever she goes."

Sounds like you, Drake thought, but kept the comment to himself.

They all chatted, and at one point in the conversation, Morgan lowered her voice and mentioned that Dreamy and Lester had won the Powerball lottery a few months ago. Drake had never met anyone who had actually won the lottery, and he found their story fascinating.

"What do you think of my place?" Lester asked, gesturing with his arm around the diner. "This was one of my purchases. Nice, right?"

"Yeah, it's great," Drake agreed.

Lester explained that he had always wanted to have his own business, but never could afford to start one. And when the diner, a place he had frequented over the last fifty years, came up for sale, he bought it.

"It was one of the most exciting things I've ever done." Lester beamed as his gaze bounced around the brightly lit space.

Drake was happy for him. So many people went a lifetime wanting something but never being able to realize their dream.

Val brought over slices of pecan pie à la mode and sat one each in front of him and Morgan, along with their coffee. The slices were as big as Drake's hand, and way more than he thought he could eat, but after two bites he had a feeling there wouldn't be any leftovers. He could see why Morgan ordered it. It was the best pie he'd ever tasted.

As they ate, Lester and Morgan flirted with each other, bantering back and forth as if they did it all the time. It was clear that she was fond of the old man, but Morgan was the one who kept snagging Drake's attention. Her laughter, her expressive dark eyes—everything about her held him captive. It was still mind-blowing that she was sitting across from him after so many years.

This moment reminded him of another time. A time back in college when they would meet up after their classes and go to an ice cream shop. Hanging out at the place wasn't what made the memory so important; it was a feeling he'd gotten while they were there one particular afternoon.

Drake's chest tightened, and he stared down at his pie as he recalled that day.

Back then, conversation had always flowed easily between him and Morgan. They could talk about anything, from their classes to politics and everything in between. Morgan had been the bright spot in his life. His refuge during a time when it felt like he carried the world on his shoulders.

That day, though, something had shifted inside of him. At one point in the conversation, Morgan stopped and fed him a spoonful of her mint chocolate chip ice cream. She would often do that, but this time while feeding him, she did it slowly as she stared into his eyes.

It was as if everything around them stopped moving, and it was only the two of them inside the shop. There weren't enough adjectives to describe the intense sensation that had flowed through Drake in that moment. It was like nothing he had ever experienced, but he knew something had changed between them. He had fallen in love with Morgan.

Morgan burst out laughing, and Drake snapped back to the present. His gaze went to her, and he swallowed hard as that memory lingered.

I've moved on, and there's no going back.

I've moved on, and there's no going back.

The words played on a loop inside Drake's mind. Now all he had to do was remember them.

"All right, I need to get back to my friends over there," Lester said, nodding at a table across the room where three older women were sitting. "That's why I'm still here this time of night."

"I should've known you were here with a woman," Morgan said and kissed his cheek.

"Not one woman, three of them, lovebug. Count them, *three*," he said, poking out his chest and wearing a smug expression.

Drake had to laugh at that, especially when Slick Lester

tugged on his suspenders and let them snap back against his chest.

"Well, I guess you better get going, because one of them keeps looking over here. I don't want her to think that I'm trying to steal her man." Morgan hugged him. "Thanks for stopping by to say hi."

"Of course, sweetheart." Lester's age showed as he slowly eased out of the booth. "Good meeting you, young man," he said, shaking Drake's hand. "You better treat her right. Otherwise, you're going to have to deal with me."

Drake didn't bother telling him that he and Morgan weren't an item. Instead he said, "Yes, sir."

Slick Lester said his goodbyes, then shuffled away, reminding Drake of Fred Sandford, grumbling, "Keep your wig on, woman. I'm coming."

Morgan shook her head. "He's a trip, and the ladies love him, and not because he has money. He's just so damn charming," she said, smiling while watching him walk away. "So, were you surprised when Gramps turned out to be my admirer?" Morgan asked, humor in her voice as she dug into her pie.

"Yeah, I was, but then I figured, since I haven't seen you in so long, you might've preferred them older now."

"Ha, ha, ha. I see you have jokes, but no, I'm not looking for a sugar daddy. Okay, we came here to catch up. Tell me about you. What have you been up to? I'm assuming you finished college."

"I did, and a few years ago I went back to get my MBA."

"Wow, impressive. My mother has been trying to get me to return to college, but I'm not interested right now."

That surprised Drake . . . well, a little. She had always had to work for her grades, often struggling to maintain a C average. Though she had never mentioned the possibility of dropping out, she had mentioned that she didn't think she was cut out for college. But still, she had seemed determined to get her degree in fashion design.

Then again, with her family's wealth, Morgan could probably live comfortably off interest alone and dabble in fashion as a side hustle.

"I haven't totally ruled out returning, but I won't be going back for fashion design. I would go back for business."

"*Seriously?* You lived and breathed fashion, and if the outfit you had on the other day was any indication, you're still very talented."

"Thanks. I still enjoy designing. I just don't plan on making it my career. My passion is helping others have a better life. Right now, I'm the chief operating officer of Open Arms, a nonprofit organization that helps teens transition out of foster care."

Drake heard the pride in her tone. "I never would've guessed you'd be interested in business or running a nonprofit. That's awesome, and I'm impressed."

"Thanks, but I'm sure you're also shocked," she said on a chuckle.

He smiled and took a sip of the steaming black coffee. "A little. Not that I don't think you're capable of accomplishing anything you set your mind to. I just never thought you'd end up doing something like that."

"Yeah, it was all part of me finding myself. While I was traveling, I had a lot of time to think . . . and basically grow up. I also did some volunteer work and realized that's when I was at my happiest."

"Volunteer work?" Drake asked.

"Yes, while I was in the UK, I volunteered at a community center. I loved hanging out with the kids, and there was this one young girl who was seventeen and in foster care. We clicked. She confided in me that she was worried about turning eighteen and aging out of foster care. Never in my life had I thought about what happened to teens when they became adults and had to leave their foster home. Thankfully, things worked out for her because her foster mother agreed to let her stay until she could afford to move out on her own. Also, the UK has services in place to provide for continuing care for those aging out of foster care."

"Is that when you came up with the idea for Open Arms?" Drake asked and sipped his coffee.

"Not exactly. I was telling my friend Isabella about that situation, and it turned out that since her schooling was in social work, she'd been thinking about trying to get something started that could benefit children. Anyway, after a few brainstorming sessions, and taking into consideration what services the UK offers to those aging out of foster care, we came up with the concept for Open Arms."

Drake nodded and listened as she spoke passionately about the work that she and Isabella were doing.

"My heart goes out to those kids. It's hard enough adulting when you've been given a good start but imagine having nothing but a few clothes, no money, no family, and trying to survive out here."

Drake picked at his pie while she explained how her organization helped some of those who showed up on their doorstep.

Morgan might've been an heir to the Redford fortune, but she never flashed her wealth and had always been selfless. That had been one of many things he loved about her. She was one of those people who would literally give the clothes off her back to someone in need.

"Open Arms is the main reason I put an offer on the Hollywood property. If I get the building, I'd lease the top two floors to the nonprofit. The current space we're in is way too small for all that we do and want to do. We can only accommodate a few of the kids who come to us for help, and it's heartbreaking every time we have to turn one of them away. Our waiting list for housing is so long, we could stand to have a building twice as large as the Hollywood one."

Drake wondered, *Why not try and find a bigger place, then?* But he didn't ask.

"I'm really hoping I get it," Morgan continued. "We'd be able to provide housing to at least a hundred kids, in addition to having retail space on the lower level. I figured, whatever commercial space we lease out, there's a good chance that jobs will be available for some of our kids. It would be a win-win.

"Anyway, even without being able to provide housing to everyone now, we can help some find work, apply for government assistance, scholarships, and anything else we can do to make their lives a little easier."

Drake's heart sank a little. Of course she had a good reason for wanting the Hollywood property. It was just like Jeffrey said, everyone who was at that meeting probably had noble intentions for why they wanted the building. Though Drake respected what Morgan and her team were trying to do, he wasn't giving up without a fight. Owning that property would be another way of preserving his father's legacy. No way would he just let someone walk away with it. Not even Morgan.

Chapter Seventeen

DRAKE FINISHED OFF HIS DESSERT AND WIPED HIS MOUTH with a napkin. Before he could call the server over for more coffee, she appeared and topped off his mug.

"I assume you're moving on to the next level in whatever this is that Mr. Kellner is doing," Morgan said, and snagged his attention when she slowly licked ice cream off the back of her spoon.

He was fairly sure she wasn't trying to turn him on, but the move was so damn sexy. It had his mind conjuring up all types of impure thoughts. He shifted in his seat and cleared his throat.

"Yeah, I heard back yesterday. You?" After hearing her story, Drake was pretty sure she was still in the running.

"Yes, I am. Now I'm just curious as to what he has in store for us come time for the meeting on Monday. I don't get why he and his team are being so secretive."

"Me either, and I'm not sure if I'm looking forward to hearing about this next step. I have a feeling it's not going to be something we'll like."

Morgan nodded. "So, what are your plans for the building if you get it?"

"My company plans to revitalize the whole property, but my reason for wanting it is mainly because of my father. He was the architect who designed the property. It was his first project."

"Oh, wow. That's pretty cool."

Drake felt a burst of pride. He often drove by buildings that his dad had designed, and in a strange way, it made him feel closer to him. That's what he told Morgan.

"I can understand that. Well, good luck. Though I hope I win the bid, if I don't, I hope you do."

"Same here," Drake said, and that was the truth. He thought it was commendable what she was trying to do, and he might even be able to help her organization in some way.

He'd keep that to himself for now, though.

"I knew you were going to be a success, but what made you go into real estate development? How'd you get started?"

"Jeffrey," he said with a smile. "He was my dad's mentor. When my dad died, Jeffrey stepped in and became my mentor as well, and helped guide me and my career."

"I figured you guys were close. I just didn't know in what capacity."

"Yeah, he taught me the ins and outs of real estate, and for the most part I listened." Drake laughed, remembering some hard lessons. "He believed in letting me learn by experience, not giving me anything, even though he was in the position to do so." He sipped his coffee. "What about you and Jeffrey? Did you know him before putting in an offer on the building?"

"Actually, he's a friend of my parents. Well, he was first a friend of my grandfather, but after he passed, Mr. Kellner and my dad kept in touch. I don't know him as well as you do, though."

They chatted like old times. Who would've thought that they'd ever get this chance to clear the air and catch up with

each other? Drake had to admit that it felt good that they were
on speaking terms, but he wasn't sure what came next. No, they
couldn't go back to the way they used to be, but could they at
least be friends? He wasn't sure.

That kiss they'd shared earlier made him want more than
friendship, but . . .

Morgan released an unladylike snort, and Drake glanced
across the table at her.

"Sorry," she said, a hand to her mouth. She held up her phone.
"Addison just texted me. She's asking if she and I can start working on her dress tomorrow. Are you okay with that? Or are you
still mad at me?" she asked teasingly.

Drake chuckled. It was a lot easier to be mad at her when she
wasn't in his presence. Now, after their evening and that kiss,
Drake couldn't stay mad. If anything, Addison gave him just the
excuse he didn't know he wanted to see Morgan again.

"Yeah, I'm fine with it, as long as you are," he finally said.

"I have to tell you, it was a shock seeing the twins the other
day. They're so big. Though I only saw Aiden from a distance,
Addison is such a sweetheart. It's clear you did a good job with
them."

Drake smiled, thinking about his siblings. "They are amazing," he said, probably sounding like a proud parent and feeling
like one. "We had some tough times early on, but we made it
through. They are my life. For years, all of my decisions were
with them in mind, and I'm just glad everything worked out.
Now that they are older, I feel like I can start living my life."

"What would that look like?" Morgan asked.

In a way, it was a loaded question because he wanted to say he
was looking to get married and travel with his wife. Instead, he
said, "It means sleeping in late. Impromptu weekend getaways,
and eventually some major traveling. I'll probably take a page
from your book and check out Europe and other countries."

"I see," was all Morgan said, and Drake left it at that.

Once she finished eating, Drake paid the bill and they left the restaurant. As he drove her home, they worked out the details for Addison's visit. By the time he turned onto Morgan's street, Drake realized that he lived only five minutes from her, on the other side of the park.

He pulled into the circle drive and then parked on the side of the driveway. The five-story stucco building was a luxury new build, and he was curious to see inside. From what he'd heard, it had a doorman, and the main floor had enough amenities to warrant the million-dollar price tag for each unit.

"Would you like to come in?" Morgan asked.

"Sure, I'll just walk you to your door, then I'd better get home."

After a slight hesitation, she said, "Okay."

Drake didn't miss the disappointment in her voice, but he didn't trust himself to keep his distance after spending so much time with her. He wanted to kiss her again, and his willpower wasn't as strong as it usually was with other women.

But of course it wasn't. The others hadn't been Morgan, and like before, she was in a class all her own.

Drake hurried around to the passenger side to get her door. "This is a nice area. I live just on the other side of the park," he said as they neared the building.

"Really?"

"Yep, I pass by here often. I'm surprised we haven't run into each other sooner."

The door to the building swung open and an older man with mostly gray hair, a deep tan, and friendly eyes held the door for them.

"Good evening, Ms. Redford. Welcome home," he said, tipping his hat to her and nodding a greeting at Drake.

"Hi, Mr. Easton. How are you this evening?"

Drake glanced around the lobby as the two exchanged small

talk. He'd been enthralled with the building's exterior, but the interior was just as impressive. The modern decor was tasteful, with neutral colors of beige, brown, and tan that created a warm and inviting atmosphere. A double-sided fireplace with a glass front and brick that went all the way up to the ceiling sat off to the right side of the room and separated a sitting area from a bar, where several people were having drinks. To his left was a café that appeared closed, a dry cleaner, and a small grocery store. Add those features to the other amenities that he'd heard about, and it was clear the developers had thought of everything.

Morgan started toward the four elevators that were straight ahead and Drake fell in step.

"Nice place," he said. "How long have you lived here?"

"About five or six months," she said as the elevator doors slid open, and they strolled inside. She pushed the button for the top floor. "Though it took me a while to decide if I wanted a house or a condo, I went with the latter. I love it here."

When they arrived at her floor, they turned left and walked to the end of the hallway. "This is me," she said, and pulled keys from the side pocket of her purse. When she turned to him, she gave him a shy smile. "It was nice hanging out with you tonight. Thanks for hearing me out earlier. I really am sorry for how things ended between us. Hopefully, one day, you'll be able to fully forgive me."

Drake nodded and slowly brushed the back of his fingers down her soft cheek. He knew he shouldn't, but he couldn't help but touch her. It still seemed so surreal that she was standing in front of him.

"I appreciate you explaining it all to me. For years, I wondered. When your friend Isabella told me that you had left the country, I'll admit I was devastated. Of course, I wish you'd talked to me . . . but I get it. I'm glad you did what you had to do for you, and it seems you're the better for it."

"I am, but if I could go back and do things differently, Drake, please know that I would. I never forgot you, and you will always have a special place in my heart."

Drake wasn't sure what to say, but deep down, he felt the same way. For years, though he hadn't realized it, he had never let a woman get close because of Morgan.

And probably never would, the little voice inside of his head said. She would always be a part of him.

Instead of saying more, he lowered his head and kissed her just below her cheekbone, near her mouth. He couldn't allow himself to get any closer to her lips; one conversation over pie was all he could take for now.

He wasn't ready to tempt fate.

"I'll bring Addison by tomorrow," he said. "Have a good night."

Drake turned to walk away but stopped and glanced over his shoulder when Morgan said, "It would be a better night if you stayed."

She was right. It would be, but it would also be a mistake. Too much had happened between them. Besides, one night with Morgan Redford would never be enough.

Maybe one day . . . maybe.

Chapter Eighteen

MORGAN CLOSED HER EYES, PLACED HER HANDS PALMS DOWN on the quartz countertop, and sighed. "What was I thinking inviting them over here?" she asked Dreamy. They were standing in Morgan's kitchen while she freaked out over the fact that Drake and Addison would be there shortly, and she wasn't ready.

"You were thinking that you wanted to help a little girl create the prettiest dress her high school friends will ever see," Dreamy said.

Morgan opened her eyes and looked at her almost sister-in-law. The woman had the nicest hair, but she often covered it up with a fabulous wig, like today. The black bob was shoulder length and had bangs that were so long, they practically covered her eyes, giving her a mysterious appearance.

She was also the most positive person Morgan knew, but right now, positivity wasn't what she needed.

"If you're not still feeling Drake, why are you so worried about seeing him again?" Dreamy asked.

Because his hard body rubbed up against mine, and I liked it. A lot.

I also liked kissing him, and I want to kiss him again, and again, and again. But Morgan didn't say any of that. Because she wasn't quite ready to admit to anyone the full extent of her feelings for Drake.

She wanted him back, but how could she prove to him that she wasn't the same person she used to be in college? She had tossed him away as if he hadn't been one of the most important people in her life. He would never let her back into his life. At least not like she used to be.

But what if he did? she thought. What if he was feeling what she felt? She had only told Dreamy about the spider disaster, the grocery store mess, the conversation and brawl at the bar, and that they hung out at the diner. She'd neglected to mention the kiss.

Dreamy and Karter's dog, Melvin, stood from his spot on the floor near the opening between the kitchen and living room. He trotted into the kitchen and over to Dreamy, then barked.

"All right, all right, we'll go outside, but then we're coming back in and figure out what your Auntie Morgan isn't telling us." She smirked at Morgan. "You have ten minutes to prepare yourself to come clean, or at least come up with a good lie."

When they walked out of the condo, Morgan continued cleaning up the kitchen. She wasn't much of a cook, but Nana had given her a simple lasagna recipe. Morgan had followed the instructions exactly, and now the lasagna was in the oven. She couldn't wait to taste it.

As she loaded the last of the dirty dishes into the dishwasher, Morgan's mind went back to thoughts of Drake. She wanted to tell Dreamy the truth about how she was feeling about him, but what if her future sister-in-law thought she was nuts?

She won't judge me, Morgan thought just as she heard the door open.

"We're baaack," Dreamy said in a singsong voice. "Start talking."

"I thought you were just coming over to pick up your wedding gown. Don't you have somewhere else to be instead of here, getting into my business?"

"Says the person who was all up in me and your brother's business months ago."

"First of all, it's because of me that you two got together." She was the reason why Karter had showed up at the place Dreamy worked, and they practically fell for each other at first sight. "Secondly, once you two were together, I backed off and minded my own business."

"Okay, that's true." Dreamy reclaimed her seat at the breakfast bar. "Anyway, I'm thinking I'll stick around here, check Drake out, then—"

"I still like him," Morgan blurted.

"I knew it! I knew you were hiding something big. I can't wait to meet him. You haven't—"

"Wait. I don't think it's a good idea for you to meet him. He and I will never be a couple again. We've made peace with the past, but I'm pretty sure he's only tolerating me because of his sister. If it weren't for her, I wouldn't be seeing him again outside of the property bid."

"Somehow, I doubt that, but I'll be able to tell once he gets here. Who knows, this might be your second chance at love. This time around, you guys might get it right. You know as well as I do that when true love comes along, there's nothing you can do but roll with it."

"I didn't say anything about love, but I *love* your enthusiasm and how you're always optimistic. Truth be told, I'm not sure if I even deserve a second chance."

For much of the night, she'd recalled the hurt on his face at the bar when she was trying to explain her frame of mind back in college. Granted, the evening turned out better than it had started, but she still couldn't get that moment at the bar out of her mind.

"At the time, I thought my reason for walking away was a good one. Now I'm not so sure."

"I understand why you left," Dreamy said. "I just think you went about it the wrong way. I'm learning daily the importance of good communication in a relationship. I really hope you get another chance with him."

"I want another chance at love, but I'm positive it won't be with Drake. He's made it clear that he's not interested."

And Morgan was fine with that. At least she hoped she was. But what if . . .

What if Drake gave her a second chance?

What if they started dating again?

What if they . . .

Just stop! she berated herself.

She didn't have time to ponder the questions or come up with answers before her phone rang. It was the ringtone she had assigned to the doorman.

She glanced at Dreamy. "They're here." After letting the doorman know that it was okay to send them up, Morgan hurried to the foyer. She stopped at the coat closet, opened the door, and gave herself one last look in the full-length mirror hanging inside the door.

Running her hands down the sides of the soft pink, low-cut T-shirt that she had paired with burgundy leggings, she looked relaxed, but still cute.

Just what she was going for.

A knock sounded on the door, and Melvin started barking, then tore into the foyer, sliding on the hardwood floor before skidding to a stop. Dreamy was right behind him, holding the long, white garment bag that held her dress.

"We're not going to stay long," she whispered, and Morgan knew what she meant by that. She and Melvin would stay just long enough to check out Drake.

She inhaled, and the scent of her lasagna flowed through the condo. She smiled on the exhale, proud of herself for cooking a meal that didn't turn into trash before she got it in the oven. She hoped it tasted as good as it smelled.

"Hush," she said to Melvin, who was standing at the door, still barking, his tail wagging a mile a minute as if telling her to hurry up.

Morgan peeked through the peephole, even though she knew who it was, and her heartbeat amped up at the sight of Drake. Back in college, he was a dream come true. Now? The man was everything sexual fantasies were made of, and her body was even more tuned in to him.

As she unlocked the door, Morgan struggled to steady her breathing.

Relax. Just relax, she told herself, then grabbed hold of Melvin's collar to keep him from running out. When she swung open the door, her mouth went dry.

Why is he torturing me like this?

She wanted to scream and tell him to stop looking so damn good.

He was dressed down in a long-sleeve T-shirt that molded over his upper body and emphasized his broad chest and muscular biceps.

How the hell was she going to focus on anything with him around?

"Ohhh, you have a dog," Addison squealed and dropped to her knees, snapping Morgan out of her trance.

"Actually, he's my dogphew," she said, but when both Drake and Addison looked at her confused, she added, "He's like my nephew, but a dog."

"Oh, I get it," Addison said on a laugh, then went back to cooing at Melvin.

Morgan opened the door wider and ushered them inside.

Dreamy stepped into view at that moment. "Hello! You must be Drake and Addison," she said in her usual cheerful voice. "I'm Dreamy, Morgan's sister-in-law. Well, soon-to-be."

"Yeah, she and my brother are tying the knot next Saturday, and she and Melvin stopped by to pick up her wedding gown."

"Cool, you're getting married?" Addison said, her cute face beaming with wistfulness. Either she excited easily or she was already a hopeless romantic.

"I am, and I can't wait. The wedding is going to be like a fairytale," Dreamy said, grinning and holding her dress close to her body as if she were afraid she'd lose it. "I have an idea," she continued. "Why don't you and your brother attend the wedding with Morgan? She doesn't have a date, and two more people won't hurt the numbers. I promise it's going to be a blast, and you might even see a few famous people."

Morgan narrowed her eyes at Dreamy, silently asking, *What the hell?*

Why would she tell them she didn't have a date? As if she couldn't find a plus-one if she wanted to.

I'm going to kill her.

"You'll let us come?" Addison squealed. "I love weddings!"

Drake frowned. "What weddings have you attended?" he asked his sister.

"None, but I've watched plenty on TV and at the movies. Like *The Best Man*, *Bridesmaids*, and oh, *The Wood* with Omar Epps. That's one of Drake's favorites," Addison said, and continued rattling off wedding-centered movies.

It was safe to say that she really did like weddings. While Addison chatted it up with Dreamy, Morgan snuck a peek at Drake, who was looking at her.

Not knowing what to do or say, she smiled and asked, "Where's Aiden?"

"At home playing video games with one of his friends," he said.

Morgan tried not to fidget under his intense stare, but she couldn't help it. Maybe he was remembering their kiss from the night before. She knew she was.

"It smells good in here," he said, finally pulling his gaze from her and glancing down at the floor, where Addison and Melvin were now playing.

"Yeah, I made lasagna," she said proudly.

Drake's eyebrows lifted skyward.

"You finally learned how to cook, huh?"

Dreamy burst into a fit of coughing and laughing, and Morgan elbowed her in the side.

"Knock it off," she said and then told Drake, "I'm learning."

Drake nodded but didn't look convinced. "Well, it smells delicious."

"It does, doesn't it." Morgan beamed. "If you stick around, I'll give you a little taste."

The moment the words were out of her mouth, she realized how suggestive they sounded.

Drake's mind must've gone in the same direction if the humor in his eyes and the way his lips twitched were any indication.

"On that note, Melvin and I better be going." Dreamy repositioned the garment bag in her hand and clipped Melvin's leash onto his collar before guiding him to the door.

"I'm going to walk her out. You guys make yourselves at home. I'll be right back."

The moment Morgan stepped out the door, she whirled on Dreamy. "What the hell was that all about? Did you not hear me say that he probably doesn't even want to be around me?"

"I heard you, but I also saw how you two were stealing glances at each other. Well, you were stealing glances while he was outright staring. Face it, you guys are feeling each other, and who knows, maybe the wedding will be just the push you both need to see if there's anything still between you."

Morgan nibbled on her fingernail as she thought about what Dreamy was saying. After a day of playing *should she, could she* in her mind regarding Drake, maybe him attending the wedding wasn't a bad option. It would give them a chance to spend time together during the reception and continue getting reacquainted.

She grinned at Dreamy. "Okay, you might be on to something."

Chapter Nineteen

IMPRESSIVE, DRAKE THOUGHT AS HE STROLLED AROUND THE first floor of Morgan's condo. He lived and breathed real estate and admired the craftmanship and the finishes of her home. The double patio doors and wall of windows next to them in the family room, dark hardwood floors throughout, and recessed lighting were only some of the features.

Morgan had always had a great sense of style, but he wondered if she'd hired an interior designer or if she'd done the decorating herself. Everything was elegant, with bright colors, yet warm and homey. Even the two white sofas facing each other in the living room that clearly said *no kids live here* seemed cozy and inviting.

Thinking of kids, he already knew he wouldn't hear the last of it from Addison regarding Dreamy's wedding invite. Dreamy had barely cleared the threshold with Morgan before Addison pounced, begging him to let her attend the *fairytale* wedding.

Morgan had seemed just as surprised as him by the invitation, and what stunned Drake was that she didn't have a date. As beautiful and fun as Morgan was, there was no doubt men were clambering over one another to spend time with her.

Hell, he hadn't been able to stop thinking about her. He had tossed and turned all night with visions of her infiltrating his dreams. Yet the fantasies of her didn't do the actual woman any justice.

Drake had attempted to convince himself that he wasn't interested, and that they couldn't pick up where they left off, but damn if he didn't want to try.

What type of fool did that make him?

Yes, they were older and were making better decisions these days, but could he risk his heart again?

He didn't really know Morgan anymore. She seemed like the same happy-go-lucky woman he had fallen in love with in college. Yet there were some subtle differences. Talking with her last night, her conversation was more confident and mature, but that came with age . . . in most cases. But for them to start over . . .

"Wow, the man in this picture looks like that old actor guy," Addison said. She was standing at the mantel with a framed photo in her hand. "I can't remember his name, but he was the dad in that one movie . . ." She snapped her fingers several times, clearly trying to remember the title.

"He looks like the guy because it is him," Drake said. "Morgan's dad is Marcus Redford."

Addison's eyes bugged out. "Get out! Seriously?" She turned to the front door as Morgan reentered her home. "Morgan, your dad is a famous actor?"

Morgan grinned as she walked farther into the room, looking like a breath of fresh air in pink.

God, she was so beautiful. It was taking all of Drake's self-control not to go to her, sweep her into his arms, and kiss her until she begged him to stop.

But he wouldn't. Especially not in front of his sister.

"Yep. That's my dad," Morgan said.

"That is so cool!" Addison set the picture down and glanced at the others. "Does that mean you get to go to all of the movie premieres? Walk the red carpet? Attend the Emmys?"

"I've gone to a few premieres. I walked the red carpet once or twice when attending the Oscars, and yeah, it was pretty cool."

She explained how each time she attended had been life changing. Even though her family was often around the rich and famous, she still had her fangirl moments. Though she enjoyed seeing the fashion and celebrities, those types of events weren't really her thing.

Drake wasn't surprised. Morgan loved a good party, but she wasn't fond of being in the public eye or the chaos that came with it. Like the media and uncontrollable fans.

"So, are we ready to discuss homecoming dresses?" Morgan asked. "We can head up to my sewing room, and I can show you some of the ideas I have."

Addison clapped her hands and hurried to the bag that she'd left on the sofa. "Yes! I'm so excited. I can't wait to show you what I've been working on. I brought some magazines that have dresses I like, and I brought my dream book."

Morgan stopped walking. "Dream book?"

"Yes, I want to be a designer one day, so I have some sketches. I also have some pictures that I've cut out and pieced outfits to-gether." She shrugged. "Just stuff like that," she said as Morgan sifted through the binder.

Drake had seen Addison's work and there was no doubt that she had talent. He was constantly encouraging her to keep prac-ticing so that when an opportunity came her way, she'd be ready.

"Wow, you drew these?" Morgan's voice held a bit of awe as she sifted through the bedazzled notebook. "You're really good."

Addison grinned, her pink braces gleaming under the lights.

She knew she was good but getting validation from Morgan made all the difference.

"I think we might be able to put a couple of ideas together," Morgan said. "Let's head upstairs, and I'll show you what I was originally thinking."

Drake followed them up until Addison stopped midway on the staircase.

"Drake, you don't have to stay. I can call you when we're done. Besides, you'll probably be bored listening to us talk about clothes," she said.

He knew she'd be fine with Morgan, but Drake wasn't ready to leave.

"I'll stick around."

Morgan gave them a quick tour of her three-bedroom, three-and-a-half-bathroom condo and, like downstairs, the second floor was just as impressive.

Once they were in Morgan's sewing room, which was twice the size of a standard secondary room, it was clear where she spent most of her time. The space looked like a small garment factory along with a clothing showroom. A female dress form on wheels was in the far corner, along with a full-length mirror, and a long counter took up the right side of the room. It held a laptop, sewing machine, and cutting board.

The space was also playing another role—dressing room. There were at least fifty pairs of shoes on racks in another corner. Add those to the closet full of footwear in the master bedroom, and you had a woman who clearly had a shoe addiction.

For the next few minutes, Addison and Morgan talked and laughed nonstop. Drake's heart warmed at seeing his sister so happy and excited, and it was as if she and Morgan had known each other forever.

He stood out of the way, leaning against one of the window-sills and watching as they dived deep into planning Addison's outfit for the homecoming dance. A dance that Drake still wasn't sure he wanted her to attend, especially with some knuckle-headed boy. He'd made it clear to both her and Aiden that there would be no dating before they were sixteen, but Aiden had told him more than once that he was being unreasonable.

Maybe he was, and maybe he was a little too overprotective where Addison was concerned, but she was his little sister. She was the sunshine in his life, and he didn't want her to grow up too fast. He only reconsidered letting her attend the dance be-cause Aiden would be with her.

Morgan burst out laughing, snagging his attention. He didn't know what the two were talking about, but whatever it was prac-tically had them rolling on the floor.

Drake loved that they were hitting it off. As the twins were growing up, and after Morgan had left the country, he'd been careful when it came to bringing women around them. He didn't want them to get attached to anyone he had no intention of being with long term.

He didn't know what would happen between him and Mor-gan. He just hoped that whether their friendship grew or not, Addison wouldn't get hurt in the long run.

"Why'd you drop out of college?" he heard Addison ask, and Drake stiffened, waiting to see what Morgan would say.

"I wasn't into college the way I needed to be. I love fashion, but I wasn't sure it was what I really wanted to do. So I took some time off to figure out exactly what type of career I wanted."

Addison nodded. "I can understand that. Besides, no sense in wasting your parents' money if you really didn't want to be there."

Damn. Sometimes his sister sounded older than her fourteen years.

Drake sniffed the air and straightened when he smelled some-thing burning, and within seconds, the smoke detector blared.

Morgan jumped and Addison released a small scream.

"Oh no!" Morgan bolted out of the room and practically leaped down all of the stairs, with Drake and Addison on her heels. Smoke filled the main floor, and it was a wonder the detectors hadn't gone off sooner.

"Whoa, it's really smoky in here," Addison said next to Drake and started coughing as they entered the kitchen.

"Nooo!" Morgan cried. She snatched mitts from a hook and pulled a dish from the oven. "It's ruined!"

While she pouted over her charred dinner, Drake and Addison grabbed dish towels. Addison stood on a chair and started waving the towel under the smoke detector in the kitchen, and Drake did the same in the living room.

"We need to get some fresh air in here," Drake said more to himself than anyone else. He moved to the double patio doors and swung them open. The alarms were still going off, but at least the space wasn't as smoky. With the loud screeching, someone would probably start banging on the door soon, but just as the thought filled his mind, the noise stopped.

He left the doors open and entered the kitchen. Morgan was standing at the counter, staring down at her food.

"My lasagna is destroyed." She didn't take her attention from the black, burned-to-a-crisp meal. From where Drake was standing, it looked like a brick or something she could use as a weapon.

He tried not to laugh, but it was hard to feel bad for her when the situation was so funny.

Morgan pointed at him. "It's your fault! You were near the sewing room door. You should've been able to smell something before it started burning."

He reared back and placed his hand on his chest. "My fault? Seriously?" He could tell she wasn't angry by the way she poked out her sweet lips. Embarrassed maybe, but not angry. "We all were in the house together. You and Addison could've smelled it too. Besides that, who makes lasagna and doesn't set the timer? I'm sorry your precious pasta now looks like a big, charred cinder block."

"Dray-Dray, stop. Now you're just being mean," Addison chastised and draped her arm around Morgan's shoulders. "Don't be too upset. When I was little, I burned my spaghetti the first time I tried making it, but over the years, my cooking has gotten a lot better. Yours will too."

Morgan glanced at his sister and her perfectly arched brows dipped into a severe frown. Then she swatted at Addison playfully. "If that pep talk was meant to make me feel better, it didn't work."

"Oh . . . sorry," Addison said, fighting back a grin.

"I guess you still can't cook, huh?" Drake cracked, then burst out laughing when Morgan threw an oven mitt at him, and then another, making them all laugh.

He missed this . . . missed her. Morgan used to be comic relief without even trying, and apparently that hadn't changed.

Could he let her back into his life, in some capacity, and still protect his heart? Drake wasn't sure, but a huge part of him wanted to try.

Chapter Twenty

"OKAY, LET ME GET THIS STRAIGHT. YOU'VE GONE FROM NOT seeing Drake in years to spending the entire weekend with him?"

"It wasn't exactly like that," Morgan said to Isabella, who was sitting in front of Morgan's desk and looking at her with wide eyes.

"And now you're planning to ride with him to God knows where to learn God knows what about how and when your offer for the Hollywood property will be accepted?"

"Yeah, pretty much."

"Okay, before I get back to asking questions about Mr. Kellner and whatever the hell he's doing with this property, let's talk more about this weekend. You actually *cooked* for Drake and his sister? Or at least tried to," Isabella said, still with a note of shock in her tone.

"I didn't necessarily cook for them. They had planned to stop by around dinnertime. I figured it would be a good idea to have food there in case they were hungry."

"And you *cooked*? Or tried to."

"Why do you keep saying it like that?" Morgan snapped. "I didn't just try. I *did* prepare a meal. It's not my fault no one likes blackened lasagna."

"Okay, okay. Touchy, touchy. I'm just trying to understand what that looked like, especially since you can't cook, Morgan. Everybody knows that."

Morgan released an unladylike snort. "Whatever. I can cook," she defended weakly.

The last few days had been interesting, to say the least, but they'd also been exciting. Morgan was still trying to wrap her mind around the fact that she had seen Drake twice in the last two days. Granted, the day before had included his fourteen-year-old sister, but still, they had spent hours together.

After the embarrassing fiasco with the lasagna, Morgan had ordered dinner from her favorite Chinese restaurant, and the three of them ate a meal together. Having Addison there made it feel less like a date—not that it was to begin with—and more like friends hanging out. Yet Morgan had enjoyed every minute of their visit.

"I'll let the topic of your love life go, but what's up with this property?" Isabella sat back in her seat and folded her arms. "I'm starting to think that maybe we should look for a different place for you to purchase."

Morgan had thought the same thing for a hot second. Kellner might be making her and other potential buyers jump through hoops, but now that she had moved on to the next stage of the process, she wanted the property even more.

When Morgan heard from Isaac, he said that if she was still interested in the property, she should meet them at eleven o'clock at the address he'd given her. It was a different location from where the original meeting had been held, and it was south of Los Angeles.

"We've come too far to give up now. I want that building." Morgan pounded on the desk. "We *need* that building, and we're going to get it no matter what it takes."

A knock sounded just before their receptionist, Audrey, pushed the door open and peeked in.

"Sorry to interrupt, but Morgan, Casey Harris, your nine o'clock, is here. I put her in the meeting room. And Isabella, the plumber should be here in fifteen minutes."

"Thanks," Isabella said.

Morgan dropped back in her seat. "Thanks, Audrey."

The moment their receptionist closed the door, Morgan groaned. "I was hoping that by now we'd have a room for Casey."

The young woman checked in every few weeks, and Morgan felt a special connection with her. She couldn't explain it. Not that the others they helped weren't special, they all were, and they were making an effort to better their lives. But there was just something about Casey. Unfortunately, the young woman was still sofa surfing, hopping from one friend's place to another.

"I hate turning these kids away when I know how much they need us."

Isabella stood and stretched her arms high above her head. "I know. We'll get there. We should probably reevaluate our budget. Maybe we can find a larger temporary space, at least until the offer on the Hollywood property is accepted. Even if it is, though, it'll take months, if not a year to renovate the place."

"That's true," Morgan said. They needed a temporary solution as well as a backup plan when it came to finding more space.

She and Isabella had agreed early on not to use their personal money to keep the nonprofit going, but Morgan wondered if they should reconsider. They had a fundraiser planned for the end of the year, but the teens waiting for housing needed something now.

"And before you even say it, I'm standing firm on us not using our personal money to pay for hotel rooms or anything like that. We're able to offer housing at minimum cost to twenty teens, which is good. In time, we'll be able to help more, but we stick with the original plan."

"Fine, for now, but our plan needs tweaking."

Isabella headed to the door but stopped and turned. "One more thing. In case I don't see you before you leave for the meeting with Kellner, I need you to remember something."

Morgan recognized the seriousness in her tone and sat up straighter. "What's that?"

"Drake is your competition." Isabella lifted her hands when Morgan started to deny it. "Let me finish. I get that you're excited about seeing him again, but the timing isn't the best. He wants that building as much as we do. Keep that in mind while you're hanging out with him."

"I don't view him as competition," Morgan said defensively, even though that's exactly what he was when it came to the building. "That property will be ours," she said with conviction.

Hopefully, she was right. Only time would tell. For now, she didn't see anything wrong with spending time with Drake. She wanted both the building and a second chance with him, and she was confident that she could separate business and pleasure.

In the end, though, she'd get everything she desired.

DRAKE LAID HIS HEAD BACK AGAINST THE HEADREST AND stared out the windshield of his Ford F-150 truck at the two-story stucco building.

What the hell am I doing?

No. He knew what he was doing. He was taking a chance on

Morgan. Taking a chance on *them*. Maybe after they got to know each other again, they'd be able to create something stronger than what they'd had before she left him. Before she tossed him away like a ratty dish towel covered in mildew.

He rarely second-guessed his decisions, but that's exactly what he was doing now that he was sitting outside the Open Arms office. When he'd called Morgan that morning to see if she wanted to carpool to the meeting, he hadn't thought out the idea completely. Instead of using his brain to deal with her return to his life, Drake was using his heart.

The damn thing got him into trouble the last time they were together, and he hoped it wasn't going to be a repeat.

That was assuming, he gave in to his feelings.

Drake wasn't just physically attracted to Morgan. It was everything about her. Her smile, her playfulness, her love for life, and more importantly, the way she made him feel. They had a connection, one that Drake had never felt with another woman. He'd felt it the night at the diner and again last night at her place. There was something still between them, and he needed to figure out what.

"I don't know if I can," he mumbled into the quietness of the car. But he couldn't deny that he wanted to see her. He also wanted to get to know the person she had become.

But hadn't he learned his lesson when it came to her? She wasn't a good fit in his life. They didn't want the same things. Drake might've been fighting the idea of dating again, but he really did want to settle down one day with a special woman.

He just wasn't sure if Morgan was at that stage in her life. Hadn't she said she'd left the country to find herself? What if she was still trying to do that? What if they got close and she took off running again?

Drake shook his head and growled under his breath, frustrated that he was still letting her past actions seep into his thoughts. He either needed to walk away or forgive her completely and give her another chance.

That was assuming she wanted one.

If that kiss Saturday night and the sexual energy pulsing between them on Sunday at her place were any indication, she did.

This is ridiculous. I'm overthinking this.

He wanted Morgan. He wanted her in every way a man could want a woman. Yet he was sitting there, letting the fear of getting hurt overwhelm him.

"That stops now."

Who knows? Today when I see her, I might not feel any of the lust I felt this past weekend.

If that turned out to be the case, then he could move on with his life and not look back.

Drake climbed out of his truck and walked the short distance to the door. When he strolled into the building, a woman with a short Afro, huge gold hoop earrings, and African attire smiled at him.

"Hi, may I help you?" she said with a subtle accent.

"Yes, I'm here to see Morgan."

"She was in a meeting, but let me see if she's finished up. Your name?"

"Drake," he said, glancing around the small but tidy area. "If she's busy, no worries. I'm a little early."

She nodded and picked up the phone.

Drake roamed around the reception area. He could understand why Morgan wanted a larger space. In his estimation, the building wasn't more than ten thousand square feet. Really small for a mixed-use property.

A tingling sensation trekked up his back. Drake didn't have to turn around to know that Morgan was near. That was how it used to be back in college. He could sense when she was close by.

He glanced over his shoulder, and his pulse amped up at the sight of her. It wasn't that she was dressed up or looked any different than the last few times he'd seen her, it was just . . . her being her.

Her presence was like a breath of fresh air, wiping out any impurities floating through the atmosphere, and the heart-rending tenderness in her gaze was like a magnet pulling him toward her.

So much for him thinking that the intense yearning for her that he'd felt over the weekend was a fluke. Morgan was still in his system, and suddenly that was exactly where he wanted her.

"Hey, you. Let me show you around before we leave," she said, closing the distance between them.

Drake glanced at his smartwatch and mentally calculated when they would arrive if they didn't leave immediately. Then again, he was curious about her place of business. Maybe they could spare a couple of minutes and not be late.

"How are you?" she asked, flashing him a sweet smile that he felt to the depths of his soul.

"I'm good now."

She awarded him with a bigger smile and looped her arm through his.

"How are you?" he asked.

"I'm great, though a little anxious to know what your mentor is up to, but we'll see soon."

Yes, they would.

Drake walked alongside her while she explained that the first floor had their offices, a family room, a kitchen, and a dining space. The upstairs had been sectioned off into two wings—one side held the men's bedrooms; the other, the women's. A game room that held a pool table divided the two areas.

"And that's our little space. What we have works, but every day we have to turn away more and more teens looking for housing. You have no idea how frustrating that is."

"I can imagine," he said, and sympathized with her, but between her sweet scent—something that smelled like roses—and the way she was holding his arm and leaning into him, Drake could barely think straight.

He appreciated the tour, but what he really wanted to do was find an empty room, pull her into it, and kiss her the way he'd done in his dreams last night, long and hard.

"Let's head back downstairs to my office. I'll grab my bag and then we can leave."

"Sounds good."

As they descended the stairs, a redheaded woman looking down at an electronic tablet in her hands was passing the staircase.

"Izzy, hold up," Morgan called out.

Isabella glanced up, and Drake marveled at how she hadn't aged. She looked exactly the same as she had back in college.

She smiled up at them and the familiar mischief that used to always shimmer in her hazel eyes was still there. Seeing the two women together, people would probably assume that Morgan was more of an influence when it came to getting into trouble. That hadn't been the case in college. Isabella was the leader in that respect. In spite of that, she was also more serious about school and had been a straight-A student.

"Well, well, well, who do we have here?" she cracked, and Drake smiled.

"Good seeing you again, Isabella," he said as they embraced. "It's been a long time."

She nodded and gave him a sympathetic smile. She'd been the one to tell him that Morgan had left the country. He just hoped she wouldn't bring it up now. He was trying hard to keep the past in the past, and any mention of it might set him back.

"So what do you think of our humble operation here?" she said instead, and he could've kissed her.

"I'm impressed. I think it's wonderful what you've set up here." They all talked for a few minutes before Isabella had to leave them to take a phone call.

Drake followed Morgan down the hall to her office. When they entered the room, he wondered how she got any work done. The space was barely able to hold a desk and two chairs, but he didn't comment. Instead, he watched as she strutted across the room to her desk.

It had been a long time since he'd seen her in jeans, and damn if she wasn't wearing the hell out of the ones she had on. They hugged her cute little ass perfectly and made him want to palm her butt cheeks and pull her against his body.

"All right, you ready?" she asked when she was standing in front of him.

Hell yeah, he was ready, but probably not for what she was thinking of.

Something intense flared inside of him, and Drake cleared his throat. "Yes, but first . . ."

He slipped his arm around her waist and crushed her against his body. Morgan gasped just as he covered her mouth with his, but she quickly recovered. Her purse dropped from her hands and landed on the floor with a hard thunk before she looped her arms around his neck.

Drake kissed her with everything in him. He wanted her to feel how much he had missed her, how much he adored her, and how much he had longed for her. He once thought that God had made her specifically for him, and still he marveled at how perfectly she fit in his arms.

Morgan clung to him as if afraid he'd stop. Drake greedily took all that he wanted while trying to maintain some level of control.

This was what he wanted. Her, in his arms, molded against him. He couldn't stop his body from reacting to her nearness, and he didn't pull away even though he was pretty sure she felt the swell of his erection against her stomach.

"Mmm," she moaned, and the sexy sounds she was making were doing wicked things to him.

If they didn't stop now, he'd be tempted to swipe everything off her desk and do something crazy like stretch her out on top of it and have his way with her. He'd have her screaming his name over and over with each orgasm.

But acting out that fantasy wasn't how he wanted to start new with her. Besides, they needed to have a talk. He needed to know if their feelings were the same, and not just physically. He already knew that physically they were perfect for each other.

Raising his mouth from hers, Drake gazed into her eyes, trying to fight the aching need to kiss her again.

"Wow," Morgan breathed, and touched her fingers to her mouth. She took a few steps away, but her eyes never wavered from his. "I love kissing you, Drake, and I know there's still something unfinished between us. But the other night after we kissed, you said never again."

Drake released a long breath and closed his eyes as he rubbed the back of his neck. Dammit. He was sending mixed signals. Not intentionally, but in his attempt to figure out his own feelings, he was going hot and cold on her.

He opened his eyes and found her standing in front of him.

"I know I hurt you," she said, "but if this is you getting back at me by playing with my emotions, please—"

"No!" He shook his head vigorously and loosely gripped her shoulders. "Morgan, I would never intentionally play with your feelings. I'm sorry if that's what if feels like, but this is all on me. I'm still trying to grasp that you're . . . back. The last couple of days with you have been fun, exciting, and surprising. They've also been scary, confusing, and sleep-stealing days."

She laughed. "Yeah, I can relate."

"I came to terms with myself this morning, decided that I would really like for us to get to know each other again."

Morgan reached for his hand. "And I assume that's where the scariness comes in."

"Yeah, partly. I'm not going to lie. I don't want to get hurt again." And he knew she had the power to do just that.

"*I'm sorry* doesn't seem like a strong enough statement to express how horrible I feel about how I handled things between us in the past. All I can say is, I'm not the same person, and I will never hurt you again. I hope you believe me."

Drake nodded. "I do. What do you say to us getting to know each other again?"

"I'd say, I love that idea, but what would that look like?"

He glanced at his watch. "I'm not sure, especially since we're competing for the same building. How about for now we play it by ear?"

"I can live with that." Morgan picked up her purse from the floor and looped her arm through his. "I'm looking forward to getting to know you again, Mr. Faulkner."

Drake smiled down at her. "Same here, Ms. Redmond. Same here."

He didn't know what the future held for them, but for the first time in a long time, he had a feeling that it was going to be exciting and full of surprises.

I can't wait.

Chapter Twenty-One

MORGAN STARED OUT THE TINTED PASSENGER-SIDE WINDOW of Drake's truck, watching as traffic crept along on I-5. They were heading to North County and were twenty minutes into the hour-and-a-half drive. She was still mentally replaying the conversation that she'd had with Drake in her office.

There had been so many times over the years that she'd imagined what it would be like to reunite with him, but the reality exceeded her expectations. Inside, she was doing a happy dance and her heart felt lighter knowing that he had accepted her apology. That he was giving her another chance with him meant everything to her. It also thrilled and scared her.

She would do everything in her power to do it right this time, but what if she screwed it up again? Because she knew there wouldn't be a third chance.

Her pulse amped up, and she rubbed her hands over her jean-clad thighs. Even though it hadn't been intentional, Morgan knew she had hurt Drake in the past. She wouldn't be able to handle it if it happened again. Of course, she had no intentions of ever hurting him, but what if . . .

"You're awfully quiet," Drake said, jarring Morgan out of her thoughts. "Are you all right?"

"I'm fine," she croaked but cleared her throat. "Thanks for the ride. I hate driving in this traffic, and I'm glad you didn't mind picking me up."

"It wasn't a problem at all. I'm glad for the company, but I have a feeling that's not what had you lost in your thoughts. Talk to me. What's going on?"

The biggest problem they'd had in the past was her inability to communicate her fears about not being enough for him or not being what he needed in his life at the time. If only she had talked to him back then, maybe things would've turned out differently for them.

She wouldn't make that mistake again.

"I'm a little anxious," she blurted.

"About this meeting?"

"Yeah, that, but mostly about us. You're giving me a second chance and I don't—"

"No," Drake cut in and reached for her hand. He linked their fingers while splitting his attention between her and the road. "I'm giving *us* a second chance. We're moving on from what happened in the past, and we're going to see where this—whatever this is between us—goes.

"I'll admit, I'm a little anxious, too, but I'm also excited to have you back in my life. I'm going to do my best to leave past hurts in the past and focus on the here and now."

A powerful sense of relief flowed through Morgan's body, and she squeezed Drake's hand. She was so grateful for his forgiveness. "Thank you for saying all of that." A goofy grin kicked up the corners of her lips, and she couldn't help the giddiness that engulfed her. "This . . . you and me together, feels good, and I'm excited about us."

"Me too, and I haven't been able to stop thinking about you since you fell back into my life, pun intended."

Morgan laughed. "I have a feeling you're never going to let me forget the most embarrassing moment of my life. Well, at least one of the most embarrassing," she said, thinking about how she'd split her pants earlier that same day.

"Nope, I'll never forget it, but I'll try not to bring it up . . . too much."

Morgan turned slightly in her seat to better look at him. Isaac had mentioned that they should dress casual for the meeting, and Drake had listened, wearing a long-sleeve shirt, jeans, and a pair of boots.

"So where do we go from here?" Morgan asked. "Are we officially a couple, or is this just us getting to know each other better?"

Drake kept his gaze straight ahead, but Morgan could almost hear the wheels in his head churning with thoughts. While she was more of a fly-by-the-seat-of-her-pants person, he was a thinker, and weighed all options before making a move. Back in the day, he would make plans on top of plans, which she loved. Because if planning dates or outings had been up to her, their time together probably would've been centered around the student lounge or making out in the back seat of his car.

They definitely balanced each other and it seemed that hadn't changed.

Drake was still holding her hand, and he brought it to his lips and kissed the back of her fingers. A tingling sensation started in her hand and charged up her arm.

When he finally gave her his attention, something inside of Morgan stirred. It was more than just being attracted to him. That was a given. This man meant more to her than she could ever put into words. Before they had started dating in college, they'd been friends. So when she walked away from what they had, not only had she lost her first love, but she had lost her friend.

Drake was one of those people who came into your life and made it a hundred times better. She knew that in college but was too young and naïve to appreciate what he brought to her life. His loyalty, his honesty, and his ability to accept a person just as they were was priceless. She might not deserve him, but she was thankful to have him back.

"Morgan Redford, will you be my girlfriend . . . again?"

Morgan couldn't control her burst of laughter. *Oh, my God.* That was exactly how'd he asked her years ago. Except then they were in a dark four-door sedan with two empty car seats in the back, and they were headed to In-N-Out Burger.

"Yes!" she squealed and fell out laughing again. "I'd love to be your girlfriend."

"Think about it before you agree," Drake said seriously even though he was smiling. "I'm a little bossy. I have two teenagers at home who are a handful, but the best kids ever. I'm not a work-aholic, however work does consume me sometimes. But I promise not to let it interfere with our time together. Oh, and I still plan everything." He released an apologetic laugh. "Well, almost everything. This proposal of sorts wasn't exactly planned."

"But I'd guess you've probably been thinking about it for at least the last twenty-four hours," Morgan added.

"And you would be right." He chuckled.

"I have to admit, though, you've mellowed out some. I assume that has to do with the twins growing up."

"Probably. I was strung tight after my parents died. You know I spent that first year trying to figure out next steps for me and the kids."

"Yeah, and you took your responsibility seriously."

"I did, but in the process, I lost a part of myself. Nothing was fun anymore because I felt I had to be focused because I had these babies counting on me to get it right. Then you came along. The responsibilities were still there, but you helped me have fun."

Then I broke his heart, Morgan thought, and some of the joy from a moment ago dimmed.

"Hey," Drake said, tugging on her hand, which he was still holding. "Look at me."

Morgan did and the compassion in his gaze punched her in the chest.

"I didn't say any of that to make you feel bad. I appreciated the light that you brought to my life back then . . . and now. I know I'm putting you on the spot with all of this, but I really do want to date you."

Morgan folded her bottom lip between her teeth. She wanted to cry and laugh at the same time. "Dang, Drake, you say the sweetest things sometimes, and I have missed you so much." Despite the seat-belt constraint, she leaned over and kissed his cheek. "I want to date you too."

Drake slid his hand from hers and switched lanes when the traffic started to open up. "Then it's settled. We're a couple."

Morgan snuggled deeper into the buttery soft leather seat as they chatted about nonessential things, like the weather, the last movie they saw, and music. They're favorite music genre was R & B, but they both also enjoyed rap. They started discussing some of Jay-Z's latest hits as the rapper's voice spilled through the speakers and he sang about legacy.

That reminded Morgan of Drake's reason for wanting the Hollywood property. Would he still talk to her if her offer was the one that was accepted? Would she still talk to him?

The latter was a no-brainer, and she temporarily pushed thoughts of the property out of her mind. Win or lose, she was confident that they'd make their new relationship work.

When GPS informed them that they were fifteen minutes from their destination, Morgan asked, "Have you ever gone through something like this before? I mean, what Kellner and his team are putting us through."

"Never," Drake said without hesitation. "I don't know what this is all about. I get that the property means a lot to him, but if it means that much, he should just hold on to it. I feel like he's up to something, and it's more than just selling the property. I just can't figure out what."

"Maybe it'll be clearer once we get to the destination."

"That's the other thing. When I mapped this trip, it looks as if the address is close to Camp Pendleton," he said, referring to the Marine Corps military base. "As far as I know, there's nothing else really out there in that area."

"If I remember correctly, Mr. Kellner is a Marine vet. I think that's how he and my grandfather met. Anyway, maybe he has some connections and we're meeting on the base," Morgan suggested.

"Maybe, but why?"

Drake wasn't really asking her, but Morgan wondered the same thing.

A short while later, Drake turned off the highway and followed the mechanical female voice that was doling out directions through the truck's speakers. Ten minutes later, when Drake pulled his truck into a graveled parking lot, Morgan tried to keep her mouth from dropping open. There in the distance stood what appeared to be some type of elaborate obstacle course.

"You gotta be frickin' kidding me," Drake mumbled.

"No way is he expecting us to run through this thing today. Is he?" Morgan asked, more to herself than to Drake. She could barely run around the block without passing out. How the hell was she going to get through an obstacle course?

"Now I see why Isaac said to dress casually. Are you going to be able to walk through the grass and dirt in those heels?" Drake asked, nodding at her favorite pair of blue four-inch Jimmy Choo pumps.

Morgan looked at the grass they'd have to cross to get to the small group of people who had already gathered.

"Well, I guess I'm going to have to figure that out. One step at a time."

When Drake opened her door, he reached for her hand and helped her out of the truck. Morgan held on to him.

"Before we go . . ." Morgan lifted up on tiptoes and covered his mouth with hers.

The moment their lips connected, Drake slid his arm around her waist and pulled her against his rock-hard body. Morgan released a throaty groan, and her arms circled his neck. Chest to chest and thigh to thigh, they were so close to each other, no one would be able to tell where one started and the other ended.

Spirals of ecstasy swirled inside of her as Drake kissed her with a hunger that engulfed her to the tip of her toes. When his hands slid to her ass, Morgan wished that they weren't restricted by their clothes. Her body yearned for him, coming alive in a way that she hadn't experienced in years, as she gave herself completely to the passionate kiss. Not until a sharp whistle pierced the air did she remember where they were.

Morgan snatched her mouth from Drake's, struggling to catch her breath. It took several heartbeats for her to peek around Drake's wide shoulders to investigate where the sound had come from. Isaac was waving his arm back and forth in the air, and heat flooded her cheeks.

"Busted," she grumbled, embarrassed that they'd been caught.

Drake chuckled, brushing some of her braids from her face. "When you kiss me like that, it makes me want to reenact some of our back-seat make-out sessions." The bass in his voice had dropped an octave, sending goose bumps up Morgan's arms.

Her body vibrated with need. The man probably had no clue the effect his touch and his mouth had on her.

Goodness.

What would happen if he kissed other parts of her body? Morgan shivered at the thought, recalling a time when he loved on her body so thoroughly that she had practically turned to mush. The idea that that could be a reality in the very near future had her squeezing her thighs together to tamp down the desire pulsing through her.

"Whew!" Morgan fanned herself, ignoring Drake's sexy grin. "Okay, we'd better get over there before they proceed without us."

Chapter Twenty-Two

THEY CROSSED THE PARKING LOT, AND MORGAN WAS FINE UN-
til she reached the grass. She hadn't taken three steps before her
high heels sank into the soil.

Refusing to let Drake see that he'd been right about her shoe
choice, she tried to act as if it were no big deal and took another
careful step. Then another. The soil was softer than she expected, but all was good until she hit a spot where her heel sunk
deeper and she almost face-planted.

"Do you need me to carry you?" Drake asked. His tone was
serious, but the comical expression on his handsome face said
that he was enjoying her predicament.

"No, you go on ahead. I'll be there in a minute."

As he slowly walked away, Morgan took a few timid steps on
tiptoes, but when she slowed, her left heel sank even deeper than
before, catching her off guard. She released a small scream when
she fell forward onto one knee.

*Dammit. This is crazy. Who has a meeting out in the middle of a
prairie and doesn't tell people to wear boots?*

Okay, maybe it wasn't a prairie, but it was close enough.

Her hands were wet and dirty from the grass and soil, and she grumbled under her breath. When she finally righted herself, she looked up to see Drake heading her way at a clipped pace.

"You okay?"

Why did he have to keep witnessing her fiascos? "Yeah, I'm just peachy," she murmured.

"Good. Let's go."

Morgan screeched when Drake lifted her off the ground and over his shoulder in a fireman's carry the way he had the other night at the bar. He swung her up into his strong arms. Normally, she would love to be hugged up against his rock-hard body where his heady cologne tantalized all of her senses, but not now. Especially not when her shoes were still planted in the ground, leaving her barefoot.

Drake bent slightly, picked up the shoes, and started moving back the way he'd come.

Oh, my God. This is so embarrassing.

"Drake, put me down. I'm going to kill you!" she seethed. "I can walk. They're going to think I'm some damsel in distress and can't hold my own."

"Well, considering you couldn't walk two feet without stumbling, I'd say they'd be right."

She socked him in the back as hard as she could, but it was like hitting a brick wall—he probably didn't even feel it.

"Ow," he barked. "I'm trying to help you here."

"You're not helping. You're embarrassing me. Now put me down," she said through gritted teeth.

He tilted her slightly and she saw the dirt and mud below her. "Are you sure you want me to put you down right here? Because I'm pretty sure your precious high heels will look like you trudged through a mud pit, and seeing as you don't have on socks, that means your feet will get dirty, Angel."

"Urgh." He knew she hated getting dirty, and that she didn't even walk barefoot around the house. "You're such a wiseass. Just go," she bit out.

Minutes later, they reached asphalt, and Drake set her shoes down, then slowly lowered her to the ground. Morgan quickly stepped into her pumps, adjusted her blouse, and dusted off her jeans. When she looked up, twelve sets of eyes were on them.

"Glad you two could finally join us," Isaac said dryly, and Morgan wanted to wipe that smug expression off his face. "If you're done playing around, I'll get this meeting started."

Drake said something under his breath, but Morgan couldn't make it out. Yet she could imagine whatever it was included *asshole* and maybe a few other choice words.

"Thank you all for joining us here this morning," Mr. Kellner said, addressing the group.

Instead of the fifteen people who had sat around the conference table a few days ago, there were now ten of them, along with him and Isaac.

"Congratulations on making it to the last and final round," he continued, his voice stronger than he looked as he leaned heavily on his walking stick.

Morgan felt even more incompetent now that she realized he must've walked across the soggy grass.

"I was touched by your letters, and all of you make good cases as to why you should win the bid for this property. I know you think what I'm having you go through is ridiculous, but like I said before, that property means the world to me. It sounds like that would be the same case for whoever walks away with the deed when this is all over."

Morgan listened as he discussed how valuable it was, and that their efforts to own it would pay off in more ways than one. Her brother Karter had told her that if she purchased the place, she would already have equity in it. The building was located in a touristy area and was considered prime real estate.

She didn't know what was to come today, but Morgan was up for the challenge.

"I still don't understand why we have to go through all of this to purchase the property," a man standing across from Morgan said. He was tall and lean, with short blond hair and startling blue eyes. "Why not just pick the highest bidder and put an end to this?"

"I could do that, but Johnathan, I want this project, for lack of a better word, to be more than just about buying and selling. I'll let Isaac explain."

Isaac seemed to pull a lawn chair out of thin air, because all of a sudden, he had one in his hands. He opened it for Mr. Kellner and helped him sit in it. Once the old man was settled, Isaac turned back to the group.

Drake was doing a terrible job of keeping his frustration at bay as he fidgeted next to Morgan. He folded and unfolded his arms while kicking at pebbles near his feet.

He wasn't alone in the irritation department. Seemed all of them were anxious to hear what else they had to do to get the property.

"As you can see from what's behind me, this round will involve an obstacle course and a—"

"There is no way in hell I'm doing that," a big, burly guy with a reddish beard said. Morgan had seen him at the meeting the other day but didn't know his name. "I didn't put in a bid on a multimillion-dollar building just so that I can run around and make a fool of myself trying to climb over a damn wall."

He had basically spoken the words that all of them were thinking. Actually, Morgan was waiting for Isaac and Kellner to tell the group that it was just a joke, but by the serious expressions on their faces, it definitely wasn't.

"Mr. Traverse, if at any point in this presentation you would like to leave and withdraw your name from the running, by all means, please do. Otherwise, I'll continue," Isaac said with authority, unfazed by the grumbling and the cursing coming from the small group.

"Some of you might know that Mr. Kellner is a war vet. He served his country through four tours. When he retired from the military, he was instrumental in getting this obstacle course built. It was originally designed as part of a program to help veterans who were battling with PTSD. Since then, it has served many purposes, including organizing and participating in fundraising events.

"Some of you might've heard of To Love a Veteran. If not, I'll explain to you what it is. It's a charity that raises money every year to help military women and men get reacclimated to civilian life once they leave the military. The charity is close to Mr. Kellner's heart.

"Each year they do a fundraiser called Titan Games. These games take place during a two-day event, and a minimum of fifty people participate. This year, as part of your financial offer to purchase the Hollywood property, you will be required to participate in this fifteen-piece obstacle course, as well as the 10K run."

"You guys have lost your mind," Drake said on a bitter laugh. "I'm with Mr. Traverse. I'm not spending multimillion dollars on a property and *then* putting on a show for you guys just for the fun of it. Nope, not gonna happen."

"Then you can leave," Mr. Kellner said with a powerful edge in his voice as he glared at Drake. "As a matter of fact, anyone who feels they can't participate in the Titan Games, now would be a good time for you to walk away. No hard feelings, just know that your offer will be taken off of the table."

"Come on. Let's go," Drake said close to Morgan's ear. Her body was so aware of his closeness, and his large hand that rested at the small of her back sent shock waves charging through her body.

But she didn't move.

Morgan wanted to leave with him, but she couldn't. She wanted this property more than anything she'd wanted in a long time, and she planned on getting it. Seeing that she could barely run down a flight of stairs without huffing and puffing, she might kill herself in the process, but she wasn't walking away.

Not only did she and Open Arms want the building, the charity sounded like a good cause. According to her father, it had taken a while for her grandfather to get reacclimated to civilian life after leaving the military, and he had suffered from PTSD. Things didn't start turning around for him until he became an actor in his early fifties.

Morgan looked Drake in the eyes. "You go. I'm staying."

Chapter Twenty-Three

DRAKE COULD ONLY STARE AT MORGAN. HER STATEMENT WAS like a sucker punch in the gut with a sledgehammer. He couldn't believe his ears. She was considering going through with this ridiculous idea.

I'm staying.

Her words played on a loop in his head. The woman he once knew didn't have an athletic bone in her body. She had an aversion to getting dirty, sweating, and exercise.

How the hell did she think she could get through an obstacle course when she wouldn't even walk up a flight of stairs?

There was no way she was capable of this type of physical exertion . . . and to run a 10K? He'd have to see it to believe it.

"You're planning to continue with this . . . this . . . farce?" he asked. Her facial expression hadn't changed, and the determined set of her body language said that was exactly what she was planning.

"I have to see this through," she said. "I'm not the same girl you knew back in college, Drake. I follow through on anything that I set out to do."

"Is that right?" he said, unable to hide the doubt in his tone.

"Stick around and you'll see." The challenge in her eyes and her sugary smile only punctuated her words.

Drake huffed out a breath and turned from her, then realized that he had attracted an audience with his earlier outburst.

"Drake, if you're bowing out, leave now and stop wasting our time. If you're staying, I don't want to hear anything else from you," Jeffrey said in his no-nonsense tone. It was the same one he used when Drake didn't do something correctly when purchasing real estate. The tone usually accompanied the word *hardheaded*.

"Yes, sir," he said, knowing he would get another earful about his behavior from Jeffrey at some point.

"And then there were seven," Isaac said as three of the ten people stomped away from the group and headed back to their vehicles. There were three women left, including Morgan, and the rest were men.

This might not be as bad as he'd originally thought. He'd get a few laughs, and based on the people who hadn't walked away yet, he shouldn't have too much competition.

"Before I give you more details, let me explain why we had you to come out here. We wanted you to actually see the obstacle course while we give you all of the details of what's involved. Also, let me say . . . this is not a place to wear your finest attire. You will get dirty." Isaac looked pointedly at Morgan, and Drake couldn't stop the snicker that slipped through. Was it childish? Probably. Did he care? Nope.

"As I mentioned, the Titan Games are a two-day event," Isaac continued. "It'll take place the first weekend of November. The obstacle course will be on that Saturday morning and the 10K, the morning after. You'll have eight weeks to prepare."

A tall man, built like a linebacker and dressed in military fatigues, approached the group and stood next to Isaac.

"This is Major Sullivan. He will be overseeing the obstacle course portion of the event. You'll have his contact information included in the packet that you'll receive before you leave today. It'll have all of the details pertaining to the Titan Games, including the rules of the competition, a schedule for doing a practice run through the course, and details about selling tickets.

"Which reminds me. Each of you will be expected to sell, not give away but actually sell, twenty-five tickets to this event. Of course you're welcome to sell more, but that's the minimum."

Grumbling started up again around the small group, and Drake glanced at Jeffrey. Even if his mentor wanted to do something grand for this charity, why go about it this way? Why attach it to the Hollywood property? Drake didn't understand, and he knew Jeffrey well enough to know that he might never share his real reasons for making them jump through literal hoops.

"I'm sure some of you are wondering why we are requiring you to *sell* tickets. Our goal is to raise money for this charity, but also to bring as much awareness to it as possible. All of you are well connected and can reach people that we might not be able to. By selling tickets, you're helping us spread the word about To Love a Veteran."

Okay, that makes sense, Drake thought, even though it all seemed like one big hassle, like he didn't already have a million things on his to-do list. But just glancing around the group and recognizing some familiar faces, he could see Jeffrey and Isaac's point. One of the people still interested in the property was a former professional golfer. He probably knew other athletes who could financially support the cause. Another guy owned several art galleries around the country, and then there was a woman who

Drake recently learned owned an investment firm. Why these particular people wanted the property was a mystery, but there was no doubt that they were well connected.

Drake continued listening as Major Sullivan discussed some of the obstacles that were part of the course, including tires, a climbing wall, a twenty-foot tunnel . . . the list seemed to go on and on. There were a total of fifteen obstacles. Some of them sounded challenging for the average person, but it was clear that everyone's physical abilities would be tested.

"The winner for both events, based on their average finish time, will win the bid for the building with their initial offer. If at that time the winner decides that they are no longer interested in purchasing the building, the opportunity will go to the second-place winner," Jeffrey explained.

"And if you're thinking about having someone else in your organization, a family member, or a friend run for you, get it out of your head," Isaac added. "You are the only ones who can represent your companies in the Titan Games."

Silence fell over the group, and Drake was pretty sure some of them had planned to do just that. Especially the older guy with a beer belly who was easily carrying an extra forty pounds on his frame.

As Drake sized up the small group remaining, there was only one person, Johnathan, who might be any competition. He didn't know the guy personally, but he appeared to be in good physical shape. Drake wasn't too worried about the golfer, since the guy hadn't competed professionally in a couple of years. The man wasn't in as good shape as he used to be, and Drake would be surprised if the other bidders even showed up for the event.

Hope blossomed within him. He saw the Hollywood property as part of his legacy, and he was starting to feel good about his prospects of owning it.

HOURS LATER, DRAKE AND MORGAN WERE HEADING BACK TO the city.

"I'm surprised you're moving forward with the Titan Games," he said. "I recognize that you've changed a bit since college, but this side of you caught me off guard."

Morgan snorted. "Some things haven't changed. I still hate working out, but I'm determined to get that building," she said, then held up a hand. "Sorry, I know you want it as bad as I do, but—"

"Sweetheart, you don't have to apologize. I get it. That property is a gold mine in so many ways. I know I tripped out at the idea of competing in this event, but it'll be fun. As for us contending against each other, it changes nothing between us."

"I don't know how this is going to work. Not the part about us dating. What I'm not looking forward to is us competing against each other. I already know it's a long shot for me to go up against you in something so athletic, but I feel like if I don't at least try, I've already lost."

"That's true. All we can do is give it a shot." Drake wasn't just talking about the competition, but also their relationship.

"I wouldn't be able to forgive myself if I didn't give it my all," she said, oblivious to the direction of his thoughts, but he hoped she felt the same about their reunion.

"Yeah, I plan to give it my all too," he said. "The fact that you're stepping out of your comfort zone says a lot about the woman you've become. It's respectable, and like I've said before, if I don't win, I hope you do."

"Same here, and hopefully I don't kill myself in the process."

"You won't."

Though Drake had every intention of winning the Titan Games, he wanted Morgan to make a good showing. He'd do whatever he could, short of losing, to make sure that happened.

Morgan turned slightly in the passenger seat to look at Drake. "If you win the competition, what renovations would you do to the building?"

"I'd like to keep the design close to what my father created, but I plan to freshen everything up. The building needs some work, and it's not operating at full capacity because of that. I want to keep the retail businesses on the ground level, and office space on the top two floors, but there are a lot of vacancies. Some remodeling will make it more appealing to those looking to lease, but I would try to maintain the overall character while also adding some modern touches."

"So you won't be just slapping a coat of paint on it and calling it a day?"

He shook his head and smiled, and her heart did a little giddyup. Back in school, Drake didn't smile a whole lot around others, but that wasn't the case when they were together. It was amazing how his smile could literally light up her world. That was one of many things she had missed about him.

Morgan had the sudden urge to touch the light scruff on his cheeks. He had the prettiest dark skin and normally his mustache and goatee were perfectly groomed. Today, it looked as if maybe he had skipped shaving, and she liked it. He was ruggedly handsome.

"Not saying that this will happen, but what are your backup plans if you don't get the Hollywood property?" Drake asked.

Morgan knew it was a long shot competing in the Titan Games, but she was a true believer that anything could happen. Besides, it would be her biggest accomplishment to date if she won. Beating Drake would be the cherry on top.

"If I don't win, I guess I'll have to look for another building. That one is perfect, though. There are so many places in that area where our clients could get jobs. If they worked and lived in the same building, it would make for a perfect commute. Most can't afford a car, so walking and the city bus are their forms of transportation."

Drake nodded. He might not have had it as tough as some of the individuals Morgan's nonprofit served, but he understood their struggle. If she didn't get that property, maybe he could help her find another one. Surely he knew of some, since he was in the real estate industry. But if it came down to it, Morgan would deal with that after the Titan Games.

"Instead of buying a mixed-use building, why not just buy up a few homes next to each other and turn them into something like group homes for the teens?" Drake asked as he coasted through traffic, which was surprisingly not as congested as earlier. No doubt that would change as they got closer to L.A.

"We've thought of that, but most of them have had to live that way all of their lives. Did you know that over twenty thousand kids age out of foster care annually?"

"Wow, I had no idea it was that many."

"Most people don't. A small percentage of those kids will have jobs or go on to college, but many of the others end up on the street. Those are the ones we're trying to save. It'll take years for us to get to the point where we can help even half of them, but one day, we're hoping to expand services across the country."

"That's pretty ambitious," Drake said.

"It is, but not impossible. We've started small, but we'll get there. We're sticking with the idea of them having their own apartments. Many of our clients see that as being out of reach. I'm sure there will be some who want a roommate, but for the first time in their lives, they'll have a choice. Though most of their rent will be paid with grants or donations, they will still have to pay a portion.

"Between leasing them an apartment for a year, helping them find employment, and teaching them how to budget their money, we're giving them a chance to get their adult life started. The apartments won't be huge, but they'll be furnished, and to them, it'll feel like luxury . . . and home."

"Sounds like you and Isabella have thought of everything."

"I'm sure we haven't, but we've tried to figure out what the minimum is that these kids will need to start their new lives."

"I'm impressed," he said, nodding.

"Don't be impressed yet. We have a long way to go."

"Yeah, but you're doing way more than most people are doing. I never even thought about what happens to those kids when they age out of foster care. I'm glad they have you and Isabella."

Heat flooded Morgan's cheeks. His praise of her work meant more than he would ever know. When she'd left him years ago, she'd had nothing going for her and no plan. It was nice that he could actually see her doing something with her life.

Drake's phone rang through the truck speakers, and Addison's name flashed on the dashboard.

"I was wondering when one of them would call. They had a half day at school today." Drake answered the call. "Hey, kid, what's up?"

Addison's voice came on the speakers. "Hi, Drake, I was just thinking."

"Oh, boy. Every time you start thinking it either costs me time or money. Which is it?"

"Neither . . . well, not exactly. Are you and Morgan still at your meeting?"

Drake glanced at Morgan with an expression that clearly stated he had no idea where this question was going.

"Yes. She's in the truck with me, and we're thirty minutes out. Why?"

"Oh, hey, Morgan! I'm glad you're there. Are you busy tomorrow night? I'm cooking dinner and I wanted to invite you. I was going to ask Drake first if it was okay, but since you're there . . ." Her words trailed off.

Morgan smiled. Talk about putting her and Drake on the spot.

"I actually like that idea." Drake beamed, and if Morgan didn't know better, she would've thought he had something to do with the invite. "What do you say? Would you be interested in having dinner with me and my siblings tomorrow night?"

Morgan might've had reservations years ago about being a part of his and the twins' lives, but that was starting to change. After spending time with Addison the other day, she was looking forward to getting to know her and Aiden better.

Her answer was a no-brainer.

"I'd love to."

Chapter Twenty-Four

"THANKS FOR PICKING ME UP FOR DINNER, EVEN THOUGH I could've driven myself," Morgan said when Drake pulled into his garage.

"I know, but I wanted to. I couldn't wait to see you, and I selfishly wanted you to myself, even for a short while."

Morgan laughed and the melodious sound wrapped around him like a gentle embrace.

He would've preferred if Addison had given him a heads-up about dinner, but he loved the idea. She and Aiden were the most important people in his life, and he was anxious for them to get to know Morgan.

He shut off the truck and reached for her hand. "You look beautiful tonight." Actually, he couldn't ever remember a time when she wasn't stunning. Morgan's natural beauty showed on her sienna-brown skin, and her eyes always seemed to sparkle no matter her mood.

"Thank you. I wasn't sure what to wear, but figured I'd go with casual."

He glanced down at her footwear; again she wore sky-high heels. "We clearly need to work on your definition of casual. The sweater and jeans fit the dress code, but heels?" He shook his head with a smile.

"I'll have you know that casual can include heels. Besides, these short booties go perfectly with my jeans."

"Fine. You look good in anything, and if at any point you need to kick off your shoes, go for it. I want you to make yourself at home."

She squeezed his hand. "Thanks. I'm looking forward to hanging out with you three. I'll admit, I was a little nervous at the idea, especially since you and I just started dating again. Addison and I get along great, but what if Aiden doesn't like me?"

Drake studied her to see if she was kidding, but soon realized that she was serious. The twins were both easygoing, especially Addison. Maybe whatever insecurities Morgan had years ago still lingered, and Drake didn't want to say or do anything that would make her think he didn't take her concerns seriously.

"They are going to be crazy about you just like I am. You're right, we're stepping into unchartered territory here, but I know my sister and brother. They go with the flow. Everything is going to be fine."

Morgan nodded. Though she didn't look nervous, she gripped his hand tightly as they strolled together to the door that led into the house. Before going in, Drake turned her and gently pushed her back against the door.

"Relax, baby. It's just us, and it's only dinner with a couple of fourteen-year-old kids. Be yourself."

"Okay, but when I take you guys to my parents' house, and you meet my mother, Kalena Redford, you remember those words. Because you're going to need all of the relaxation techniques you can conjure up to meet her."

"Hmm . . . so you're planning to introduce me to the family, huh?"

The corners of her scarlet red lips tilted into a grin. "Yeah. You're important to me. Well, actually, you've always been important to me. Though we didn't get around to meeting family members last time, this time I want you to meet mine."

When they'd dated in college, she never suggested he meet her family. If he was honest, he'd been okay with that. With all the responsibilities he'd had at the time, he liked it that way. For just a little while, he could pretend that he was like other college students whose only responsibility was showing up for class and getting a passing grade.

Drake lowered his head and covered Morgan's lips with his. He told himself that it was to help relax her, but in reality, he selfishly wanted to taste her sweetness again. The brief kiss that they'd shared at her place minutes ago hadn't been nearly enough to satisfy his desire for her.

"Mmm," she moaned and slipped her hand around the back of his neck and pulled him closer, deepening their kiss.

Oh yeah, this was something he had missed. He would never get enough of kissing her. Or touching her, he thought, as he slipped his hand beneath her sweater and caressed her silky soft skin.

The door suddenly swung open, and Drake lost his balance as the two of them crashed into the house and landed on the floor of the mudroom.

"Dang, Drake. You can't even let her into the house before shoving your tongue down her throat. What the heck? Are you looking for her tonsils or something?" Aiden's words penetrated the temporary fog in Drake's mind.

"Oh, my goodness," Morgan murmured, then started laughing as she pushed against Drake, trying to get untangled.

As they got up and dusted themselves off, Drake decided that it wasn't going to be easy dating with kids around. Especially when one of them was a smart aleck like Aiden.

"Morgan!" Addison squealed from the kitchen, then plowed through the mudroom and threw her arms around her as if they hadn't just seen each other a few days ago.

Morgan laughed and would've toppled over had Drake not had a hand on her back.

"I'm so glad you came. I hope you're hungry." Holding her hand, Addison pulled her into the kitchen. "There's plenty of food. Would you like a glass of wine?"

Morgan's brow went up in surprise.

"Don't worry. I never touch the stuff," Addison said with a straight face. "But Drake said that you like red wine, and he bought your favorite."

Drake chuckled. His sister was on a mission to play her version of a matchmaker even though he and Morgan had already agreed to give their relationship a second chance.

Morgan flashed him one of her seductive smiles that he felt to the soles of his feet. He had wanted her to feel welcome in his home, and it felt like they were off to a good start.

"It smells amazing in here," she said and glanced around the kitchen that Addison had insisted he remodel the year before. It was the least he could do since she loved cooking for him and Aiden. Several food dishes covered the countertop, and she had stacked dinner plates and glasses on another counter.

His sister had been busy, determined to make everything perfect. She had marinated four steaks overnight and started preparing the side dishes when she'd arrived home from school.

It was evenings like today that he appreciated Ms. Lawson. She was an older woman who used to live next door when they were in an apartment. Not only had she babysat on occasion, she also taught both kids how to cook. Since then, Addison had enhanced her skills by watching cooking demonstrations on YouTube.

Addison put them all to work. Aiden tossed a salad while she had Morgan set up the dining room table, an area of the house they rarely used. Drake was responsible for opening wine for him and Morgan.

Once they were sitting down at the table, general conversation flowed, except Aiden was quieter than usual. He kept his head down and shoveled food into his mouth as if he hadn't eaten in days.

"Addison, everything is so good. Thank you again for inviting me to dinner. I would offer to cook next time, but we already know how that would probably turn out."

Drake smiled, glad she could make fun of herself. He loved that she was there, and looked forward to many more family dinners that included her.

Throughout the meal, he struggled to keep his hands off Morgan. If he wasn't touching her jean-clad thigh, he was playing with one of her microbraids. Each time they were together, it felt like the first time.

Everyone's attention shifted to Aiden when he slammed his fork down and it clattered against the plate.

"What's wrong with you?" Drake asked.

"So just like that y'all are lovey-dovey? Aren't you afraid Morgan is going to cut out again and dump you? Or once wasn't enough?" Aiden asked around a mouth full of food, and silence filled the room.

Anger swam through Drake as Morgan sat frozen next to him.

He wiped his mouth with his napkin and pushed back his chair, ignoring the way the legs scraped across the hardwood floor. Pointing at Aiden, he said, "In my office . . . now!" He squeezed Morgan's shoulder, hoping that his brother hadn't totally ruined the evening.

Addison scrambled to her feet as the two of them started to

move from the table. "Wait a minute. Drake, Aiden didn't mean—"

"Finish eating, Addy," Drake said and followed after his brother.

When he reached the office, he stormed inside and slammed the door closed.

MORGAN SAT STUNNED, STARING DOWN AT HER PLATE AS THE fellas stomped out of the room. Part of her wanted to go after Aiden and explain what she'd been going through years ago, but why bother? He was right. She had treated Drake horribly, as if he hadn't been the love of her life. The man she absolutely adored.

She released a long, frustrated sigh, and when she looked up, Addison was watching her with tears in her eyes.

Morgan's heart broke. This was only supposed to be a fun, get-to-know-you-better family dinner, and she had ruined it.

"I know you're not the same person who hurt Drake when you guys were in college," Addison said. "But why did you leave him without saying goodbye? Was it because of me and Aiden?"

"Oh, sweet girl, no." Morgan hurried out of her seat and sat next to Addison in the chair Aiden had vacated. "You and Aiden had nothing to do with my leaving. It was all me. I needed to do some growing up, and I didn't think I was good enough for your brother at the time."

Morgan shared part of the explanation that she'd given to Drake the other day. She was surprised that Addison, and apparently Aiden, knew how things had ended between her and Drake. Or at least part of the story. They were so young at the time— had they overheard him telling someone what had happened? Had he told them himself?

She doubted the latter. Knowing Drake, he probably didn't tell anyone. So how had they found out? At this point, it didn't really matter. What mattered was that she made it clear that their relationship didn't end because of the twins.

"You really thought you weren't good enough for my brother?" Addison asked. Out of all that Morgan had told her, that was the part that she latched onto. "He loved you. That means you were more than good enough for him."

"Are you sure you're only fourteen?" Morgan asked, hoping to lighten the moment. Addison was so mature. It was easy to forget she was a teen when she acted like a grown woman at times.

Addison smiled. "I read romance novels. Don't tell Drake," she whispered. "At least I know why he didn't want another serious relationship. He didn't want to get close to anyone else after what happened between you and him."

Damn. Just twist the knife in even deeper.

"I left to become a better person. I wasn't as wise as you, and I made some mistakes. Mistakes that caused me to lose the only guy I really loved."

"When you left, were you planning to come back to him at any point?"

Morgan wondered if Addison already suspected the answer.

"No, and it wasn't because I didn't love him. I thought he was better off without me. Besides, so much time had passed between us. I didn't think he would want me back."

"I think he would've. He's been happier since you're back in his life. Just think of the time you've wasted. You could've had a few kids by now, and I could be an auntie," she said breezily.

Kids?

Morgan wasn't sure if or when something like that would happen. Drake might've been marriage material, but during one of their conversations, he'd made it sound like having kids wasn't on his radar. Why would it be when he had already given up so much of his life to raise his siblings?

Morgan returned her attention to Addison. "You would make a wonderful auntie."

But Morgan wasn't sure if she could ever see herself as anyone's mother.

Chapter Twenty-Five

"WHAT THE HELL WAS THAT IN THERE?" DRAKE ROARED THE moment they were in his office with the door closed. He stood in Aiden's face. "What were you trying to accomplish? Morgan is a guest in our home, and she's very important to me. How dare you talk to her like you're talking to one of your peanut-headed friends. Have you lost your mind?"

Aiden shoved past him. "You're the one who's acting all brand new, like you've forgotten what she did to you. How can you pretend like nothing happened?"

Drake shook his head, feeling as if he had missed part of the conversation. "What are you talking about?"

"I'm talking about how she kicked you to the curb when me and Addy were little. She treated you like crap, and now you're taking her back? Aren't you afraid she's going to run away again? Do you really want to go through that a second time?"

Drake just stared at his brother, who looked as miserable as Drake had felt years ago when he first learned that Morgan had left him. There were times when Aiden and Addison could feel each other's pain, their hurt. If he didn't know any better, he'd think that was happening between him and Aiden.

"Who told you about that?" Drake asked, already knowing the answer. There was only one person who knew how much he loved Morgan back then. Well, maybe two, but Jeffrey never knew Morgan's name.

After a long hesitation, Aiden said, "Uncle Matt. He's worried that Morgan is going to make you fall in love with her again, and then toss your ass away like she did when you guys were in college."

Drake snorted, knowing that part of that comment was probably a direct quote. Normally, he'd reprimand Aiden for cursing, but decided to let it slide this time.

As for Matteo, it wasn't that his friend didn't like Morgan. He did. He had once told Drake that he thought she was the perfect balance to his serious, rigid side. Still, he hadn't liked the way she had taken off and he hadn't hesitated to share his opinion on the subject. They'd always been closer than brothers, but in this instance, Matteo had overstepped. It was not his place to tell the kids anything about Morgan.

"Listen, you don't have to worry about me," Drake started, and walked to the nearby sofa, expecting Aiden to follow. He sat on the edge of the cushion, but his brother stayed rooted in place. "It's my job to worry about you and Addy. Not the other way around."

Aiden stomped over to the sofa and pointed at him. "See, that's where you're wrong. I know sometimes you think I'm just some goofy kid who is always clowning around, but I look out for you and Addy. You guys are all I have and there is no way I'm letting somebody come around and punk you again! Not even Morgan."

Aiden rarely raised his voice. Out of the three of them, he was most like their father with his calm demeanor. It was clear that the Morgan situation bothered him.

"Have a seat." Drake nodded to the upholstered chair next to the sofa. After a slight hesitation, Aiden dropped down in the chair. "It wasn't Morgan's intent to hurt or *punk* me. She had her reasons for leaving, and though I didn't know them at the time, I know them now. Matteo didn't tell you the whole story because he doesn't know it."

Drake had no intention of telling Aiden everything, because technically it wasn't any of his business. But he did share parts of what Morgan had told him the other night.

"I could be real intense back then, and I was driven. That's not who Morgan was, and instead of me making her feel like she was a part of my future, she felt intimidated."

They talked for a few minutes longer before Drake said, "You hurt her feelings with what you said in there, and that's unacceptable. How do you plan on apologizing?"

"What, you don't think sorry is enough? I have an extra spider that—"

"Dude, if you bring out one of your stupid toys and even think about giving it to her, I'm going to knock you out. Then I'm going to hide your body somewhere no one will find it."

Aiden laughed, and the tension in the room dissolved. "That's not going to work. Addison would find me. You know we have that twin telepathy thing going. Not even a six-foot-deep grave could shut that down."

Okay, this was getting a little too morbid. Instead of keeping the nonsense going, Drake said, "Duly noted."

"So, you and Morgan, huh?"

Drake leaned forward with his elbows on his thighs and linked his fingers. "Yeah. Maybe I should've talked to you and Addy before Morgan and I—"

"Actually, you don't owe us an explanation. You're grown. You can do whatever you want to do."

Drake chuckled. How many times had he said that to the twins whenever they thought they were adults? He'd tell them that when they got grown, they could make their own decisions. Until then, he was the boss.

He studied his brother, who was slouched down in the chair. Aiden was a mystery. Some days he acted like a grade schooler while other days he acted like the intelligent young man Drake knew he was.

"Thanks for looking out for me," he said. "No matter what happens between me and Morgan, I'll be fine. She and I were practically kids when we hooked up back then, and we've both matured since. We're going to be okay, even if we end up as just friends."

Drake might've spoken the words, but deep down, he would always want Morgan as more than a friend.

Aiden leaped up all of a sudden. "Okay, let's get out of here before you get all mushy. I'm not in the mood. I gotta come up with an appropriate apology for your hottie girlfriend."

"Hey, what did I tell you?" Drake barked, knowing that Aiden was only trying to get a rise out of him. "Show some respect."

"Yeah, yeah, yeah. She's still hot, but I'll try not to steal her from you. Most women can't resist my charm."

Drake shook his head and looked heavenward.

God, give me strength with this kid.

MORGAN WAS CLEANING UP THE KITCHEN WHEN DRAKE AND Aiden returned. The two of them hadn't finished eating, but she'd decided to get started on the cleanup. Then she would leave. The last thing she wanted to do was cause a rift between

Drake and his siblings. If it meant breaking things off with him to keep his family together, she'd say goodbye.

It wouldn't be easy to walk away again, but she'd do it for them.

Without a word, Drake placed a kiss against her temple and headed back to the dining room. Aiden stayed in the kitchen, and Morgan debated about what to say to him. She didn't know him, not like Addison, and she wasn't sure where to start.

"Listen," she said. "I'm sorry if—"

"You don't have anything to apologize for," he said, leaning against the counter. "I was way out of line. I knew that even before Drake ripped me a new one in the office."

Morgan's brows went up, and she tried to stifle her laugh at the seriousness of his tone and expression. She wasn't exactly sure what had gone on in that office, but she had to respect Aiden for coming to her like an adult.

"I'm sorry for what I said to you, and I honestly didn't mean to hurt your feelings. I just . . . I guess I don't want Drake to get hurt. He's great and has done a lot for me and Addy. He gave up his life for us."

"I know. He's the best, and I don't want to say or do anything that will ever come between you two."

Aiden nodded. "Yeah, I know. My brother has good taste in women, even if he acts like an old dude sometimes. He wouldn't have brought you around me and Addy if you weren't cool."

"Thanks for saying that. I know you don't know me," Morgan said as she went back to rinsing a pot, "but I'd like to get to know you and Addy better."

"Okay, but first, I need to officially apologize." He headed to the nearby pantry before she could tell him that they were good. After moving stuff around, he emerged with a small brown paper bag.

Morgan's curiosity was piqued.

Aiden glanced over his shoulder as if checking to make sure no one was entering the kitchen. "Here's a peace offering. Don't tell my brother and sister where you got it from even though they'll probably figure out it came from me."

Morgan accepted the paper bag and peeked inside. Her mouth started watering before she even pulled out the clear container.

"That's from my secret stash. I have to hide junk food from Drake and Addy. Otherwise, they'll eat it as if it were their own."

Morgan laughed as she opened the cupcake container. She had a feeling it was the other way around, that he was the one who ate everyone's stuff, but she didn't say anything.

"My lips are sealed."

She took a huge bite of the chocolate cupcake and couldn't stop the moan from slipping through as the delicious treat practically melted in her mouth.

"No wonder you hid this. It's *sooo* good," she gushed, and took another bite.

Someone cleared their throat, and Morgan's gaze leaped toward the opening to the kitchen.

Addison marched over to them and put her hands on her hips. "I know you two aren't in here eating my cupcake. Seriously, Aiden! How'd you even find it?"

Morgan choked on a piece of cake that went down wrong and pounded her chest as she glared at Aiden. It wasn't like he noticed, since he was doubled over laughing.

"I thought you would be okay with our guest eating it," he said as his laughter grew louder, and he stumbled out of the kitchen without further comment.

"Addison, I am so sorry I ate your dessert. I had no idea it was yours. Your brother said it was his."

"No worries. At least his greedy self gave it to you instead of eating it." Addison went to the pantry. "Good thing I bought two, just in case. He got me once, and I've learned my . . . Wait. Where's my other cupcake?"

Morgan had a sinking feeling she knew, and what started as a chuckle from her, turned into uncontrollable laughter. She was going to have to keep her eyes on Aiden. He was a sneaky one.

"Aiden! You better run, because it's about to be on!" Addison bolted out of the kitchen like something or someone were chasing her.

Drake strolled in seconds later. "Well, it looks like things are back to normal." He pulled Morgan into his arms. "Are you good?"

Morgan smiled up at her handsome man. "Yeah, I'm better than good, but your brother might not survive the two women in your life."

He chuckled. "Probably won't because he always has some nonsense going."

Morgan grinned. As the baby of her family, she'd never had younger siblings and it was clear that Aiden and Addison would keep things interesting. Now she was looking forward to more family dinners, especially since she wouldn't have to cook them.

Chapter Twenty-Six

ON DREAMY AND KARTER'S WEDDING DAY, DRAKE ENTERED
the stately church that boasted an ornate design; cathedral ceil-
ings; and elaborate, stained-glass windows. He marveled at the
elegance of the sanctuary that was slowly filling up.

Morgan had informed him that though Dreamy had wanted
a small and intimate gathering, her soon-to-be mother-in-law
had insisted on something grand. Actually, *grand* was putting it
mildly.

The scent of roses greeted him the moment he stepped into
the sanctuary, and he understood why. From the ends of the
church pews to the huge vases along the perimeter of the space
and the elaborately decorated wedding arch, deep burgundy and
white roses were everywhere. That, along with millions of clear,
twinkling lights hanging on the walls of the enormous space,
created a magical and romantic feel.

Drake sat on the bride's side since Dreamy had been the
one to invite him. Arriving early in order to get a seat close to
the center aisle had been his plan, but it seemed everyone had

the same idea. Luckily, he was still able to find a spot near the front.

He was glad he'd worn his tuxedo. Men and women strolled in dressed to the nines and made it clear that this was no ordinary wedding. While most men wore tuxedos, the women were decked out in evening wear befitting a royal wedding, with diamonds and other gems dripping from their ears and hanging around their necks.

Anybody who was anyone was in attendance, from famous actors to some of the wealthiest business moguls, but Drake only cared about seeing one person—Morgan.

Weddings weren't really his thing—especially ones like this, since he'd spend the next hour or so on his own. Addison and Aiden had opted out, choosing to hang with friends at a birthday party sleepover, and Morgan had already warned Drake that they wouldn't get to spend much time together until the reception. When he'd suggested that he not attend and wait to see her after the festivities, she'd insisted that she wanted him there.

"Excuse me."

Drake glanced up to find two women standing at the opening to his row.

"Are you saving seats?" the one with long, reddish brown hair and false eyelashes that could've passed for spiders asked.

It was hard not to laugh at the way she kept batting her eyelashes. Drake wasn't sure if she was flirting with him or trying to keep the lashes from falling off.

"No, I'm not." He stood and stepped into the aisle to let them pass before reclaiming his seat.

While he waited for the wedding to start, Drake checked his phone and saw the text from his sister.

Addison: Are you having fun yet?

Drake smiled. Considering how much she'd wanted to attend, it hadn't taken much to change her mind.

He sent her a quick text back with an emoji eye roll, only to receive four identical emojis—the one of the face laughing with tears.

She knew he was kidding about the eye roll and that he couldn't wait to spend time with Morgan. Especially with their busy work schedules.

They were still getting adjusted to their new relationship. Drake was glad that the twins had a chance to get to know Morgan. The family dinner might've started off rocky with Aiden's surprising outburst, but the night had turned out to be one of the best evenings Drake had had in a long time. By the end of it, everyone was getting along.

After dinner, they'd watched a movie. Well, it started off as the four of them watching. Then Addison made a big production of yawning and claiming how tired she and Aiden were, and they excused themselves.

It was fine with Drake. He and Morgan snuggled together, drank wine, and exchanged heated kisses for much of the night. It had been hard to take her home when what he'd really wanted to do was take her upstairs to his bedroom.

All in good time, he thought to himself.

The music started, and Drake glanced around to see that the church had filled up. He hadn't attended a wedding in years and was glad that this one was starting on time.

A couple of people were escorted down the aisles by ushers, and Drake knew immediately that the first one was Morgan's mother. The resemblance was uncanny, except Mrs. Redford had an air of arrogance about her that he had never noticed on Morgan.

When the music changed, Drake turned toward the back of the church, and his heart galloped like a horse racing around a track. The sight of Morgan slowly walking down the aisle stole his breath. His gaze traveled the length of her. She was one of those women who could make a burlap sack look good on her. Today was no different. *Stunning* wasn't a strong enough word to describe her appearance. Actually, there were no words.

He'd seen the bridesmaid dress the first time when he and Addison were at her condo. On a hanger, the outfit had looked like any other dress, but on her, it looked like a million bucks. The woman was breathtakingly gorgeous.

The strapless garment was the color of red wine. The front of the dress stopped just above her knees, giving him an unobstructed view of her legs. The back was a little longer and swung back and forth with each step she took. Her customary high heels were the same color, and the jewel-encrusted strap around her ankles enhanced her long, shapely legs. Legs that he imagined would wrap around him tonight.

Drake might've been trying to take their reunion slowly, but he wanted her. Wanted her like he had never wanted another woman in his life.

As she moved down the long aisle, the soloist at the front of the church sang "Conversations in the Dark" by John Legend.

Drake couldn't take his gaze from Morgan as he absorbed the lyrics to the song. He had heard the piece a hundred times, but not like this. Not when it seemed Legend had written the song with Drake and Morgan in mind. The words depicted her thoughts and beliefs about herself that she had shared with him the night they'd met at the bar.

He still found it hard to believe that his strong, gorgeous woman had ever had the type of insecurities that she had described. It broke his heart. She thought she hadn't been worthy of him, and that her flaws would somehow lessen what he felt for her back then.

It was a great reminder that everyone had insecurities. Some that only they could see. All it would've taken was a conversation between them, and they might've been able to start their lives together years ago.

Anything meant to happen will happen. Jeffrey's words rang in Drake's ears.

He had never been a believer in fate, but to what else could he attribute running into Morgan after so many years?

As Morgan moved closer, Drake didn't think she could get any more beautiful, but it seemed she did every time he saw her. When she neared the row that he was sitting in, their eyes met, and she gave him a sweet smile as her long lashes swept over her high cheekbones, then back up again. She puckered her lips in a motion of a kiss.

After she passed by, he was grinning like an idiot, but he didn't care. He felt like he was a teen again and the prettiest girl in school had just noticed him.

Murmurs flowed through the sanctuary, and the wedding march started. Everyone stood. Dreamy and her grandfather, Slick Lester, stood in the doorway. Though Morgan was the most beautiful woman in the building, Dreamy looked stunning in the champagne-colored gown that was like something out of a magazine. It was no wonder Morgan's family was pushing for her to go into fashion design. The woman had skills.

Drake glanced at Karter Redford standing at the front of the church next to his brother, the best man. Karter might've been standing tall and looking fearless, but he couldn't hide the emotions on his face.

Chuckles in the sanctuary caught Drake's attention and he turned back to Dreamy and her grandfather, who had started walking down the aisle. The old man should've looked out of place since he was dressed differently from the other men in the wedding. But the tailcoat suit and top hat fit his personality. Slick Lester walked with his chest poked out proudly, and he stopped occasionally to kiss the hands of a few women, leaving them giggling. All the while, Dreamy smiled and shook her head as if she was used to the show.

When she was finally presented to her soon-to-be husband, Drake's gaze slid over to Morgan. As if sensing his eyes on her, she looked at him, and his pulse beat a little faster. The adorable smile she cast him pierced his chest. In that moment, he was positive that he and Morgan were going to make it. He couldn't explain the sudden feeling of rightness inside of him, or how he knew for sure she would be his forever. He just knew.

Drake could count on one hand the number of weddings he had attended in his lifetime, and he'd never realized how much they tugged on the heartstrings. Then again, maybe it wasn't so much the wedding as it was the idea that this could be him one day, marrying the woman of his dreams and vowing to spend the rest of his life with her.

"HEY, HANDSOME. YOU CLEAN UP WELL," MORGAN SAID WHEN she came up behind him. Drake turned and snaked his arm around her tiny waist, crushing her to him.

"Dance with me," he said, not giving her a chance to respond. He pulled her onto the dance floor and wrapped her in his arms. "Finally, I get you all to myself. I had no idea how involved your bridesmaid duties would be with this wedding."

"Me neither! I thought once we got Dreamy down the aisle and married, that would be it. But between keeping people from stepping on her train, posing for fifty million pictures, hunting down her comfortable shoes, and a hundred other things, I'm wiped out. I can't wait to cut out of here. This has been the longest day that I can remember. I'm going to be knocked out the moment my head hits the pillow tonight."

"Speaking of your head hitting the pillow, how do you feel about coming back to my place when we leave here?"

Morgan's steps slowed and she leaned back and looked at him. "Your place?"

"Yeah, the twins are at a slumber party, and I'll have the place to myself." He wiggled his eyebrows, enjoying the way she giggled. "I was thinking that maybe you and I can have our own sleepover."

As they continued swaying on the dance floor, she brushed her thumb slowly over his bottom lip. He captured it in his mouth, and a moan slipped from her. The heat in her eyes said more than words ever could.

"I like the way you think, Mr. Faulkner. I might even be able to leave early. Then we can get our night started, but what exactly does a sleepover at your place entail?"

He gave a slight shrug then lowered his lips to her scented neck and nibbled. "I'm thinking a little bit of this. A little bit of that," he mumbled against her soft skin. "And a whole lot of something else."

"I see, but you're going to have to be a little more specific. Will we be watching movies, eating popcorn and a whole lot of junk food, and staying up way past our bedtime?"

"Yes, yes, and hell yeah. We'll definitely be staying up past our bedtime."

"In that case, let's get out of here," she said excitedly. "But before we leave, how would you like to—"

Drake covered her mouth with his, unable to wait any longer to kiss her enticing lips. As their tongues tangled, her erotic sounds only spurred him on more. Yeah, they were definitely going to need to get out of there, and sooner rather than later.

A throat cleared, and Drake ripped his lips from Morgan's and lifted his head. A chill rushed through his body when his gaze met Marcus Redford, Morgan's dad. The older gentleman was around Drake's height, but not as wide. Standing next to him with her lips pursed and her eyes narrowed was Mrs. Redford.

"Daddy, Mom, I was just coming to find you two. I want you to meet someone," Morgan said as if the moment wasn't awkward as hell. She slipped her hand in his. "This is my boyfriend, Drake Faulkner. Drake, these are my parents, Marcus and Kalena Redford."

Drake hadn't been called anyone's boyfriend since college, and he wasn't sure how he felt about the title. It sounded a little juvenile, but how else would they describe their relationship?

Mr. Redford stuck out his hand and gave Drake a genuine smile as they shook. "Nice to meet you, young man."

"Same here, sir, and Mrs. Redford. It's a pleasure to meet you both."

Kalena cast Morgan a disapproving look, and Drake's protective instincts went up before the woman could say anything.

"Darling, I wanted to introduce you to a designer. He was admiring Dreamy's dress and wants to see if you'll be interested in an apprenticeship. Instead, I find you kissing this . . . this man."

Morgan sighed. "I'm not interested in an apprenticeship, and you already knew that. Besides, I'm not talking shop tonight, and me and Drake, *my man*, were getting ready to leave."

"Surely, your young man can wait until after introductions are made," Mrs. Redford said, softening her tone. "This is your future we're talking about."

Morgan huffed out a breath that had a growl dangling on the end of it. Drake wouldn't want to pull her away from any opportunities, but even he knew that Morgan wasn't interested in fashion design professionally. Her mother knew too. Yet she kept pushing.

"Ready?" Morgan asked him.

"Whenever you are," he said, and slipped his arm around her waist. He always liked it when she leaned into his touch.

"Morgan, this is no time—"

"Kalena, let it go," Mr. Redford said. "You kids have a good evening."

"I will not let it go. She's throwing away her future."

"Goodbye, Mother," Morgan said with disappointment in her tone, and placed a kiss on her parents' cheeks. "Bye, Daddy."

Without another word, she slipped her hand into Drake's and they walked out of the hotel ballroom.

"I'm going to need you to take my mind off of my mother and her pushiness."

Drake pulled her to his side and placed a kiss on top of her head. "Challenge accepted."

Chapter Twenty-Seven

MORGAN HELD ON TIGHT AS DRAKE INSISTED ON CARRYING her into the house through the garage. Without the twins there bickering and laughing, the place was eerily quiet. She had only visited one other time since their first family dinner and had gotten used to their noise level. But she was glad that she and Drake had the place to themselves tonight.

"Ow," Morgan yelped when her leg made contact with a wall. It didn't hurt but had caught her off guard.

"Oops, my bad. Are you okay?"

"Yeah, I'm fine, but maybe you should turn on some lights. It would also probably help if you put me down. I don't know why you insisted on carrying me when I'm perfectly capable of walking."

"I know, but I like carrying you. Besides, it's all a part of my seduction scene. We don't need lights. I've walked through this house a hundred times without—"

"Ouch!" Morgan squeaked when her shoulder rammed into a door, again catching her off guard more than causing pain.

"Okay, this is absurd," she said, unable to stifle a giggle at the ridiculousness of them walking through a pitch-black house. "Put me down. Your seduction game needs help."

"Nah, nah, baby, I got you." He chuckled and kept moving. "I promise, I won't run into—"

The clatter of books and metal slamming to the floor pierced the quiet of the house.

"You were saying?" Morgan said on a laugh, and Drake joined in.

"I was saying that maybe I should turn on a light." He leaned to his left slightly, close to a wall, and within seconds the kitchen was illuminated.

They both glanced down at the floor, which was now littered with cookbooks, a metal napkin holder, and loose napkins, strewn all over.

"I'll take care of that mess later. Now, where were we?"

"You were about to put me down. That'll probably help with your lousy coordination. At this rate, you're never going to get laid because I'm going to be too banged up to—" Her words died on her lips when he covered her mouth with his.

Drake kissed her slowly and tenderly, and everything inside of Morgan melted. Her arm was already around his neck, and she placed her hand on the back of his head and pulled him even closer, deepening the kiss.

God, she was crazy about this man and felt like the luckiest woman alive. They had found their way back to each other and were getting a second chance to make it right. Morgan was going to cherish every delicious moment with Drake.

"Now, you were saying?" he said when the kiss ended, and he moved out of the kitchen and toward the stairs.

"I was saying, hurry up so that I can get you out of this tuxedo and have my way with you."

"That's what I'm talking about!"

Drake rushed up the stairs, moving a little too fast for Morgan's comfort, but she didn't say anything. Being hugged up against his hard, muscular body was no hardship. She just held on tight and enjoyed the ride.

When they reached his bedroom, Morgan inhaled. The scent of Drake's intoxicating cologne filled the air. The space was dark except for a little light filtering in through the sides of the window blinds.

Drake touched the light switch on the wall, and the room was softly illuminated by the bedside lamps. Within seconds, soft jazz filtered through hidden speakers and Morgan smiled.

"Well, all right now. Maybe your seduction game doesn't need as much work as I originally thought."

He chuckled and didn't stop moving until they reached his huge, four-poster bed. A quick glance around his masculine personal space revealed dark gray, bare walls; large mahogany furnishings; and a cozy reading area in the corner.

Morgan liked the space, and it fit Drake's personality perfectly. He was a simple man who preferred functionality over appearance.

"Thanks for the lift," she cracked when Drake finally set her on her feet.

"Anytime, Angel."

Hearing the nickname he'd given to her years ago made her heart squeeze. He'd only used it a few times since they'd been back together. She wasn't even sure he realized it, but hearing it meant the world to her. There had been a time when she thought she would never hear *Angel* spoken from him again.

Drake brushed the back of his fingers down her cheek as he studied her. "Usually, the bride outshines everyone at the wedding, but I can honestly say, you stole the show, baby."

The corners of Morgan's lips kicked up. "Wow, you're really

turning on the charm tonight," she said, and slowly slid her hands up his torso. The material of his tuxedo jacket felt like silk under her touch. "I hope you're as ready as I am to get reacquainted."

"Beyond ready, which is why I took the liberty of stopping by the drugstore earlier. I'm prepared." He pulled a plastic bag from his inside pocket. It was the same bag that she'd seen him retrieve from his glove compartment before climbing out of the truck.

Morgan's grin widened when he pulled out a box of condoms. "Always prepared . . . still. I guess we should put those to good use."

He ripped the box open, pulled out a strip of condoms, and set everything on the nightstand, saying "Let me get your zipper."

Morgan turned her back to him and shivered as he slowly slid the zipper down. Getting her undressed wouldn't take long since all she had on underneath was a thong.

The strapless dress skimmed down her body and pooled around her feet. Drake held on to her hand while she stepped out of the garment. He picked it up and set the outfit on the bench at the foot of the bed.

His appreciative gaze traveled the length of her semi-naked body and lingered on her bare breasts before going lower. As he silently studied her, he made quick work of undoing his bow tie and getting out of his dress shirt.

Drake was left in a white T-shirt that hugged his sculpted upper body, and Morgan's mouth went dry. Everything inside of her came alive at the way the material highlighted his wide chest and huge biceps. Within seconds, he had stripped down to his boxer briefs that emphasized his well-endowed shaft.

The man was even more built than she remembered. Gone was the college boy who she had fallen for immediately. In his place was the man she was falling for all over again.

"Those are the sexiest shoes I've ever seen," he said as he approached her. "Part of me wants you to keep them on, but the other part of me wants you completely naked, and that includes the shoes."

Drake gripped the back of her thighs, picked her up, and set her on the bed. He lifted her right leg, and Morgan trembled under his gentle touch. The erotic feel of his lips on the inside of her thigh had her swallowing hard, and she moaned in pleasure as he placed feathery kisses down her leg.

If he was trying to turn her on even more than she already was, it was working. The delicious ache between her thighs was growing stronger, and her need for him was off the charts. Yet he took his time getting both her shoes off.

She really did love the fact that he was trying to take things slow, but she didn't need slow right now. She wasn't known for being the most patient person in the world, and with him barely clothed, doing what he was doing to her body, her impatience was growing.

"I get that you have this whole seduction thing playing out, but . . . oh . . ." She moaned and closed her eyes when he started kissing his way up the inside of her other thigh. He didn't stop until he reached her damp panties.

Damn. Just that almost had her flying apart. She hadn't been intimate with a man in a long time. It wasn't going to take much tonight to get her off.

"You smell so good," he said.

When his fingers replaced his lips at her core, Morgan released an unsteady breath and dropped back onto the bed. The delicious ache between her thighs was growing more intense with his touch. Even more so when he pushed her panties aside, and his fingers made contact with her slick folds.

"Goodness," she breathed. Her back arched and her hands fisted the bedcover on each side of her as he entered her with one finger and then a second one.

Morgan whimpered and when the pad of his thumb teased her clit, her hips moved up and down of their own accord. Her head swished back and forth against the comforter as her heart pounded faster. Her breathing was loud enough to drown out the music playing overhead, and she was nearing her limit as her muscles tightened around Drake's fingers.

"Ohhh," she groaned, rocking against his hand as a tsunami of sensations swirled inside of her, pushing her closer to her release. His thumb teased her mercilessly as his fingers continued stroking her, intensifying the sensation as he increased the pace.

"Drake, I can't hold on," she muttered, and gripped his arm as she chased her orgasm. What he was doing to her felt too damn good, and she didn't want it to be over . . . not yet.

"It's okay, baby. Let go," he crooned.

His words and the way he continued working his fingers tugged something deep within, and the sensations swirling inside of her detonated. They pushed her to the brink and then sent her careening over the edge of control. Her thighs locked around Drake's wrist, holding his hand in place as her body trembled uncontrollably.

"*Oh* . . . my goodness," she mumbled, her eyes tightly closed as she struggled to catch her breath. Her nails dug into Drake's arm while aftershocks continued rocking her body until she finally regained some control. But she was left spent and still breathing hard.

Drake hovered above her and kissed her lips. "You okay?" he asked quietly.

Morgan barely had enough energy to ease her eyes open, and when she did, his smoldering gaze held hers. Instead of responding, she framed his face with her hands and pulled him closer. So many emotions swirled inside of her, but her words wouldn't come. So she kissed him and let her lips do the talking.

THEIR KISS GREW MORE INTENSE AS DRAKE THOROUGHLY EX-
plored the inner recesses of her mouth. He could kiss her all day
and all night, and he planned to, but right now he wanted to
explore the rest of her body. Watching her fall apart under his
touch was hot as hell. He wanted to get her to that point again . . .
and again.

"We're not done," he said when he finally broke off their kiss.

He scooted to the edge of the bed, then stood. Morgan's gaze
followed his every move. The intensity of her stare had his dick
throbbing with need as he pushed down his boxer briefs and
kicked them the rest of the way off. All the while, Morgan's attention was still on him. Clearly, she liked what she was seeing.

While Drake watched her watch him, he gripped his dick and
started stroking himself. He didn't miss her audible intake of
breath as he slid his hand slowly up and down his erection, growing harder with each stroke. The heat radiating in her gorgeous
eyes only made him that much harder, and though he felt like he
was going to explode, he didn't stop.

She likes this. And for the rest of the night, he planned to give
her whatever she wanted.

Morgan got on her knees. The sight of her slowly crawling
toward him like a lioness seeking her prey was sexy as hell. Especially the way her breasts swayed back and forth as she moved.
As she got closer, a groan rumbled in his chest and the desire
burning in her eyes matched what he was feeling inside.

"I want you inside of me," Morgan said, her voice low and
throaty.

Yeah, he wanted that, too, but he still wanted to refamiliarize
himself with the rest of her body.

Morgan stopped when she reached the nightstand, and she

snatched up a condom, then ripped it open with her teeth. When she started rolling the condom on him, Drake slipped his hand to the back of her neck and pulled her against him.

He kissed her and divine ecstasy charged through his body. The need to be buried deep inside of her was unbearable, but he wanted to make this last. At least a little longer.

Drake urged her back onto the bed and hovered above her, kissing her hungrily. He couldn't get enough, but he wanted to make this good for both of them and needed to regain some control.

He eased his lips from hers and placed kisses over her cheek and worked his way down. Morgan wiggled beneath him as he sucked on her neck, sure to leave a mark, before he moved even lower. She shivered with every touch of his lips on her skin, and the sensual sounds she was making did wicked things to him.

But he moved even lower, continuing to kiss his way down her gorgeous body. When he cupped her breasts, pushing them together, she moaned with pleasure as his thumbs brushed over her perky nipples.

"Drake, I don't think I can take mu . . ." Her breath caught when his tongue swirled around one of her nipples. He sucked, tugged, and sucked some more while also squeezing and teasing the other.

Morgan's erotic moans grew louder, and she gripped the back of his head.

"Drake," she panted.

"Yeah, baby?" he said when he released her nipple and moved to suck on the other one. With each lap of his tongue, his need to be buried balls deep inside of her intensified.

"Please," she whined.

That one word lit another spark inside of him. Her nipple popped out of his mouth as he moved to get between her legs.

Heat charged through him as his shaft nudged against her opening before he slowly entered her sweet heat, inch by inch.

Drake sucked in a breath and willed himself to maintain control when her interior walls contracted around him. Damn, she was tight, and he loved the feel of being inside of her. Every nerve in his body was heightened as she adjusted to his size.

He covered her mouth with his, kissing her hard as he started rocking his hips and moving inside of her. Slowly at first, but as she caught his rhythm, he moaned into her mouth and picked up speed.

He lifted his mouth from hers. "God, I've missed you," he murmured.

"Me too, baby," she said, and kissed him again as he continued driving into her.

Morgan rocked her hips and moved with him as their tongues dueled and their moans floated through the air around them. They were each taking what they wanted, and with each thrust, passion built inside of him, threatening to break free.

"Oh, yes!" Morgan wheezed as she tore her mouth from his. "Drake . . ."

Her fingers dug into his shoulders, and both of their breaths were coming in short spurts as Drake increased the pace. His moves grew more jerky as pressure built inside of him, and he struggled to hang on. He could tell Morgan was nearing her release.

Hell, they both were, and as soon as the thought entered his mind, Morgan tightened around him, then screamed his name as her body spasmed beneath him.

With one last, powerful thrust, Drake was right behind her. His release ripped through him and sent him spiraling out of control. He collapsed on top of her, his chest heaving as he struggled to catch his breath.

Still panting, Drake rolled off her and onto his back. He pulled her closer and tucked her into his side as they continued gasping for air.

Earlier, saying he missed her was an understatement. When Morgan had disappeared, he didn't think he could live without her. One thing he knew for sure—he was never letting her walk out of his life again.

Morgan was his. Forever.

Chapter Twenty-Eight

HOURS LATER, DRAKE WALKED BACK INTO THE BEDROOM carrying wineglasses and a snack tray of cheese, crackers, and grapes. He held a bottle of white wine under his arm but could feel it slipping, and he hurried to the bed.

"Here, let me help you," Morgan said and hurried to the edge of the bed, wearing one of his T-shirts. She reached for the chilled bottle just as it slipped out of his hold. "Why didn't you tell me you needed help? I could've come downstairs and carried some of this stuff up."

"I thought I could handle it, until I got up the stairs and everything started shifting. But hey, I made it."

Drake sat the tray in the middle of the mattress, then climbed back onto the bed while Morgan fluffed pillows behind them. Once she was situated, he pulled the try between them.

"This looks great and I'm starving," Morgan said, snatching a couple of grapes and popping them into her mouth. "So, how often do you get the place to yourself?" She set cheese on one of the crackers and fed it to him.

Drake munched on the delicious snack as he opened the wine and poured them each a glass.

"Not that often, but I don't really need the place to myself. This is the first time I've brought home an overnight guest."

"Wow, I feel special."

"You are special. Very special." He lifted his wineglass and she followed suit. "Here's to more sleepovers in our future."

Morgan giggled. "I'll drink to that." She sipped from her glass and set it on the bedside table closest to her. "And during our sleepovers, if you're not naked the whole time, I want you dressed like you are now—shirtless with your pajama pants hanging low on your hips."

"That can be arranged."

Drake shivered when she reached over and placed her hand on his chest. He made his pecs bounce up and down, and Morgan gasped. She snatched her hand away, then burst out laughing.

"Oh, my God! How do you do that? Do it again."

He did and she laughed even harder.

Drake shook his head and grinned. He grabbed a couple of grapes and popped them in his mouth, then one into hers.

"I've only seen the actor Terry Crews do that," she said while chewing. "Is it hard to do?"

"Not really. It took a little practice, but now it's no big deal." He shrugged and they dove into the food like they hadn't eaten in days.

"You said the kids had a party to attend tonight. Do they usually go to parties together?"

"Surprisingly, yes. They have a lot of the same friends, which I'm glad about. For the last few years, some of the parents have been doing more coed parties since several of them have sons and daughters that are the twins' age.

"I'll admit that I really don't like the idea of Addison going to parties just yet, especially coed sleepovers. And before you call me a chauvinist or something, I'll accept that title. I worry about both of them, but especially her. Addy is just so . . ." he started, trying to find the words he was looking for to describe his sister.

"Sweet, kindhearted, impressionable," Morgan finished.

Drake chuckled. "Exactly. She's also a girl, and she's my little sister. I tend to be more protective of her than I am of Aiden. Actually, we both are protective of her because we don't want people to take advantage of her kindness."

"I can totally understand that. She's lucky to have you two."

"She reminds me a lot of you," he said, brushing one of her braids away from her face. "You two have some of the same qualities."

"I'm flattered because I think she's amazing."

"So are you." Drake placed a lingering kiss on her mouth and tasted the wine on her lips.

After two rounds of amazing sex, he still couldn't stop touching her, or kissing her, or staring at her. Having her there felt like a dream come true. A dream he never wanted to wake up from.

"Did I mention that I think you're doing a fabulous job raising the twins?"

"I think you might've mentioned it once or twice," he said, and nudged her lips apart with a piece of dark chocolate. Then he kissed her on those luscious lips.

It had been a long time since he'd felt so relaxed and fulfilled, and it had everything to do with her. It wasn't only about the sex, which was amazing, it was about her presence in his life. It made him want to sit back and just enjoy the moment.

"Since you don't do overnight guests, does that mean you're one of those guys who insists on spending the night at the woman's house?"

Drake sensed she was searching for more information than

what she was asking. He was sure she didn't want details of his relationships with other women, but maybe she needed to know more about his dating life.

"In case you're wondering if I hop from one bed to another, you don't have to worry. I don't date much. I don't have time."

"We always make time for the things we really want to do," she countered, popping a grape into her mouth.

"That's probably true. I guess I haven't wanted to do a lot of dating, but it's not because of lack of effort on my sister's and Matt's part. They've tried to push me out there into the dating world. I just hadn't found anyone I wanted to spend time with, until you."

"Boy, you're really pouring it on thick tonight, but I feel exactly the same about you."

She fed him a couple of grapes, and yelped when his lips gently latched onto her finger, sucking it into his mouth.

Morgan snickered and eventually escaped, then kissed him sweetly. When she started to pull back, Drake held her in place. He wasn't done loving on her mouth. Actually, he would never be done with her, and the way she returned his kiss had him ready to lay her back and take her lush body again.

Oh, yeah. I can definitely get used to this.

When her stomach growled, she chuckled against his mouth and eased away.

"I guess you did say you were starving. I need to feed you. Do you want more than these snacks? I can go down and cook something."

"No, this is fine. My stomach sounded hungrier than I actually am. Besides, it's one o'clock in the morning, way too late to be cooking."

They went back to talking and eating. As Drake leaned against the headboard, he reveled in how perfect the moment felt.

This was what he wanted all the time. Him. Morgan. Together. Forever.

"We've briefly discussed my dating life. Tell me about yours. Am I going to have to beat someone's ass when they realize that you're taken?"

She laughed. "Hardly. I haven't dated much over the years, either, and the few guys I did hang out with didn't last long. According to Isabella, I compared every man to you. It made it hard to get serious with anyone since there's no comparison. You're one of a kind, Drake."

"If you keep talking like that, I'm gonna have to show you again how much I've missed you."

"Actually, that sounds like something I wouldn't say no to," she said, and Drake laughed when she batted her long eyelashes at him.

He lifted the tray from between them and set it on the floor next to the bed.

"You were saying?" He didn't give her a chance to respond. Instead, he started feasting on her lips.

The logical side of his brain insisted that he was moving too fast, that *they* were moving too fast. But the part of him that had missed her like crazy didn't care. They had years to make up for, and Drake had learned a long time ago to never take any day for granted. He'd also learned to cherish those who held a special spot in his heart.

"I need you naked," he said, and within seconds he had Morgan out of his T-shirt. He tossed it to the floor and added his pajama bottoms to the small pile. When he turned back to her, she was sitting up on her knees and her nakedness was on full display.

"You have an incredible body," she said and pushed him back on the pillow before straddling him.

"Funny, I was just thinking the same thing about you." He loved having her bare ass on top of him with her gorgeous breasts in his face. He ran his hands over the smooth skin of her back, and shivered when she started kissing her way down his neck.

"I haven't explored every inch of you the way you've done me," she said between kisses as she slowly worked her way down. "You've had me so distracted tonight, that I—"

The house alarm blared, startling them both.

"What the hell?" Drake sat up so fast, he bumped heads with Morgan.

"Son of a—"

"Ouch!"

Rubbing his head, Drake scrambled out of the bed, but his foot got caught in the covers. He hopped on one leg, trying to get the other free, but crashed to the floor.

"Oh, my God!" Morgan screeched.

Her eyes were wide with horror when she glanced over the bed at him. But that horror suddenly turned to amusement when she saw his bare ass sprawled out on the floor.

"Are . . . are you okay?" she asked and started snickering before slapping her hand over her mouth.

Drake growled at her and ignored the pain in his butt as he snatched up his pajama bottoms. He hurried into them and dashed to the door just as he heard three beeps and the alarm stopped.

That could only mean one thing. Either the kids were home or Matt was there. They were the only others who knew the code. Before he could open the door, he heard Addy's voice downstairs.

"What's going on?" Morgan asked, scrambling out of bed. She hurried back into the T-shirt that he ripped off of her moments ago. The only other choice was her bridesmaid dress, which would've taken twice as long to get on.

"The kids are home, but what I don't know is why."

Drake heard them coming up the stairs, and he grabbed a clean T-shirt from the dresser drawer. He could've sworn he heard crying, which only made him get dressed faster.

When he opened the bedroom door, Addison screamed, and her hand went to her chest.

"Drake, what are you doing here? You're supposed to be with Morgan. Please don't tell me you ruined the date."

Drake ignored the comment. "The question is what are you two doing here? You're supposed to be at a sleepover. Why are you home?"

He looked from Aiden to Addison and then back to Aiden. His brother glanced at their sister but didn't say anything, which was so unlike him.

"One of you better start talking, now! How did you even get home? Please tell me you didn't walk back here at this time of night."

"We didn't walk," Aiden said, and rubbed the back of his neck the way Drake often did during stressful situations. "Addy didn't want us to call you, so I ordered an Uber."

Drake's gaze went to Addison, and he didn't miss the smudged eye makeup. Tears welled in her eyes, and all his protective instincts kicked in. Something bad had happened.

"Come here." He pulled Addison to his side and kissed her temple. "Tell me what happened."

"You wouldn't understand," Addison said on a sob.

"Try me. I can't help if I don't know what's going on." He looked at his brother, waiting for one of them to respond, but Aiden stared at Addison. It was clear he'd been sworn to secrecy.

They always stuck together, which Drake loved. Yet, during times like these, he hated when they enacted part of their twin code—your secret is my secret.

Drake sensed Morgan behind him before she came into view.

"Is everything okay out here?"

Addison gasped and pushed away from Drake. "Morgan!" Before Morgan could respond, Addison launched herself into her arms. "I'm so glad you're here," she said in a small voice, her face buried against Morgan's chest.

Morgan's eyes widened. She held Addison tightly while looking lost and concerned when her gaze met Drake's.

She was out of her element. Wanting to soothe both of them, he rubbed Morgan's back, then spoke to Addison.

"Tell us what's going on. One of you needs to start talking."

Seconds ticked by and Drake was starting to lose patience when his sister finally lifted her head. Morgan kept her arms around her.

"I got into a fight," Addison said.

"What?" Drake barked, and shock vibrated through him. "What do you mean you got into a fight? Are you hurt? What happened? And where were Layla's parents?"

One question after another pounded through his mind, and he couldn't get his words to form quick enough.

"There was this guy . . ."

"What?" Drake roared. "If you tell me that some punk-ass kid tried to push up on you, and Layla's parents didn't step in, I'm going over there and raising holy hell." He whirled on Aiden. "And you! You're supposed to look out for your sister."

"Drake, chill! It's not what you think," Aiden said, his volume matching his older brother's.

"You guys stop arguing!" Addison said. "I'm okay. Everything is fine."

Morgan got between Drake and Aiden. "Okay, time-out. We're not getting anywhere like this. Let's all calm down, and then we're going to let the kids tell us what happened," she said, looking pointedly at Drake.

She turned to Aiden and Addison. "First, we're going to get

dressed, and then we'll meet you two downstairs. I'll even make everyone some hot chocolate."

"Umm, that's okay. I'll make it," Aiden volunteered. "I heard about the lasagna fiasco. Wouldn't want another fire."

Drake didn't miss the humor in his brother's tone, but Morgan's mouth dropped open. Aiden didn't notice as he trotted down the stairs.

Addison's eyes widened, but she didn't laugh, not like Drake did.

"I'm sorry," he said. "I didn't mean to laugh, but come on. You got to admit, it was kind of funny."

"Urgh. I can't with you guys," Morgan said, folding her arms. "I burn one lasagna and you think I can't cook. I was just distracted that day! Just wait, I'm gonna show all three of you how great my culinary skills are, but right now, I'm going to get dressed." Morgan marched back to the bedroom.

"Do you think we hurt her feelings?" Addison whispered.

Drake wrapped his arms around her and kissed the top of her head. "Nope. She's fine. She knows she's a terrible cook."

"I heard that!" Morgan shouted. Drake and Addison laughed.

His heartbeat slowly went back to normal, and for the first time in the last ten minutes, he felt like he could breathe. It was always a good sign when Addison laughed, but for a minute there, he really did think he was going to have to kill somebody.

"Apparently, I need to add some soundproofing to this place," he cracked, then turned serious. "Are you okay?"

"Yeah, I'm fine. I got into it with one of my friends over a stupid boy. It's nothing."

Drake was sure there was more to the story that she wasn't saying. Addison wasn't a fighter, and he needed details, but he wouldn't push an interrogation right now. He'd wait to talk as a family downstairs.

"I hate that I messed up your date," she said. "We wouldn't have come home if we knew you guys were here."

"Sweetheart, whether I'm on a date or not, if you need to come home, you come. And if ever you're in trouble, you know you can always call me, *no matter what*."

"Me too!" Morgan called out again. "No matter the day or time, call one of us."

"Yep, definitely need some soundproofing," he whispered close to Addison ear, making her laugh again. "But seriously, she's right. Don't ever think you can't call or come to us. Understand?"

Addison nodded and smiled up at him, and it was as if the sun was coming out after a rainy day.

"Now, go wash your face and get your pajamas on. We'll meet you downstairs in a minute."

Drake reentered the bedroom just as Morgan was putting her braids up in a ponytail on top of her head. He leaned against the closed door and just looked at her.

His heart was heavy with the love he felt for this woman. It wasn't just because she was so damn cute; it was everything.

She filled a void inside of him that no other woman could ever fill. It thrilled and scared him. He'd loved her years ago, but it was nothing like what he was feeling right now.

More than anything, Drake wanted them to make it this time around. He wanted to scream to the world that his baby was back and that he loved her to death. But professing his feelings to Morgan would probably scare her and might even send her running again.

No, he had to tread lightly. The last thing he wanted to do was lose her so soon after finding her again.

Drake pushed off the door and strolled over to her. "You are an amazing woman, and I'm glad you're mine."

Morgan sighed as if relieved. "Oh good, because for a minute there I thought you might've been mad at me for overstepping. I really should've stayed in here and let you handle the situation, but I heard the tears in Addison's voice and . . . Well, I couldn't just sit in here and do nothing. I wanted her to know that I was here for her if—"

Drake crushed his mouth over hers and smothered the rest of her words with a kiss.

He already felt overwhelmed with love for her, but to know that she cared about the twins meant more than Morgan would ever know. He would never be upset with her for trying to comfort his siblings. She had just proven what he already knew, she had the capacity to love unconditionally, whether she realized it or not.

No mommy gene my ass.

When the kiss ended, Drake didn't release her, only stared into her beautiful brown eyes. "I'm glad you're here, but are you sure you're up for teenage life? Because I'm pretty sure you're going to get a taste of it more often than you'd prefer."

She placed her hand on his strong jaw and he leaned into her touch. "I'm ready, and I'm in this for the long haul."

Chapter Twenty-Nine

I HAVE TO STOP. I CAN'T DO ANY MORE, MORGAN THOUGHT AS sweat dripped down her face. She plopped down on the hard ground, then laid back on the grass. She and Drake were jogging through the neighborhood park and the sun was slowly rising, wiping away the darkness of the early morning.

After the wedding, she had vowed to start training first thing Monday. But that was before she knew Drake ran every day at six o'clock in the morning.

It was also before Morgan knew she'd be spending Sunday with him and the twins. She couldn't remember the last time she'd had so much fun. After the kids had showed up at the house, they'd all talked over hot cocoa, which Aiden made from scratch. That in and of itself was a surprise, but it was even more shocking that it tasted good enough to sell in restaurants.

Addison and Aiden finally came clean about what had happened during the sleepover. It turned out that Addy and one of her friends liked the same boy, who happened to be at the party. The friend got mad when the peanut-headed boy, as Drake called him, liked Addison more. Words were exchanged, and a fight broke out. Though Addy won, according to Aiden, she felt awful about fighting.

Morgan was impressed with how Aiden had gotten her out of the situation. Granted, he'd lied to Layla's mom by saying that Drake was picking them up, but he'd been determined to take care of his sister. Addison had wanted to leave the sleepover immediately but hadn't wanted to call Drake.

The love those three had for one another warmed Morgan's heart.

"Are you kidding me right now?" Drake barked and Morgan startled.

She lifted her head slightly to look at him. She was wondering when he would notice that she wasn't running behind him.

Drake stood over her with his muscular arms folded across his chest. His thick biceps bulged from under the sleeves of his T-shirt, which molded over his upper body. Damn. The man was the epitome of sexy and fit. He also looked like a drill sergeant ready to whip her into shape.

"Get your lazy self up. We haven't even gone a mile yet, and you're acting like we ran a marathon."

"Wait a minute. That wasn't a mile?" Morgan whined and dropped her head back onto the ground. Chest still heaving. Heart palpitating. She struggled to catch her breath. She could've sworn they'd run at least five miles.

"We barely have seven weeks to get into tip-top shape. So stop clowning around and work with me, Morgan."

"Who's clowning? I'm serious. Drake, are you sure you measured those miles correctly? Because I'm telling you, it felt longer."

"Did you hit your head on a rock or something? Your ass only ran a mile, if that. Now get up! Even if we don't run two miles this morning, we're at least walking them."

"Can't you just carry me?" She batted her eyelashes, trying to get a rise out of him. Nothing.

Normally, he loved carrying her around, but even when she gave him her puppy-dog face, he continued glaring at her. Nothing was working. His stone-faced expression was unwavering.

"Come on, baby," Morgan grumbled. She really was tired. "Carry me the rest of the way. Then your upper body workout for the day will be done."

Her gaze traveled the length of him from the top of his head covered with a Dodgers baseball cap to his black running shoes. The man was built like a stallion. Hell, he *was* a stallion when it came to the bedroom. That thought sent unadulterated lust nipping at every nerve in her body, and she suddenly didn't give a damn about running. Unless they were running back to her place to make mad, passionate love.

But the way he was still glaring at her, it was safe to say that not even that enticing invitation would lighten his mood.

"You know what? With a body like yours, you could—"

"Morgan, get up." He huffed out a breath. "Do you want me to leave you here?"

She didn't, especially since the sun hadn't completely broken through the clouds yet. Besides that, she wasn't kidding when she told him she was tired.

"Okay, give me five minutes. No, make that ten."

"Morgan, if I have to drag you behind me, I will."

"Well, before you start dragging me, can you put some casters under my butt? I don't think I can move without them."

"Fine, stay there." He started jogging in place. "But that slimy worm crawling toward your head is going to get lost in all of those braids."

"Worm? Worm!" Morgan screeched and leaped to her feet.

She frantically brushed off her head, her back, and her butt, hoping that Drake was kidding. Morgan wasn't taking any chances. Even after she dusted herself off, it felt like something was crawling down her back.

She despised dirt but truly hated creepy-crawlies even more.

"I think something's on my back." She shivered in disgust and turned, begging Drake to inspect it. "Come on, Drake. Get it off!"

He released a laugh for the first time that morning. "I just can't with you." He turned and started jogging, leaving her to check and recheck that there were no slimy worms on her.

"Drake! Don't leave me!" she screamed like a banshee and ran after him.

Morgan ignored the irritated looks from a group of older women who were doing yoga in the park. They were all in a lotus position, and it was safe to say that she had ruined any sort of Zen that they were trying to reach.

Huffing and puffing, she ran past two women who were walking, talking, and laughing.

How was that even possible? Who in their right mind would be up that early in the morning, hanging out for the fun of it?

Morgan wished that she was in the park running for pleasure and not out there trying to get into shape to compete for a commercial property.

I hate jogging. I hate jogging. I hate jogging.

The chant played on a loop inside her mind as her feet pounded the pavement. She wasn't moving very fast, but she didn't stop until she finally caught up to Drake.

"Well, it's about time," he said, keeping a steady pace as his bare arms glistened with sweat. "I'm telling you now. If you don't get serious about this competition, you're definitely going to lose. But me? I'm in it to win it."

Morgan didn't bother responding. He was right. It was already a long shot that she would even come close to winning, but the least she could do was make a good showing.

———

DAYS LATER, MORGAN AND ISABELLA STROLLED INTO A GYM where they were scheduled to meet with a personal trainer. It was Isabella's idea. She was the most competitive of the two, and according to her, Morgan wasn't taking the training seriously enough.

Okay, maybe she wasn't, but who had time to train four hours a day, which was what Drake wanted them to do? For her to go from never working out to a rigorous training schedule was impossible. Which was why she told Drake that she would run with him in the morning, but that was it. She needed to enlist the help of a professional—a personal trainer.

What was even better was that Isabella agreed to train with her since she had just as much at stake. Her friend might not be able to participate in the Titan Games, but this was a way to feel like part of the process and give Morgan support.

"Hi, can I help you ladies?" the woman at the front desk asked. Her name tag said *Brianna*. It was safe to say she had a solid workout plan since she looked as if she could bench-press Morgan with little or no problem.

"Yes, we're here to see Stanley. We have an appointment with him."

"All right, I'll get you checked in. Your names?"

They gave Brianna their names and answered a few additional questions that Morgan hadn't been asked when she signed up online. Unlike Isabella, who was already a member, Morgan had to buy a membership before she could pay for the personal training.

Normally, she would've wanted to meet the person before signing up, but Dreamy had used this guy for several months before getting married. She swore that he was a miracle worker and even claimed that she was more fit than she'd ever been in her life.

"You two are all set," Brianna said. "Stanley will be up here shortly to get you."

"Thanks," they said in unison.

"Feels like I haven't been here in, like, forever," Isabella said as they glanced around. Though she had a membership, she preferred jogging outside as opposed to running on the treadmill. "Let's go over here and check out the trainers' bios."

Morgan followed her to a wall with framed photos.

"Wow, that's Stanley?" Isabella said with interest, and pointed to a picture of a man with a military buzz cut, a deep tan, and light gray eyes. "If he looks this good in person, I might have trouble focusing on toning my muscles if I'm too busy ogling his."

Morgan had to agree that he was good-looking. Her gaze skirted over other photos; there were at least twenty trainers. She shouldn't be surprised, though. The gym was huge, and Californians were serious about staying in shape.

Hearing people behind them, Morgan turned back to the registration desk. Brianna was talking to a man and pointed toward her and Isabella.

"Do you believe in love at first sight?" Isabella whispered next to Morgan, who laughed.

"You already know I do," she said.

She had fallen in love with Drake the moment she crashed into him in the hallway in college. Even the years apart hadn't diminished the strong feelings she had for him.

"Okay, then in that case, I think I'm in love."

Stanley gave them a small wave as he approached, and his movie-star smile was on full display. His photo hadn't done him justice. He was a giant of a man with double-wide shoulders that were practically bursting out of his T-shirt, and biceps that were bigger than Morgan's thighs. Speaking of thighs, his were on full display since he was wearing shorts, and his legs looked like tree trunks.

"Yep, definitely in love," Isabella murmured, then stepped up to him. "Hi, I'm Izzy and this is my best friend, Morgan."

For the next few minutes, Stanley showed them around before they entered a small office. It held a desk that was equally small, a bookshelf full of fitness gadgets, and a guest chair.

"Hold on, let me grab another chair." He left them in the room and Morgan poked Isabella in the arm.

"You're making a fool of yourself. You're going to scare the poor guy away if you keep finding excuses to touch his arms," Morgan said out of the side of her mouth. She had never seen Isabella go gaga over a man. At least not like this.

"I can't help it. His body is calling to me," she whispered.

"Okay, here we go," Stanley said, carrying a chair in. He set it down and nodded for them to have a seat.

"So based on what you two have told me, Morgan," he said, pointing to her, "is competing in an Ironman competition of sorts, but doesn't work out on the regular."

"Correct," she said. "Isabella agreed to train with me, which is why she's here."

He nodded and cast Isabella a smile. "I've seen you here before."

Morgan watched as the two discussed the type of workout Isabella usually did, and it was obvious that the attraction was mutual. If nothing else came out of the training, at least there might be a love connection.

For the next few minutes, Stanley asked Morgan a slew of questions, including whether she had any restrictions or limitations. Once that was done, they went to the cardio room, where he set them both up on a treadmill to warm up. They ran at a sprint for ten minutes, and Morgan wasn't off to a good start. She was already proving that her stamina needed work.

Although Drake hadn't complained the night before when he'd stopped over and brought dinner. One thing led to another, and before she knew it, they were naked and rolling around in her bed. It all started the moment he stepped into her place wearing a designer three-piece suit that made him look strong, powerful, and totally irresistible.

She had been turned on immediately and practically jumped him the moment he stepped across the threshold. Some women fell under a man's spell because of his money, his career, or hell, even his scent. Apparently, her sexy man in a nice suit did it for her.

Stanley escorted them past the bikes and treadmills, and they slowed when he pointed out a couple of rowing machines. Both were occupied, but he assured Morgan and Isabella that they'd return to them before their session was over.

Morgan groaned when they reached the weight room.

"I was hoping that I could get in shape with just cardio," she said, eying the free weights and machines warily.

"Nope, you need to strengthen your muscles too. That'll help with stamina," Isabella said before Stanley could respond. "Oops, sorry, I forgot. You're the expert."

He flashed her a wide grin. "No problem. You're right. Tonight, with a few exercises, I'll figure out where you both are as it relates to your flexibility and strength."

"I can show you how flexible I—" Isabella started, and Morgan jabbed her in the side with her elbow.

"Knock it off." She laughed at her friend's attempt at flirting. "We have work to do."

Isabella nodded vigorously. "Right. Right. You're right. I need to stay focused. Carry on, Mr. P.T."

Morgan was sure the personal trainer was used to being hit on, especially if the attention he was getting from other women at the gym was any indication. If they weren't trying to start a conversation with him, they were posing in front of him wearing some of the skimpiest workout wear that Morgan had ever seen.

If Isabella noticed, she didn't say anything, but how could she when she hadn't taken her eyes off the guy? Morgan had never seen her friend like this, but in her defense, Stanley was *fine*. The man should've been modeling and posing for the cover of a fitness magazine instead of hanging out in a gym.

"Let's go over there to that corner. I want to see how many push-ups you both can do without stopping."

Morgan snorted. "I don't even have to show you. I can tell you. *Zero*. I never could do a push-up or a pull-up."

"O-kay," he said slowly, tapping something into the electronic tablet he was carrying. "Well, humor me and give it a shot."

He pointed to the pile of red and blue mats, and they walked over to grab one. "I don't know about all of this, Izzy. I don't think I'm made for exercising." Morgan yanked down a thick blue mat, but three more came with it. She lunged forward, trying to catch them, but the weight of them overpowered her, sending her to her knees.

"Whoa!" Isabella said, grabbing the last one before it landed. "Damn, girl. You might be stronger than you think if you were able to pull all of those out at once."

Morgan released an unladylike snort. "Yeah, that's it, I'm strong." She flexed her minuscule biceps. "It had nothing to do with me being clumsy."

Isabella shook her head and smirked as she replaced the mats they didn't need. They made it back over to Stanley and dropped onto their mats. Super athlete that Isabella was, she started doing push-ups before Morgan even got into position.

While Isabella did the traditional ones, Stanley instructed Morgan to get on all fours, placing her hands shoulder width apart. She crossed her ankles before he had her bend her elbows and lower her chest to the floor.

Morgan managed to do three before her puny arms gave out and she crashed to the floor.

"Are we done yet?" she asked, rolling onto her back to look up at Stanley. "That should be enough for today, right?"

"Not even close, warrior," he cracked before turning to Isabella, who was still going. "All right, Izzy. You can stop. You've given me a good idea of where you are fitness-wise."

"Show off," Morgan mumbled and started to stand.

"Stay down there, warrior. Let's see how many sit-ups you can do without stopping."

"Stanley, if I didn't know any better, I'd think you were trying to kill me," Morgan mumbled, but got into position.

For the next thirty minutes, they did one exercise after another, their personal trainer being incredibly patient with her the entire time. According to him, if she wanted to be ready for her competition, she'd need to run every day and work out with him at least three times a week to do strength training.

By the time the personal training session was over, Morgan knew two things. One: she was the weakest person on the face of the planet. Two: Stanley had his work cut out for him.

Chapter Thirty

ALMOST THREE WEEKS LATER, AND AFTER WORKING OUT
every day, Morgan was finally able to run four miles without
passing out.

"I never thought we'd actually be able to jog together without
you complaining the whole time," Drake cracked as they ran
along the trail through the park. "Especially this early in the
morning. Granted, I wasn't thrilled about you having a male personal trainer, but Stanley is a miracle worker."

"Whatever," Morgan said as her tennis shoes pounded the
wet pavement in rhythm with his.

Wearing white tennis shoes with a yellow jogging suit might
not have been one of her better ideas, but she hadn't realized it
had rained the night before until she was outside. Good thing
they were able to get an early start today since there was a threat
of more rain to come. Which was good for the city, considering
how dry it had been.

"Yup, he's definitely a miracle worker," Drake repeated as he
casually picked up speed.

"And I'm telling you that I'm the one who did the work," Morgan said, puffing out a breath as she ran alongside Drake, matching him step for step. "All Stanley is doing is torturing me."

"Maybe, but look at you now. You might actually stand a chance at winning this thing."

She cut her eyes at him, half expecting him to be looking at her with a wicked grin on his face. "Are you trying to be funny or are you serious?" They both knew that he was going to be hard to beat.

"No, I'm serious. Weeks ago, you could barely run up a flight of stairs without practically passing out. I'm surprised, in a good way, at the transformation."

Morgan couldn't believe her progress either. She still had to work her way up to a six-mile run in the next few weeks, but it seemed attainable now. Not only did she have the stamina to do it, she was also stronger thanks to weight training.

"That doesn't mean you're going to beat me, though," Drake added. "I'm planning to take it all, but I'm glad that you'll at least make a good showing."

"Oh, so you want to start talking trash? You already know I can go toe-to-toe with you in that regard. You think you're all big, bad, and powerful, but those qualities aren't going to help you when you have to get through that twenty-four-inch diameter tunnel. Whereas I'm going to fly through that baby."

Morgan gave herself a virtual pat on the back when those words shut him up. Drake was a beast. He ran laps around her without even breathing hard, but she was staying positive knowing that anything could happen. There were several obstacles on the course that were going to kick his butt, and she couldn't wait. Yeah, he might be faster, but she was going to use her size and smarts to one-up him during the competition. After weeks of training, she felt fully confident that she could win.

"Besides all of that, I think you were trying to kill me those first couple of days."

After the first time they'd gone running, Morgan knew training with Drake wasn't going to work. He wanted them to train all day, every day, and wanted her to change her eating.

"Drinking raw eggs was not going to kill you. That was to help you build more muscles," Drake said, defending himself.

"Are you kidding me? Just thinking about drinking that concoction you cooked up made me want to stick my head in a toilet and flush."

Drake let out a laugh that sounded like it was mixed with a snort. "Okay, maybe that was a little extreme, but on a serious note, you're impressing me more and more every day. You look amazing and happy. I don't think I've ever seen you smile as much as you have lately. But that's probably coming from me putting it on you real good every night."

Morgan sputtered a laugh. "Arrogant much?" She tried to punch him in the arm, but he dodged her attempt without missing a step. Morgan caught up to him. "I'll admit, you might have something to do with my joy, but I've noticed you've been whistling more. I'm sure that me and all of this," she waved her hands up and down her body, "have everything to do with that."

Drake flashed the sexy smile that always made her heart beat a little faster. He didn't agree with or deny her claim. He didn't have to. They both knew the positive effect they had on each other. It wasn't just that they were physically compatible, it was everything. They clicked.

She was so glad they were back together again, and the last few weeks had been some of the best of her life.

"Two more miles," Drake called out when Morgan fell behind again. "You gotta keep up, babe. Otherwise, I'm going to leave you."

He threatened her with that every time they ran together, but Morgan knew he never would. Still, she pumped her arms and kicked her legs until she caught up. If she didn't think about how tired she was or the sweat dripping down her back, then the running wasn't so bad. Besides, getting up early every morning gave her that much more time to spend with her man.

My man.

Whenever Morgan thought about how they'd found their way back to each other, her heart turned over in her chest. She was happier than she'd ever been in her life. They had always got along well and never had problems with intimacy, but the last few weeks with him were like a dream.

God, she loved him.

Neither of them had said the three magic words, but there was no doubt in Morgan's mind—she was crazy in love with him. That's what she'd told Isabella the day before during lunch when her friend questioned the relationship.

Morgan recalled the conversation.

"What do you mean you're in love with him?" Isabella said. "You guys have been together for two seconds and you're in love?"

"To be honest, I never stopped loving Drake," Morgan said. "And I get along great with Aiden and Addison. They are so amazing, Izzy. Super smart, sweet, kind, and just . . ."

She didn't know what else she could say. Drake and the twins meant the world to her, and it felt like they had all been together forever.

"Oh, and I didn't tell you about Addy's dress for homecoming. It came out perfectly. The design was mostly her creation. She definitely has an eye for fashion. I only added a few touches here and there."

"Did she have a date?"

Morgan explained how adamant Drake was about the kids not dating, but he bent his rule a little. He only agreed that Addison could attend with a boy because the two of them would be hanging with Aiden and Kira. He had also insisted on taking them and picking them up from the dance.

"Anyway, Aiden and his friend Kira looked so cute together. Remind me to show you pictures because I took a ton of them. I hope that girl knows how lucky she is. Aiden is already a sweetheart. He's so frickin' sweet and charming and . . ."

"Okay, okay, I get it. You're crazy in love with Drake and his siblings. You guys sound like one big happy family, but are you sure you're ready for this, Morgan? The last time you got close to Drake you—"

"I know what I did, and I'm trying to forget it," she said, probably a little more forcefully than she needed to. "I'm not the same person, Izzy."

"I know that, but I just want to make sure you're going into all of this with your eyes wide open. You can't have Drake without his siblings. Basically, if you two end up getting married, you'd be like their mother. Would you be ready for that type of responsibility?"

Morgan had never imagined being anyone's mother even though she loved kids. Did the idea scare her? Heck yeah. Was she up for the challenge? Maybe.

"All I know is that I love them all so much. I can't imagine my life without them."

"Aww, my little girl is growing up. I'm so proud of you," Isabella cooed. "But still . . ."

"Look out!" Drake and someone else yelled.

Morgan snapped back to the present, shocked to see a man on a bike barreling toward her. She screamed and put her hands up and out in front of her, thinking they were going to collide.

At the last second, she went right, and the guy jerked his bike to the left, but Morgan lost her footing and stumbled sideways into the wet grass. Her arms flailed as she slid and slipped, practically doing the splits as the ground seemed to rise up to meet her. She barely saw the puddle of mud before she landed in the middle of it.

"Morgan!" Drake sprinted back to her and skidded to a stop on the edge of the trail. "Are you okay? Are you hurt?" he asked in a rush, gingerly stepping onto the wet grass.

"Oh, my God! Oh, my God!" Morgan screeched when mud drenched her face and body.

A nauseating feeling of humiliation shattered the happiness she'd felt moments ago, and the harder she tried to get up, the worse the situation got. She wanted to cry, looking at the muddy mess on her yellow jogging suit and her snow-white running shoes.

"Argh!" she screamed in frustration.

When she looked back up, Drake was doubled over laughing, and annoyance and embarrassment warred within Morgan.

"It's not funny!" she fumed. "Look at me! Look at my shoes," she sobbed, and cringed at the brownish muck soaking into her clothes.

"Are you hurt?" Drake asked, struggling to pull himself together.

"No! Just help me!"

"O-Okay, I will." Drake used the back of his hands to wipe at his tears. "But first, I have to get a picture because no one's *ever* going to believe me without proof."

"Urgh, I can't stand you!" she yelled at Drake. He was as bad as the twins when it came to whipping out his phone to capture a moment. "I'm sitting in mud . . . like a pig! And you're messing around." She gathered a handful of the yucky muck and threw a mudball at him.

Drake jumped out of the way and held up his phone. "Oink. Oink. Smile, baby. Just think. Falling in mud can be considered part of your training," he rationalized as he snapped photo after photo. "Now you know how it'll feel if it happens while you're running the obstacle course."

A few joggers slowed to see what the commotion was about but kept going, and that only made Morgan angrier.

"I hate this," she sobbed. "I hate mud. I hate rain. I hate training, and—and just—just get me out of here!" That only made Drake laugh harder.

I can't wait until this contest is over. I'm never running again.

Chapter Thirty-One

TUESDAY NIGHT HADN'T COME FAST ENOUGH, DRAKE THOUGHT as he entered Morgan's building. He missed his baby. He and Morgan had both been busy with work for the past week, and it seemed everything came before their relationship.

But not on Tuesdays.

The day had been dubbed their date night over a month ago, after they officially started dating. And short of a natural disaster, there would be no canceling. Tuesday nights were sacred. Even the twins had gotten on board. They already knew that if they needed him to do something or take them somewhere, it couldn't be on date night unless it was an emergency.

Longing swirled inside of Drake as he pushed the button for Morgan's floor. If he could, he would spend every waking hour with her, but that wasn't practical. Being their own bosses, with tons of obligations, made it difficult and kept them apart more than he preferred. Like this past weekend.

He had traveled to San Francisco for a meeting and while he was there, he'd also looked at a potential property that his company was considering purchasing. All the while, his mind was on Morgan.

He had tried talking her into traveling with him, even suggested that they stay an extra day to play tourists, but she already had plans. A board meeting on Friday and a family event on Saturday night that she couldn't miss.

Thank goodness for cell phones. Morgan was the first person he talked to in the morning, and the last one at night, but this weekend it hadn't been enough. It wasn't the same as seeing her, touching her, and holding her in his arms.

Tonight, Drake would rather stay in and love on her, but he had promised that they would go out for dinner and dancing. Something they both enjoyed but didn't get to do often.

Excitement simmered inside of him as he neared her floor. He had to laugh at himself for feeling like a kid going on his first date. If a few days away from her did this to him, he would have to assign someone else to travel in his place going forward. Just one more thing he needed to deal with. Maybe after the Titan Games.

The Titan Games. The closer they got to the date, the more anxious he was getting. Not that he was concerned about losing. That hadn't crossed his mind. It was the fact that he was competing against his woman.

That would never be okay.

It didn't sit right with him, but they both agreed that they would see the competition through to the end. Win or lose, it wouldn't affect their relationship, but they both were in it to win it.

But how would she handle the situation if she didn't win?

Drake shook the thought free. Tonight, he had vowed not to think about the competition, work, or anything else except for Morgan.

When the elevator stopped on her floor, he exited and strolled down the hallway with his duffel bag hanging on his shoulder and a bouquet of orchids in his hand. He stopped in front of her door and huffed out a cleansing breath before he knocked.

When several minutes ticked by with no answer, concern replaced his excitement. She should've been home, but he hadn't bothered calling before coming over.

He readjusted his duffel bag on his shoulder and pulled his cell phone from the front pocket of his pants. Just when he was getting ready to call her, the door swung open.

Drake's heart skipped a beat, and for a moment, all he could do was stare. She was literally breathtaking.

His hand went to his chest at the sight of her in a short black dress. Not just any dress, but a one-shoulder outfit that skimmed over her shapely body, fastened on her left hip, and stopped mid-thigh.

If he'd thought the shoes she wore for Dreamy's wedding were the sexiest, it was because he hadn't seen the ones she had on now. They had a strap across the toes with a small black-and-white bow. Then another strap that spiraled halfway up her legs. The five-inch heels screamed *do me*, and in that moment, that was all he wanted to do.

"Hey, baby. I'm sorry it took me so long to answer the door. God, you are a sight for sore eyes. Get in here," she said.

Drake heard her talking, but he had a one-track mind as he entered and shut the door with his foot. He let his duffel bag drop to the floor and instead of handing her the bouquet, he set the flowers on the table in the foyer.

Her brows dipped into a frown. "Are you okay? What's wrong?"

"I'm fine and you're *gorgeous*. I've missed you so much," he said, his voice thick with emotion.

"Aww, babe. Thank you, and I've missed you too."

She stepped into his arms, and though he wanted to devour

her, he just kissed her lips and held her close, loving the way her body molded against him.

Feeling all her curves hugged up against him made his need for her spike. His hands slid down the sides of her body and around to her perfectly round ass. Palming her butt, he pulled her even closer, then lowered his head and captured her lips.

The kiss was originally meant to be a greeting, to let her know how glad he was to see her, but it quickly climbed out of control. Not seeing her for several days had Drake all worked up, and though he knew they had to leave now to make their reservation, he needed her like a starving man needed food.

Morgan's hands slid to his butt and gripped him the way he was palming her. When she broke the kiss and lifted her head, she stared into his eyes, then smiled.

"Now, that's how you say hello," she said, grinning harder.

Drake backed her farther into the house and up against the closet door. "There are more ways I want to say hello, because when you come to the door looking like a gift from God, I can't help but want to unwrap this dress on you."

She laughed. "I see what you did there—unwrap my wrap dress—cute."

Drake returned her smile, but instead of voicing how much he needed her, he unhooked the clasp that was holding the dress closed and let it fall open.

"Oh, so you were serious about unwrapping me."

"As a heart attack," he said as she stood before him with her shoulders back, her chest out, and her hands on her hips.

Drake sucked in a breath and his gaze gobbled her up. "I should be concerned that you were about to step out of here without a bra, but I can't even be mad. Easy access. Just the way I like it."

His eyes took in his woman's sexy body. Her perky breasts

called to him while her dark nipples stood proud as if demanding that he suck them.

His attention went lower to the tiny strip of black material covering one of his favorite parts of her body, and his mouth went dry. She was always well-groomed, but it was safe to say that she was bare down there, because her panties weren't hiding much.

Drake stepped to her and lowered his mouth to her delectable neck while sliding his hand up her torso until he reached her breast.

"You know if we don't leave now, we're going to miss our dinner reservation," she said, and hissed when he tweaked her nipple.

"I know, and right now, I don't give a damn. Food can wait. All I want is you."

She felt so good, and touching her like this—squeezing and teasing her breasts—sent a ripple of desire charging through him. He was so hard, he was sure his shaft was going to break through his zipper at any moment, and all he wanted to do was bury himself deep inside her.

"Well, if food is off the table . . ." Morgan said, her words trailing off when she went for his belt buckle and then his zipper.

Now Drake was the one hissing and cursing under his breath as she reached into his briefs and cupped him. He was already on the brink of losing control, the way her soft hand stroked, squeezed, and tugged on his dick, he didn't stand a chance at lasting long.

"Babe," he groaned and staggered a little, dizzy with desire as he stood to his full height. He eased out of her grip and quickly dug his wallet out of his back pocket, while watching her dress slide off her body. And man . . . what a body.

Drake's pants dropped to his ankles, and he was in so much of a hurry to sheath himself that he didn't bother kicking them off. By the time he had the condom on, Morgan was standing naked in front of him.

A growl rumbled inside his chest. "*Damn*, baby," he said tightly and backed her to the wall.

It would probably be just as easy to carry her to the bedroom, but he couldn't wait. He bent slightly, gripped the back of her thighs, and lifted her.

He had slid inside her before she could wrap her legs around him good.

With the wall at her back, Drake pounded into her like a man possessed. Her hold around his neck tightened as he pumped into her, and she slid up and down on his shaft.

Her sexy sounds rolled through him like fuel, sparking him to thrust faster and harder, going deeper . . . and deeper with each thrust.

His mind whirled. His pulse pounded in his ears. And his body vibrated as Morgan's eager response matched his. Passion and need soared through him as they picked up the pace.

"Oh, yeah, that's it, baby," he said, the words tumbling out of his mouth as their movements grew more frantic.

Hold on, *man. Hold on*, he told himself. He always wanted to make sure Morgan reached her release before he did, but right now . . .

"Drake!" Morgan screamed, her arms tightening around his neck and practically choking him as her body convulsed uncontrollably and her inner muscles squeezed his shaft.

That pushed Drake to his breaking point, and he growled her name as something akin to an electric shock scorched through his body, almost bringing him to his knees.

"*Oh, my goodness. Oh, my goodness*," Morgan whispered over and over again, and her forehead dropped to his shoulder before her body went limp in his arms.

Suddenly struggling to keep them both upright, Drake braced a hand and her against the wall while he struggled to breathe.

Long minutes ticked by as he continued panting for air, and involuntary tremors rocked him every few seconds. That was so intense he could barely think straight while he tried to pull himself together.

That was . . .

Morgan kissed his sweaty neck. "I missed you too," she whispered, and Drake sputtered a laugh.

"Not as much as I missed you." He shook his head, feeling as if his brain was cloudy. "That was . . . Man, I have no words."

Morgan lifted her head and kissed him. "Yes, it was, and I can't wait to do it again."

Drake chuckled, and he stared into his woman's bright eyes. His heart squeezed as so many sensations warred within him— anxiousness, exhilaration, possessiveness, and . . . love. His love for her was almost overwhelming and his chest tightened as the emotion seemed to expand. "I love you so much, Angel, and I can't imagine my life without you in it."

"Oh, Drake," she whispered. "I think I fall more and more in love with you every day, and I'm not going anywhere. You're it for me."

He kissed her hard, wanting her to feel every emotion swirling inside of him. "I'm glad to hear that because I'm never letting you go."

Chapter Thirty-Two

THE NEXT MORNING, DRAKE STROLLED INTO HIS OFFICE BUILD-ing whistling and feeling like a new man. He'd give anything to have his days start out the way it had that morning—with Morgan naked and joining him in the shower.

Just the thought had him smiling like an idiot. They'd never made it to dinner the night before. Instead, after a couple of rounds of sex, they'd ordered in, then ended up feasting on each other all over again.

To say it was an extraordinary night was an understatement, and he wasn't letting anything, or anybody, rain on his good mood. So when he walked into his office to find Matteo sitting on the sofa and looking at him bitterly, Drake kept his night with Morgan at the forefront of his mind.

"I'm not accepting any bad news today. If that's why you're in here looking like someone kicked your puppy, I suggest you table whatever conversation you want to have with me."

"Oh, so it's like that?"

"Yes. Now, let's start over. Good morning. How was your trip? When did you get back?"

Matteo had spent the last few weeks in San Diego where they had a few projects going on. He had worked a vacation into the trip during his last week there, and based on his tan, he'd spent some time hanging out on the beach.

"It was amazing and productive. I got back yesterday."

"Cool. Glad it was a good trip."

Drake strolled across the office and went through his usual morning routine. Setting his laptop bag on the desk, he placed his cell phone on the charger and dropped his keys into the top drawer.

"I was going to go over this at our Friday meeting, but it can't wait. We have some issues that are costing time and money."

Drake sat in his desk chair and rocked back. "Did you not hear me when I said don't bring me no bad news?"

Matteo rolled his eyes and continued as if Drake hadn't said anything. "That Malibu project is over budget, and I've been in contact with Hector," he said of the project manager.

"How much over?" Drake asked. It wasn't unusual for some projects to exceed their initial budget, but this one surprised him. It hadn't needed as much work.

"Fifty-five thousand." Matteo lifted his hands to stop Drake from speaking. "I know I give him a hard time, but in his defense, we hadn't figured on the time and money involved with the zoning issues. Add that to the damaged sewer pipe, and I can see how the project went over."

For the next few minutes, they discussed next steps with the project and possible ways they could recoup the overage. Unfortunately, this was the second time in six months that Hector had gone over his proposed budget.

"Also, instead of allowing us to build fifteen homes on the

plot of land in Woodland Hills, the county is only approving ten."

"What?" Drake yelled. It had already taken almost a year to go through the approval process, and now that they had, the county was causing them trouble. "Come on. At this stage in the game, they—"

"I've said it before, and I'll say it again, we should sell that land. Otherwise, it's going to take years before we turn a profit."

Drake shook his head. "We've dumped too much money into it already to turn back now."

"I'm telling you, man. With all the delays, it's costing us. I don't think we should hold on to it. Cut our losses and get out."

Drake released a noisy sigh and rubbed the back of his neck. "No wonder we got that property for cheap. I wouldn't be surprised if the previous owners had gone through the same mess."

"Probably," Matteo said, studying Drake as if seeing him for the first time.

"What? Why are you looking at me like that?"

Matteo folded his arms across his chest. "What did you do this morning?" he asked.

"I did what I usually do. I went for a run, then took the kids to school. Why?"

"Because something is different about you. Your tie is askew, you have shaving cream next to your ear, but what's most noticeable is, you're glowing."

Drake snorted and opened his laptop. "Man, you're crazy. Hell, I don't even know what that means. People don't glow," he said, but then remembered when his assistant was pregnant. She really did seem to glow, and he assumed it had everything to do with the fact that she was having a baby after years of her and her husband trying.

"Did you see someone today?"

Drake narrowed his eyes at his friend. "Yeah, I saw a lot of people," he said, then logged into his computer. "What's wrong with you? Why all the questions? Rough morning? Bad night? What's up?"

"No, my night was incredible. I went to an amazing restaurant, had some good food, and woke up with a smoking hot babe in my bed. So yeah, it was great. But we're not talking about me right now." He placed his hands on the desk and leaned forward. Seconds ticked by without either of them speaking, and then Matteo's brows dipped into a frown. "It's Morgan, isn't it? You're finally getting some on the regular, huh?"

Drake's gaze shot up and onto Matteo. How the heck did he know that? Surely, he couldn't tell what he and Morgan had done just by looking at him.

Matteo nodded without Drake saying anything.

"I knew it!" He banged his hand against the desk before sitting in one of the guest chairs. "You're all disheveled, and you *never* walk out of the house without being totally put together. But why? Why would you hook up with her again, especially now?"

Drake studied his friend for the longest time. Matteo prided himself on dressing to impress in the finest, most expensive suits and shoes. His motto was that you never knew who you'll run into, so always look your best. One other thing about his friend— he rarely missed the smallest detail.

"Don't even try and deny it. Your ass walked in here like you didn't have a care in the world. When normally, you would've rushed in here with your cell to your ear, and probably be on your second or third conference call by now. I'll ask this a different way. What's up with you and Morgan?"

"None of your business," Drake said.

He had torn into Matteo about talking to the kids about Morgan, especially when he didn't have all the facts. He'd also mentioned to his friend that he and Morgan had made peace.

He just hadn't told him that they were officially dating. Although Drake was pretty sure Matteo had figured it out.

Drake skimmed through his emails. It always amazed him how fast they accumulated. It wasn't even nine o'clock and already he had a hundred of them to read through.

"Dammit, man! Morgan is the enemy right now. You need to stay clear of her, at least until this property situation is handled."

Drake chuckled. "Aren't you being a little dramatic? Sure, we're going for the same property, but I already know it's going to be mine. I'm not worried about that."

"Well, you should be. That woman is your kryptonite. She has some type of control over you, and if you let her get close, she's going to snatch that property from right under your nose."

Drake sat back in his seat and steepled his fingers. "You honestly think she's going to beat me at the Titan Games? Seriously? I'll admit, she's putting in the time needed to prepare, and I think she's going to do great. But Morgan doesn't do sweat, dirt, or mud. All the things involved in the obstacle course. And the other contenders don't stand a chance, except for maybe this one guy. He's in great shape, but I don't think he wants this as much as I do. Don't worry," Drake said, pounding his hand against his chest. "I got this."

He was in the best shape he'd ever been in, and over the last few weeks he'd gotten even faster and stronger. He had no doubt that he'd win.

Matteo sat back and sighed. "You're talking all big and bad now, but I wouldn't get too confident if I were you. When Morgan pulls out all of her feminine wiles on you, it'll be like taking you out at the knees. You're going to be good for nothing. I get keeping your enemies close, but—"

"She's not my enemy!" Drake said with more force than intended. "Yes, we're going after the same property, but that's business. It has nothing to do with our personal life."

"And if you believe that shit, you're already a goner. Couldn't you have waited a few weeks before hooking up with her? Why now? Why get into her panties now and risk ruining everything?"

"Don't speak about her like that, man."

Matteo threw up his hands and stood. "Here we go. This was how it began the last time. She smiled in your face, made you feel invincible, then she left without a trace. Crushing you in the process."

Drake didn't say anything because he had vowed to leave the past in the past. Besides, Morgan wasn't the same person, and neither was he.

"For the record, Morgan and I are together. Things are great between us, and that's how it's going to stay. If you have an issue with that, keep it to yourself because I don't want to hear it."

"Fine," Matteo snapped.

They were like brothers and could argue without causing a problem between them professionally or personally. Drake was counting on that being the case today.

"Since you know what you're doing, I'm heading back to my office to get some work done."

"Before you go, there's something I want to talk to you about. Just don't freak out."

Matteo huffed out a breath. "Dude, whenever someone starts a conversation with *don't freak out*, it means I'm going to freak out."

"You might not, but . . . anyway, I'm thinking about buying the Hollywood property myself, and not have the company purchase it."

From the time he'd heard that Jeffrey was selling it, Drake had gone back and forth on whether to buy it through the company or purchase it outright himself. The day he'd submitted the bid was the day he had decided that he wanted the building in memory of his father. Like he had mentioned in the letter, it was a part of his legacy.

The problem was, Drake hadn't shared that decision with Matteo or the board.

Matteo studied him for the longest time, and for a moment, Drake wasn't sure he'd respond.

"What, you gon' buy it and then give it to your girlfriend?" he finally said.

"Not exactly."

Drake had been thinking about this long and hard, and if he won, he wanted to somehow share the property with Morgan. That's what he explained to Matteo.

What he didn't say to his friend was that he wasn't sure what exactly that would look like, or if Morgan would even go along with the idea. She wanted the building to be her first commercial property that she purchased on her own. Granted, Karter and Dreamy were putting in some up-front money, but they wouldn't own it. Morgan planned to pay them back within three years.

"What does your girl think of this idea of yours? She doesn't come across as the handout kind of person."

"It wouldn't be like that, and I haven't mentioned the idea to her." Drake was still mulling it over and wasn't sure when or if he'd bring it up to her. "We both have good reasons for the property bid. It could be a win-win proposition and . . . I believe in what she's trying to do."

"Which is?"

Drake told him about Open Arms and their goals for the future. No one could deny, not even Matteo, that what they were doing for those teens was greatly needed. Another option would be to find her a different place near her preferred area.

"What I want to know is how are you going to explain that at the next board meeting?"

"By that time, I will have found another property with the

same price tag and potential for the business. You already know why I proposed we get the Hollywood property. Yes, it's exactly what the company would normally purchase, but there are plenty of other properties out there we can get and accomplish the same goals with that we laid out for this one."

"You act like it's so simple when we both know it's not. Unless Jeffrey has another property to sell you that's just like the Hollywood one and in the same area, this ain't gon' fly."

"Well considering all that I'm going through for the Hollywood property, I should have the right to decide what happens with it. Right now I'm planning to purchase it myself."

Matteo shook his head. "I get why the building means so much to you, Drake, but . . . I hope you know what you're doing."

"I do. I'm investing in my future."

"Yeah, you just keep telling yourself that," Matteo said as he strolled out of the office.

Drake no longer had doubts about his and Morgan's relationship, and he loved the idea of them owning a property together. It would be a great way to kick off their future. He just hoped he wasn't getting ahead of himself.

Only time would tell.

Chapter Thirty-Three

MORGAN LOVED EVENINGS LIKE THIS ONE, WHERE SHE AND Drake could lay around and just enjoy each other's company. After dropping the twins off at Karter and Dreamy's house so that they could spend the weekend with Nana, he came over with dinner and a change of clothes.

They'd eaten and made love, and now were lying in her bed watching television. Well, Drake was watching a basketball game, while Morgan struggled to keep her eyes open.

"Going to spend the night with Nana and Melvin was all Addy and Aiden talked about until I dropped them off. I don't know if I'll be able to get them to come home again," Drake said as he stroked Morgan's arm, practically lulling her to sleep.

She smiled at his comment. Morgan had visited Nana a couple of weeks ago and had taken the twins with her, and they had had a blast. Probably because Nana doted on them the whole time, the way she did with Morgan and her brothers when they were growing up. The kids loved hanging out with Nana and especially Melvin.

It worked out well that Addison and Aiden enjoyed going

over there, especially this weekend while Karter and Dreamy were out of town. Nana lived with them and didn't much like being in that huge house alone. Even having Melvin, their dog, there, the house was still too big for one person.

This was also the perfect time for them to visit because it was the weekend for the Titan Games. Eight long weeks of training, and the big day was tomorrow.

She and Drake had wanted to spend time together the day before it started, and Nana had offered to watch the twins.

"Nana loves the company," Morgan said. "Since my brothers and I are all grown now, she doesn't have any kids to spoil."

"What about your brother Randy's kids? Do they spend time over there? He has girls, right?"

"Yeah, identical twins, and yes, they go by there often. Just not often enough for Nana. If it were left up to her, that house would be full of people all the time."

Before Drake came back into her life, Morgan had thought about asking Nana to move in with her. Karter and Dreamy were always busy with their jobs, and Morgan figured she could keep Nana company better. It was probably good that hadn't happened since Morgan was just as busy now as they were. Besides, Nana probably wouldn't have left Karter. He was her favorite, even though she always said she didn't have favorites.

"You doing okay?" Drake asked, pulling Morgan out of her thoughts.

She glanced up to see him watching her. "Yeah, I'm fine. Why do you ask?"

He ran the back of his fingers down her cheek and her eyes drifted closed at his tender touch.

"It just seems like you've been dragging today. Especially earlier."

"Oh, that was probably because I had some bad sushi for lunch. Messed my stomach up pretty good."

Drake sat up in the bed. "Why didn't you tell me? How do you feel now? Do you need me to go to the drugstore and get you something?"

"Nope. I'm good now. Just a little tired. Between the extra hours at work and training every day, it's all starting to take its toll."

That was putting it mildly. By the time she got home at night, she barely had energy to climb the stairs.

"And I guess me keeping you up late some nights hasn't helped."

He laid back down, wrapped his arm around her, and she rested her head on his chest. "You're actually the highlight of my days. For some reason, whenever I'm with you, I miraculously have more energy."

He chuckled and kissed the top of her head. "Funny how that works, huh?"

"Yeah, every time." She sighed and wrapped her arm around his waist and snuggled closer. "I'm glad that I'm in better shape, but I can't wait until this competition is over. I'm tired of training."

"I know, baby. Tomorrow is the big day, then you can go back to being a bum."

She laughed and pinched him in the side.

"Ow." He tried pulling away, but she held on to him until he settled back. "Seriously, though, I'm so proud of you. I'll admit, I didn't think you could do it, but running with you this week, I know you've got this. You're going to do great."

"Yeah, let's hope."

"TODAY IS THE DAY," MORGAN MURMURED.

She rubbed her hands up and down her arms to warm herself as she stared out at the course. Though the weather was dreary and overcast, with a slight chill in the air, everyone seemed to be pumped about the Titan Games. She and the rest of the participants received a walk-through of all the obstacles, and Morgan was already tired just looking at them.

I should've taken advantage of the trial run that they offered a couple of weeks ago.

Now that she was seeing it up close and personal, there was no way she could go through with it. Besides that, she didn't feel all that great. Even after a good night's sleep, she was exhausted, and all she wanted to do was go home and crawl back into bed.

"I can't do it," she whispered and leaned her head against Isabella's shoulder. Izzy and Dreamy were there for moral support, despite the early hour and chillier than usual temperature.

"You can, and you will," Isabella insisted. "You have worked your butt off. There is no way that you're not ready."

"This will be so much fun. You're going to crush this thing!" Dreamy encouraged her from Morgan's other side.

Always the optimist, it was easy for her sister-in-law to be excited. She wasn't the one who was getting ready to possibly embarrass herself and break a bone or two.

"You got this, girl. You have trained for two months, and you're tougher, stronger, and faster. There is no way you're not going to win."

Even though Stanley and Isabella had created a makeshift obstacle course at the gym that she'd done well on, it wasn't the same. This was much bigger and more intimidating.

"I'm kicking myself for not coming out here and practicing when I had a chance. God, I'm going to make a total fool of myself."

"Not totally." Dreamy wrapped her arm around Morgan's shoulder. "You're going to go out there and be the badass that I know you are. I have complete confidence in you."

"On that note, it looks like they're about to get started. Let's go over here so you can get warmed up," Isabella said, and started toward a grassy area off to the side.

Morgan slowed when she spotted Drake walking toward her wearing a long-sleeved T-shirt that molded over his upper body and showed off his thick biceps. But how he wasn't freezing in his basketball shorts was a mystery to her.

Her pulse pounded a little harder the closer he got to her. They'd been together for months now, and each time their gazes met, desire still roared through her body.

He looked so good, and his confident swagger probably had every participant on edge, knowing that he would be their biggest competition.

And I'm supposed to beat him?

Normally, Morgan was confident in her abilities, but this was so far outside of her wheelhouse. She might've trained for this and could make a good showing, but seeing the intimidating course had her nerves twisting into knots.

What had she been thinking? She wasn't an athlete. She didn't run through water, or crawl through mud, or even swing from ropes. What made her think that she could do this?

Without a word, Drake gently pulled her into his arms, and she rested her head against his chest. This was home for her. Even without speaking, he had the ability to calm her nerves and relax her instantly.

Morgan wrapped her arms around his waist and inhaled his familiar fresh scent. "I love you," she said, the words muffled against his chest.

He tightened his hold. "I love you more."

Even if they were competitors, she was glad he was there. Preparing for the event had brought them even closer together, and knowing that they were both going through a major milestone made the competition that much more special. They would remember this day for the rest of their lives.

She was so proud of both of them, but especially of herself. Never in a million years did she think she could ever get into top physical shape and compete at this level. Sure, there had been sweat and tears involved, but she made it through a grueling training, and it was about to pay off.

Whatever the outcome, she was already a winner. She just had to remember that.

And I have to complete this course no matter what.

"You got this, baby," Drake whispered in her ear. "Don't start doubting yourself now. Be safe, and I'll see you at the finish line." He gave her a squeeze, kissed the side of her head, and strolled away.

Alrighty then, she thought. *Let's get this thing started.*

She strolled over to where Dreamy and Isabella were standing.

"Okay, so they created the groups," Dreamy said as she stared down at the paper that she'd picked up from the check-in desk.

Since there were over fifty people participating, the organizers divided everyone into six groups.

"Oh, this should be interesting. It looks like you're in Drake's group."

"Of course I am. Now I get to make a fool of myself right in front of him."

"Girl, knock it off. That man is so in love with you. Just do your best," Dreamy said.

"And who knows, maybe he'll be eating your dust and won't see a thing," Isabella added, but was doing a horrible job trying not to laugh at her own joke.

"Whatever." Morgan slipped on her weight gloves, hoping they'd help her keep her grip on some of the apparatuses. "I just want to get this over with . . . and win."

It was time she tapped into her competitive side and did everything in her power to make a good showing. Her goal was to come in first, but if not, second might work too. Out of the fifty participants, seven of them were competing for the building. The Titan Games organizers planned to combine the time that it took them to finish the course with the finish time of their 10k tomorrow.

She had a chance.

She just had to give it her all.

THIRTY MINUTES LATER, THE EVENT BEGAN.

The moment it started, Morgan took off for the first obstacle—the monkey bars. This had been crazy hard for her when she first started training, but now that she had built some muscle and was stronger, it was one of her favorite obstacles.

Her hands gripped the steel bars, and even with gloves on, the cold seeped through, but that didn't stop her from moving. She swung from one rung to the next, cycling her legs with each swing and moving at a quick but controlled speed.

No way was she stopping.

She was pumped.

When she got to the end of the monkey bars, she dropped down and took off for the tires. Her easiest obstacle. Morgan learned early on that her small feet gave her an advantage of getting through them quickly. She kept her head down, got into a rhythm so her feet barely touched the inside of the tires, and flew through them.

It was one of several obstacles that she could beat Drake at. That one as well as the tunnel were a struggle for him.

A couple of people were ahead of her, but others hadn't passed her yet. It didn't matter; she had to stay focused on what she was doing and get to the end.

Morgan ran through a maze that was built with cones but must've been too hasty because she suddenly tripped over her feet, falling hard in the dirt.

Dammit.

"At least it ain't mud!" She heard Isabella scream, and Morgan couldn't help but laugh. But it was just the encouragement she needed, and she jumped back up.

She made it through and cleared the next obstacle but struggled through the one after that.

Keep going. Keep going.

The chant played on loop through her mind as she kept moving.

Breathing hard while trying to stay relaxed, Morgan sprinted to the hang-over wall, praying that she could get over it on the first try. She grabbed on to the rope, which was rough in her glove-clad hands, and planted her feet on the wall.

Go, go, go, she told herself, and climbed halfway up. Panic swirled inside of her when she couldn't pull herself all the way over.

Come on, don't let go. Don't let go.

But no amount of self-coaching could get her up and over the wall, and she cursed under her breath when she slid back down inch by inch.

"Come on, girl. You got this!"

"Don't give up. Keep going."

She heard Isabella and Dreamy screaming from somewhere nearby. Knowing them, they were probably running along the side of the course, at least as far as they could.

After a second attempt at climbing the wall and failing, Morgan had to dig deep to try again. She couldn't use up what little energy she had on one obstacle. She also couldn't move onto the next one until she got over the wall. Otherwise, minutes would be subtracted from her final time.

Don't give up. Don't give up. Don't give up, she kept telling herself.

I can't give up.

———————

DRAKE COULD PRACTICALLY DO THE COURSE WITH HIS EYES closed, but he had one problem—Morgan. Every few minutes, he glanced back to see how she was doing. It was hard to watch her struggle, stumble, and even fall on one of the obstacles. His biggest fear was that she'd hurt herself before it was all said and done.

He was proud of her, though, and loved how hard she tried, but at the rate she was going, she wouldn't cross the finish line in second or third.

He was worried about her. Not just because of the course, but because of how tired she'd seemed the day before and this morning. Normally, she was a light sleeper. Not today, though. It had taken him several tries to wake her up.

It was clear that she was mentally and physically exhausted, but she hadn't complained. Well, not much.

Drake kept telling himself to focus. He was halfway through the course, but he couldn't leave Morgan behind. At least not too far behind. Before climbing the rope obstacle, he ran back to the wall where she was struggling to get over.

He saw the hopeful expression on two people's faces as he passed them on the way back. They were thinking this was their chance to get ahead, but he planned to turn it up once he got Morgan over that wall.

"Okay, baby. You're getting over this wall. Now," he said when he reached Morgan, and he almost laughed at the surprised look on her dirt-covered face.

"Drake, get out of here! Remember, one of us has to win this. Go!"

"Not until you're over the wall. Come on. One more try."

The determination on her face as she gripped the rope squeezed at his heart. She was going over.

"Go!" he yelled, and she took off, pulling herself up. When she started sliding back down, Drake planted his hands on her perfect ass and pushed.

Morgan started giggling. "Don't be trying to cop a feel, Drake Faulkner, when I'm struggling up here."

He chuckled. "Angel, stop talking and get over the damn wall. I need to get back to work."

"Yes, sir," she mocked him, and made it to the top.

As she went over it, Drake sprinted back to the rope obstacle.

He had dropped into second place, but he was determined to regain the lead. One of the hardest obstacles for him was the thirty-foot tunnel. He had a tough time getting through it without getting stuck along the way. Once he got through that obstacle, though, it would be smooth sailing through the rest.

He just had to stay focused, and more than that, stop worrying about Morgan. She could hold her own.

Ten minutes later, he approached the red finish line ribbon, and broke through it with his arms held high. Cheers erupted from the crowd, including Dreamy and Isabella, who congratulated him.

"Now our girl has to get across," Dreamy said as they all waited for Morgan.

Come on, baby.

She was a few people behind, but lucky for her, several of the individuals in the group were older and slower. Some had also skipped a few obstacles, meaning that they'd be penalized and their final time would be affected.

"Come on, Angel!" Drake yelled, clapping as she caught up with the participant who was on the second-to-last obstacle. If she could pass them, then she'd cross the finish line in second place.

Come on, baby. You can do this. Just keep moving, he said in his head as if he had the same telepathy that the twins seemed to share.

When Morgan passed the last participant and reached the final obstacle, Dreamy and Isabella started jumping up and down and screaming her name.

Drake's heart swelled with pride as she breezed through it and ran toward him at the finish line. Her momentum had her going so fast, she slammed into him, sending them both to the ground.

The breath whooshed out of Drake when she landed on top of him, but he burst out laughing.

"We have to stop meeting like this," he said and they both laughed.

"You did it, Angel. You did it!" he yelled, barely hearing himself over the cheers as other participants started crossing the line.

"I did it," she panted, sweat dripping down her face. She laid her head on his chest. "We made it."

"Yes, we did, baby. Yes, we did."

Chapter Thirty-Four

HOURS AFTER FINISHING THE OBSTACLE COURSE, DRAKE stood at the window behind his desk, chugging an energy drink. He hadn't planned on coming into the office, even though he often worked Saturdays, but it couldn't be helped. He had contracts to look over and sign before Monday morning.

What a day it had been so far. He'd been operating on adrenaline earlier, and now all he wanted to do was go home and chill. Better yet, he probably should've followed Morgan to her place to make sure she got home all right.

The obstacle course had totally worn her out. Despite that, she'd been in good spirits and had insisted that after a hot shower and a nap, she would be as good as new.

The main reason he hadn't followed her home was because Isabella was planning to hang out with her for the rest of the day.

Drake had just reclaimed his seat when his office door burst open, and Matteo stormed in.

"You've lost your mind, haven't you?"

Drake frowned. "What are you talking about?"

"You risked losing that race this morning, and the property, because you went back to help Morgan. You do realize this is a competition, right? I get that you're crazy in love, and that you're thinking of doing something different regarding that property, but come on, man. You're going to mess around and she's going to steal that building right from under you no matter what you're planning on doing with it."

Drake ran his hand over his mouth and down his goatee, trying to think before he spoke. Matteo was like a brother. He was family, but right now Drake wanted to pound him into floor.

Matteo had been there for Drake when Morgan left him back in college. He understood why his friend was concerned about him moving too fast when it came to her. He even understood why he was worried about Drake losing the property. What he didn't understand was why Matteo couldn't trust his judgment. Drake's business decisions had been solid over the years, so he could only assume that this whole issue had everything to do with Morgan.

"It's happening again," Matteo said.

"What is?"

"Morgan's control over you. It happened in college and it's happening again. You have been planning for that Hollywood property for years. She's been back in your life for a few months, and you're changing the plans. That's not like you. At least not like the adult version of you. She's reeling you in."

"My dad taught me a lot of lessons before he died," Drake started. "One being to always put people, especially family, before *stuff*. When I saw Morgan struggling this morning, I couldn't help but go back and help her. You know why?" Drake stared his friend down, making sure he had his full attention. "I'm in love with that woman. She's my heart, man. I will *always* put her first."

Matteo huffed out a breath and dropped into one of the guest chairs in front of the desk. "Even at the risk of losing this competition? The building?"

"Let's just say that if I ever have to choose between Morgan and the Hollywood property, I'm choosing her. I'm choosing *us*. But for the record, and I've said this before, I won't lose the Titan Games."

Matteo ran his hands over his face. "I don't know, man. You're willing to sacrifice everything for her. Aren't you afraid that the next time things get tough, she'll bolt? She did it before. What's to keep her from doing it again?"

Drake would be lying if he said that he hadn't thought about it, but he trusted Morgan. He trusted her to come to him if she had a problem, whether it was about them or anything else. He also knew she regretted the way she left back then, and the Morgan he knew now was different. She wouldn't do that to him again.

"Matt, when you find that one special person, you'll understand. Until then, you'll just have to trust that I know what I'm doing—professionally and personally." Drake pushed away from his desk and stood. "Come and let me show you how sure I am about my love for Morgan."

Matteo followed him to the drafting table in the far corner of the office. Drake unrolled the blueprints that he had received yesterday from one of their architects and spread them out on the table.

"I recently had these plans drawn up to show my new ideas for the Hollywood property." Originally, when the company was going to buy the property, he and Matteo had worked together on the plans. The place could be a gold mine, and they would've been able to make a profit within a year after renovations were done and it was at full capacity. Many of the original concepts were still included, but Drake had made some major changes.

"Apartments?" Matteo asked as he studied the blueprint. "How many?"

"There will be thirty one-bedroom units and ten two-bedroom units."

He explained Morgan's vision for the building, and how he wanted to stay as close to it as possible while also maintaining some of their original business ideas. The property was going to make money either way. With these new plans, Drake and Morgan would both get what they wanted.

She and Isabella would have to keep Open Arms's current location since the Hollywood property wouldn't have office or meeting room space for them, only apartments for their clients, but it was still a win-win. They could remodel their current facility and turn it into an administrative building of sorts, while still keeping a couple of the bedrooms for emergency situations or even temporary housing.

"I'll admit, the plans look good. You've put a lot of thought into this." Matteo turned to him and folded his arms. "I know I've given you a hard time about her, but just know, it's only because I'm looking out for you."

Drake gripped his friend's shoulder and squeezed. "I know, man, and I appreciate that. Just know that I'm not going into this lightly. Not only am I thinking about her and me, but I also have the twins to consider. Right now I'm doing everything I can to secure a future with Morgan and to provide for Addy and Aiden."

Matteo nodded. "In that case, you have my blessing. What does Morgan think?"

"I haven't mentioned any of this to her yet."

"Why not? What are you waiting for?"

Drake released a long sigh. He wasn't a hundred percent sure why he'd held back. He said, "I'm waiting for the right time."

MORGAN LAY FACEDOWN ON HER BED AND STRUGGLED TO keep tears out of her eyes. Every inch of her body ached, even her hair. She might've made it through the obstacle course, but how was she going to get through the 10K? She needed more than twenty-four hours to recuperate.

"Okay, get up. I can't believe you're lying on the bed, considering how filthy you are," Isabella said.

Morgan could feel her friend's energy filling the room. Too bad she couldn't figure out a way to soak some of it up.

"I made you some tomato soup, and I have salmon in the oven and other foods to get you and your body ready for tomorrow. Oh, and I have a few ice packs for you," Isabella said.

"Thanks," Morgan said without moving.

"Actually, why don't you shower first?" Isabella continued. "Then we'll get to work on getting you in tip-top shape for tomorrow."

"Tomorrow?" Morgan sobbed. "I don't even think I can get through the next couple of hours. There's no way I'll be ready to run a 10K. I feel like my arms and legs are detached from my body. I think—"

"There's no way we're letting Drake win that property," Isabella interrupted. "Now, are you going to get your ass up and into the shower, or do you need me to drag you in there?"

Drake.

The mention of his name reminded Morgan of how he had come to her rescue during the obstacle course. There was a good chance she wouldn't have finished without his help. She had told him she owed him, and he said they were even. Surely, he hadn't been talking about when she gave him tips on getting through the tires. It wasn't like he wouldn't have figured it out on his own eventually.

"Chop-chop. Get up. You don't want your muscles to cramp. Jump in the shower, then I'll meet you downstairs so that you can eat."

Morgan slowly turned onto her back. It was too late. Her

muscles were already screaming. She doubted a shower would help at this point.

"I'm more tired than hungry," she said as Isabella headed to the door. "I'll eat after I take a nap."

"Nope." Isabella grabbed her hand and pulled her into a sitting position. The woman was a lot stronger than she looked. "Let's go," she said, practically dragging Morgan to the bathroom.

"Iz, I appreciate what you're doing, but I think my body is about to crumble into a million pieces," Morgan sobbed. "Between exhaustion and pain, I don't think—"

"Don't think. Just get in the shower. I promise you'll start to loosen up." Isabella turned the shower on full blast and within minutes, steam filled the bathroom. "Don't make me throw you in there with your clothes on . . . Get. In. There!"

Morgan groaned as she watched her friend march out of the room. As steam built behind the glass enclosure, it was as if the shower was calling to her.

Morgan stripped out of her clothes as fast as her achy muscles would allow and stepped into the shower. She could almost hear a chorus of angels singing when the hot water slapped against her skin. She closed her eyes and turned her face up to the showerhead. She could already feel her muscles loosening.

Izzy was right. This was exactly what I needed.

As she started to relax, thoughts of Drake filtered back into her mind. She never knew she could love someone as much as she loved that man. It was scary how much she'd grown to depend on him being in her life, and she was going to do whatever was necessary to make sure they stayed together.

She laid her forehead against the tile as weariness seeped deeper into her bones. She didn't want to be one of those people who started something and didn't finish it, but damn she was exhausted.

Morgan startled at the pounding on the door before it opened.

"Let's go, MoMo! We got to get you into shape so that you can win that 10K tomorrow," Isabella said, sounding more like a drill sergeant than a director of a nonprofit. "Hurry up."

"Oh, good grief," Morgan mumbled. "You should get out of the nonprofit business and join the military. The army could use a few good women like you."

"Yeah, yeah, whatever. Just get a move on. I'm giving you five more minutes, and then I'm going to drag you out of there."

"Yes, sir!" Morgan mocked. "I mean, yes, ma'am."

Isabella rolled her eyes and closed the door.

I am not a quitter, the little voice inside of her head screamed. *I am not a quitter.*

With that in mind, she hurried through the rest of her shower. Her body still felt as if she'd been run over by a reindeer, but no way was she quitting.

"I'm making it to the finish line even if it kills me."

Chapter Thirty-Five

MORGAN TRIED NOT TO MOAN AS SHE STRETCHED OUT HER hamstrings. It was the morning of the 10K and once again all she wanted to do was curl up on her eight-hundred-thread-count bedsheets. Instead, she was getting ready to run the longest race she'd ever run.

As of the week before, she was able to do seven miles at a decent time without falling on her face. She needed to drum up that same energy and determination to do it again. At least the weather was cooperating. This part of the event was being held in Los Angeles, and it was seventy degrees and sunny. That alone should give her extra energy.

"Are you ready?" Drake asked. He performed calf stretches next to her, looking scrumptious in a tank top that showed off his chiseled chest and arms.

"I'm as ready as I'll ever be, but I want to talk to you before we do this."

Morgan wasn't sure what he heard in her voice, but he stopped stretching and moved closer.

"What is it? Are you okay?"

"Yeah, I'm fine, but I want us to agree on something before we start."

"I'm listening."

"I'll only agree to run with you if you promise not to let me slow you down."

When he'd picked her up from home that morning, he had posed the idea that they run together. Morgan thought it was a horrible idea. He was twice as fast as she was on his worst day. She would definitely slow him down, but he didn't want to hear it. Now she needed to take a different approach in convincing him.

"You're not going to slow me down. We ran together all last week. You've got this. Besides, two of the competitors dropped out overnight. That increases our chances of one of us winning."

"That's another thing. I want you to win." When he started to speak, she lifted her hands. "I'm not dropping out. I'm still going to run, but Drake, you're going to be the one with the fastest time. That means if I slow down, you're going to have to keep going."

"I'm not leaving you behind, even if I have to carry you across the finish line."

"Then you're guaranteed to lose. Remember what we said when this whole thing started? If I don't win, I want you to win, and vice versa. You have a real shot at this. Besides, remember, this is about your family's legacy. I didn't know your father, but I would bet that he would be ecstatic if you owned one of the buildings he designed, especially the first one."

Drake didn't respond. He pulled one arm across his chest, and then the other, limbering up. All the while, his gaze stayed on her. He didn't have to say anything for her to know what he was thinking. He heard what she said, but that wouldn't change anything.

I guess I'll just have to keep up.

"Are you sure you're feeling okay?" Drake asked as they took off. That was the second or third time since she had arrived that he'd asked her.

"I told you, I'm fine. Why do you keep asking me that?"

"Because you don't look fine, Morgan. There are dark circles under your eyes, you've lost weight in the past week, and you look like you can barely stay upright. I'm worried about you. What's wrong?"

She laughed and shook her head. "What's wrong? I'm exhausted. I've been busting my butt to get to this point, and it has almost killed me. I'm not an athlete. This competition has taken every bit of energy I have, and I almost dropped out this morning."

"What? After all the hard work you put in?"

"Yeah, but I knew you and Izzy wouldn't let me. So I'm going to finish what I started, but I'm never running or doing anything more athletic than taking out the trash ever again. And even that's questionable."

He started laughing and pulled her into a hug. "Well, I am so proud of what you've accomplished. You never cease to amaze me."

Her heart melted a little at his words. "Thank you, baby. That means a lot."

"Maybe you can take a few days off this week," he said.

"There's no maybe about it. I'm staying in bed for at least three days straight."

"Hmm . . . I like the sound of that. I might have to join you some of those days," he said and kissed her sweetly.

Morgan slid her arms around his waist and molded against him. There were days when she didn't know what she'd done to deserve him, but she was so thankful he was back in her life.

"All right, you two, knock it off," Isabella said as she approached. Morgan and Drake eased apart. "You guys have a race to win. Quit playing kissy-face and get to the starting line."

Drake saluted her. "Yes, ma'am."

"Dang, she's bossy," Morgan said as they joined the other runners.

There were at least fifty people at the starting line, if not more. She and Drake, as well as the other three individuals who were left and competing for the property, greeted and wished one another luck. There didn't seem to be any animosity among them. Maybe like her, the small group had come to the conclusion that either Drake or Johnathan would win the right to purchase the Hollywood property.

"Runners, on your mark," the announcer said through a bullhorn after the participants were in place. "Go!"

Drake set a moderate pace and Morgan kept up easily. It was the perfect day for a run. Mild temperatures, birds chirping, and a light breeze kissing her heated skin. The event organizers had done a great job with logistics. Streets were blocked off and along the route there were drink and snack booths. There were even first responders mixed in. The organizers had thought of everything.

"You doing okay?" Drake asked as they hit the two-mile mark.

"Yeah, I'm good," Morgan said, her breath coming in short spurts. "You?"

"I'm great, especially since I get to hang out with you. What more could a guy ask for?"

She gave him a smile. The last couple of months had been exciting as well as exhausting. It would probably take her a good week to feel her legs again, and after that, she couldn't see herself ever stepping back into a gym.

Three miles in and Morgan was panting harder, but she kept going. She had come too far to stop, and she had every intention of finishing the race. No sooner had the thought popped into her mind than she stumbled, but caught herself and kept moving. Drake, on the other hand, slowed.

She glanced over to find him looking at her.

"I'm okay," she said quickly before he could ask.

He really needed to pick up the pace. She had lost track of the other competitors. For all she knew, they were miles ahead of the two of them.

"Drake, please don't hang back for me. You probably could've finished this race by now." He could run a six- or seven-minute mile, while she was still around the ten- or twelve-minute mile mark. "You have to win."

Instead of responding, when they passed a water table, he swiped a bottle and opened it.

"Here. Drink," he said without missing a step.

Morgan had to admit she was a little thirsty, but she hadn't wanted to slow down for water. During her training, she could run for an hour without hydrating, and so far, they'd only been running for thirty-five minutes.

Still, she took a couple of gulps as they continued moving, then tried to hand it back to him.

Drake shook his head. "Drink some more."

Morgan growled under her breath but didn't argue. Considering she was getting a little tired, she did as she was told, hoping it could give her a little boost of energy.

They were four and a half miles in when she started to slow down. Nausea bubbled inside her. Though she was trying to push herself, her energy level was fighting against her. Before Morgan realized what was happening, her head started spinning and she staggered, even bumping into another runner.

"Dammit," she heard Drake say, and he grabbed her around the waist just as she felt her legs give out.

"Drake," she said weakly, struggling to even keep her eyes open. The bagel she ate earlier wrestled inside of her stomach, begging her to throw up.

"I've got you," he said, and rushed her off to the side of the running path. He lowered her to the ground and leaned her back against a tree. Morgan didn't even have the energy to protest.

"I don't feel good," she murmured, and slumped against him, despite trying to keep her head up.

"I know. I've got you," Drake said again.

He put a couple of his fingers into his mouth and whistled. The sharp sound pierced the air, and he started waving his arm.

Morgan assumed he was calling for help, but she couldn't seem to get herself together to look. People talked around her as Drake barked for someone to get him a sports drink. Before she knew it, he was practically pouring it down her throat.

"Drake . . . please," she said, pushing his hand away.

"Baby, I need you to drink some more. You're dehydrated."

"No. You have to go. You have to get to the finish line," she managed to say. "I'm fine. Please . . . go."

"Not until I know you're okay," he fired back. "Drink some more."

Morgan drank a little more, but still felt light-headed. There was no way she was finishing the race, but she had to get Drake moving. If he didn't win or didn't finish, he probably wouldn't blame her, but she would blame herself.

"I feel better." She pushed the bottle away. She had drunk at least half of it. "Please, Drake, go. Finish the race. You can win. I know you can."

He shook his head before she could even finish her sentences. "I can't leave you."

"Yes, you can. I'll stay right here."

"No. I can carry you."

"Then you won't win, dammit! Would you just go?" Frustration gnawed inside of her. "I swear I'm okay. Just come back here *after* you win. Or better yet, I'll call Izzy. She can come and stay with me."

"Angel . . ."

"Do it for me, Drake. If you don't finish, I'll never forgive myself. You have to leave me, and your ass *better* win that property."

That got a slight smile out of him. Her speech was working. "I promise I'll be fine right here. Please . . ."

"Okay, but don't move." He waved one of the female volunteers over.

"Should I get an EMT?" the woman asked. She had water and snacks in her hand, and concern radiated in her eyes as she looked at Morgan.

"No," Morgan said. "I'm all right. I just need to rest."

"She needs one of those bottles of water and give her a breakfast bar," Drake insisted.

The volunteer handed both items to Morgan.

"Drake," Morgan ground out. "Go!"

"Okay. I'm going." He kissed her hard before standing. "I'll be back to get you."

He took off in a sprint, and Morgan prayed that he'd make good time to the finish line.

DRAKE HAD RUN THOSE LAST FEW MILES LIKE HE WAS BEING chased by fire, all the while thinking about Morgan. She had scared him to death when she almost passed out. He should've stopped her sooner. He'd seen that she was fading but thought that after some water, she could keep going.

"Nice job, man," Johnathan said as he approached.

"Yeah, you too. Good job," he said as they shook hands.

Drake had crossed the finish line a few minutes before Johnathan, but they wouldn't know which one won until the times were calculated. He still didn't know who'd had the better time for the obstacle course, meaning first place could go to either of them.

The other participants vying for the property hadn't finished yet, and it was safe to say they were out of the running. But at this point, it didn't matter to him. All he cared about was getting to Morgan.

He jogged back to where he'd left her and was surprised to see her and Izzy walking toward him. She should still be sitting down somewhere, not moving around.

"I told you to wait for me," he said.

"I wanted to be at the finish line with you," she said. Her eyes were droopy with dark circles beneath them, but she seemed steady on her feet.

"Come on. Let's get you somewhere where you can rest."

Drake scooped her up into his arms without her protesting, and when she laid her head against his chest, he definitely knew she wasn't feeling well.

"When will we know if you won?" she asked. Her voice was so quiet, he could barely hear her over all the activity going on around them.

"We should know in a little while. Johnathan and I were the first ones in our group to cross the finish line."

"*Okay,*" was all she said, and instead of taking her to the tent where Jeffrey and Isaac were waiting, Drake made a beeline to the EMTs.

Chapter Thirty-Six

"DRAKE, BABE, YOU CAN STOP HOVERING," MORGAN SAID.

They had arrived back to her place hours ago, and he hadn't let her out of his sight. Except for when she insisted that she use the bathroom alone.

She loved him so much, and hated that she had scared him and Isabella, but she was fine. After the EMTs treated her for dehydration, she felt much better. Yet that wasn't enough for Drake. He'd wanted to take her to the hospital to make sure nothing else was wrong.

"I'm not hovering," he grumbled and climbed on top of the covers instead of getting into bed with her. "I'm taking care of my woman."

"Call it what you want, but waking up to find you staring at me with your face only inches in front of mine kinda freaked me out."

He laughed and scooted up higher on the bed until his back was against the headboard, then pulled her against him. "Sorry. I was just checking to make sure you were still breathing. How was I supposed to know that your eyes would pop open in that moment?"

Morgan shook her head and smiled. She really was glad he was there with her. He could be somewhere else celebrating his big win. He had won the right to purchase the Hollywood building and she couldn't be happier for him.

"What comes next with purchasing the property?" she asked, making circles on his chest with her finger. "Is Jeffrey going to make you jump through more hoops?"

He released a noisy breath. "Nope, sounds like he's done torturing me, but I have to say, there's one good thing that came out of all of this."

"Besides you buying the first property that your dad designed?"

"Besides that." He turned slightly and lifted her chin, forcing her to look at him. "I found you. I never imagined that you would one day stroll back into my life. It all feels like a dream."

"It does, doesn't it? And just think, it all started with a hairy spider." They both laughed. That day seemed a lifetime ago. Morgan couldn't have planned a better reunion if she tried.

"You have Aiden to thank for the spider incident. Actually, I'm a hundred percent sure he's going to bring it up every so often. He'll probably claim that he's the reason why we got together."

"Actually, Addison is already taking credit for that. She mentioned it the other day. Saying that had she not asked about my dress, we would still be glaring at each other."

Morgan released a noisy yawn and snuggled closer. She might've been feeling better, but she still felt as if she could sleep for a week.

"I love those kids," she said, the words coming out before she could think about them.

"And they love you. Not as much as I do, but close." He kissed the top of her head. "I need to go and pick up the twins from Nana's before it gets too late."

"Oh, that's right. By the way, I heard that she might become the kids' nanny."

Drake chuckled. "That's what I heard too." She smiled, not missing the humor in his voice. "It was Addison's idea. She offered Nana the job, telling her that she wanted her to raise them the way she did you, Karter, and Randy."

"Oh, my goodness." Morgan laughed. "Those kids . . ."

"Yeah, I know. Their idea is a bit much, especially since they won't need a nanny in a couple of years. But I'll be talking to her this week because I love the idea. I don't know if she'll go for it, but according to Addison, she's thinking about it."

"Karter will have a fit, but he'll get over it. She's more of a mother to him than our own mother, and he loves having her live with them. *But* since he and Dreamy are traveling more, I think it's a wonderful idea, and you have the space for her to move in."

"And if she does, that would mean you and I can start having a few weekend getaways."

He kissed the top of Morgan's head and she hugged him tighter. "I can't wait."

They sat in a comfortable silence until Drake said, "Are you sure you don't want to come home with me?"

"I would love to, but I think I'll stay here tonight. Do you still have to go to Phoenix?"

He released a noisy sigh. "Yeah, I do, but it will be the last trip for a while. I hired another project manager, who starts in a couple of weeks. That'll take some responsibilities off of me."

"Good," she said, already missing him.

He had asked her to travel to Arizona with him, but once again, she couldn't. After spending so much time training, she was behind at work and needed to catch up.

Morgan snuggled into him more, her head resting on his chest and her arm across his waist. Her eyes drifted closed as the steady beat of his heart against her ear relaxed her. This was what she wanted every night—to fall asleep in his strong arms.

"Angel?"

"Hmm . . ."

"I'm going to head out. I'll check on you in the morning. If you can, eat some more before the night is over. Food will help build up your strength. You barely touched your chicken burrito. I left it in the refrigerator."

"Okay," she said, but knew that she wasn't getting up again. All she needed was sleep.

Morgan groaned when he sat up to put his shoes back on. She really didn't want him to leave, but she knew he had to. He hadn't seen his siblings all weekend, which was rare.

Drake stood and then leaned over the bed and kissed her. "You call me if you need me, all right?"

"I will."

"And Angel . . ."

She met his eyes. "Yeah?"

"Now that this competition is behind us, and once I return from Arizona, I want us to discuss our future."

A giddiness bubbled inside of Morgan, and she reached out and cupped his cheek. She wasn't sure what the future held for them, but she was optimistic that whatever it was would be amazing.

She leaned toward him and kissed his lips. "I look forward to that conversation."

SEVERAL DAYS LATER, MORGAN WAS BACK AT THE OFFICE, BUT she still didn't feel a hundred percent. Either way, she was determined to catch up with some of her work. Starting with figuring out how she could help Casey, one of the teens on the waiting list for housing. They sat in the small meeting room together.

"Ms. Redford, I just don't know what else to do," Casey said. "I can find the jobs, but I can't take them because they don't pay enough to live on. If I work two jobs, then I won't be able to attend school."

"And if you don't attend school, you can't pursue the career you want," Morgan added.

"Exactly, and I can only take one class at a time, because I can't afford to attend school full time. I don't know what to do. I can't catch a break."

Tears filled the girl's light brown eyes, and her fair complexion became blotchy. Morgan could feel herself getting choked up. Normally, she wasn't so emotional, but she kept seeing the same vicious cycle with so many of the those they served. She grabbed the box of tissues sitting on the bookshelf behind her and snatched out a sheet for herself before handing the box to Casey.

What could she tell the young woman that she hadn't already said the last two times they met? Open Arms still didn't have a room available. The grant they had applied for to put toward some of the clients' tuitions hadn't come through yet. And Morgan's hands were tied when it came to shelling out her own money to help.

What could she possibly tell this girl?

Instead of saying anything, she skimmed through Casey's file. When individuals came to them for assistance, looking for housing or for work, they had to take an assessment test. The evaluation gave Open Arms an idea of what career fields they might excel in.

Casey had done extremely well with the organizational skills section, as well as Microsoft Office skills. She wanted to be an office manager or an executive assistant.

As Morgan skimmed the information, an idea came to mind.

"You know what, Casey? I'm going to make some calls this week to business owners I know personally and see if anyone is hiring. If they are, I'll find out if they offer tuition reimbursement and I'll put in a good word for you. I know that doesn't help you in this moment, but—"

The girl leaped out of her seat and wrapped her arms around Morgan, almost knocking her out of the chair.

"Thank you, thank you, thank you for believing in me. If one of your associates hires me, I promise I won't let you down. I'll do a good job."

"I know you will."

They talked for a few minutes longer, and once their meeting was over, Morgan headed back to her office.

The meeting with Casey gave her a couple of ideas. Open Arms needed to set up some type of partnership with organizations. That way when superstar kids like Casey came along and needed a job, they could slide them into open positions at those companies.

Morgan wasn't sure how exactly she would set it up, but this was the type of magic Dreamy pulled off all the time. All it would take was for Morgan to call her sister-in-law and pick her brain.

Morgan entered her office and walked around her desk just as a wave of dizziness seized her. She gripped the edge of the desk to steady herself before sitting down. That was the second time in a matter of days that she'd gotten dizzy. It reminded her of the time when she'd had a middle ear infection.

She propped her elbows on the desk and held her head for a moment until the dizziness passed. The icky feeling could also have something to do with her dehydration issues the other day, as well as overexertion.

"Still not feeling good, huh?"

Morgan lifted her head as Isabella strolled across the office.

"I feel better than I did after the race, but I'm still feeling a little yucky. I might have an ear infection."

"Well, maybe you'll feel better if you eat something. I brought your favorite," she said, holding up the white paper bag. "Loaded potato skins."

"Oh, that sounds so good. Gimme, gimme. I'm suddenly a little hungry."

Morgan opened the bag and started to dig in when she got a whiff of the food, and suddenly, bile rose to her throat.

"Oh . . . God." She bolted out of the office, holding her stomach, and ran down the hall to the bathroom. She barely made it to the toilet before emptying the contents of her stomach.

What the hell was going on with her?

She startled when she heard the bathroom door open, but she didn't bother getting off her knees. Not yet. Not until the room stopped spinning.

"You know," Isabella said from the doorway of the stall, "I have a feeling that what you have is way more than an ear infection."

Chapter Thirty-Seven

"I CAN'T BE PREGNANT."

Morgan stared down at the little white stick in her hand that said otherwise. It was a good thing she was sitting on the edge of the bathtub in her master bedroom. Otherwise, the shock of this news would've knocked her to her knees.

When Isabella had suggested that they pick up a pregnancy test after work, Morgan thought she was crazy. Being pregnant had never crossed her mind. Not until Isabella mentioned it.

"How could this have happened? We've been so careful."

"Well, apparently there was a slip up along the way," her friend said on a chuckle.

Isabella's words triggered a memory that included hot, sweaty sex in the shower. Morgan shook her head. They were usually always so careful, but that one time . . .

"I can't believe you didn't know," Isabella said. She was standing in front of Morgan and leaning against the bathroom vanity with her arms folded across her chest. "When was the last time you had your period?"

"You know my cycle has always been irregular. I never thought . . ."

Morgan groaned and closed her eyes, still trying to process that she was having a baby. What the hell was she going to do? After raising his siblings, Drake wasn't interested in having kids. Heck, she wasn't even sure she was ready for this type of responsibility, but this was happening whether she was ready or not.

"How am I going to tell Drake? We've only been back together a couple of months, and all of a sudden we're having a baby? He's going to hate me," she sobbed, her heart breaking at the thought.

"Oh, girl, please. That man worships the ground you walk on. He's going to love this baby just like he loves you and the twins. I say just tell him."

Morgan wasn't ready to just tell him. It was a blessing in disguise that he was still out of town. They talked on the phone a few times a day, but there was no way she could tell him something like this over the phone. Besides that, there were some major changes at work that had him a little stressed. The last thing she wanted to do was add to the craziness.

"I can't do this right now. I need time," she said.

Isabella frowned. "For what? Wait, you're not considering an—"

"Oh no! Of course not! That never crossed my mind. I need to see a doctor and make sure that I'm pregnant before I turn Drake's world upside down. And . . ." She started but stopped as so many thoughts rolled through her mind. "It's just that Drake . . . Izzy, he has raised two kids already. He told me that now that the twins were older, he was looking forward to finally having a life with freedom to come and go as he pleases. He wants to travel and have weekend getaways, and I'm sure he doesn't want a baby in tow."

Morgan stood slowly, still feeling like crap. When she walked over to the double sinks, she wrapped the white stick in a tissue and set it on the counter before washing her hands.

"The twins are finally independent enough to allow Drake to have a social life. He can travel and do all the things that he hasn't had a chance to do. Things that most single people were able to do in their twenties. And here I come along and strap him with another kid."

Her pulse amped up as she thought about the conversation they had to have. Tears filled her eyes as one scenario after another played out in her mind. Drake might not hate her after he found out, but he was going to be so disappointed.

This wasn't even just about him. What was she going to do? She was just getting her career started, and now she was bringing a baby into the mix. And her mother . . . God, she would disappoint her mother yet again.

Morgan lowered her head and shook it. She would never be ready for another one of her mother's speeches.

When are you going to grow up and make better choices, Morgan?

Why can't you think before acting, Morgan?

You're such a disappointment, Morgan.

"I need to lay down," she said, and left the bathroom. She climbed into bed and sighed. "I might've ruined everything. Drake and I were planning to discuss our future. He was looking forward to us sneaking away for long weekends. Now that's not going to happen."

"Aww, sweetie, you're overthinking this," Isabella said and sat on the edge of the bed. "Being pregnant won't keep you from doing anything. You guys can do all the things you usually do and plan to do. This is not the end of the world, Morgan."

"Yeah, if you say so. We'll see what Drake says about that."

THE NEXT DAY, AFTER LEAVING THE DOCTOR'S OFFICE, MORGAN went into work. She was operating on less than two hours of sleep, but she wasn't planning to stay in the office long. She

needed to talk to somebody, and Isabella was her only choice—
nobody else knew about the baby yet.

Drake had called Morgan the night before like he usually did
at the end of the day. It had been hard not to burst into tears
when he asked how she was doing, but she had played it cool.
Acting as if all was well. There was no way she would tell him the
news over the phone, especially since at the time she hadn't been
a hundred percent sure that she was pregnant.

But now she knew.

"Well, what's the verdict?" Isabella asked when Morgan
walked in and closed the office door. "Are you?"

Morgan sighed and sat in the chair in front of the desk. "Yes.
I'm about three weeks pregnant."

A slow smile spread across her friend's ruby-red lips.

At least someone was happy about the news because right
now Morgan wasn't sure what to feel. Excitement, fear, and concern all warred within her, and she hadn't settled on one emotion.

"So, what did Drake say? How'd that conversation go?"

"I talked to him, but I didn't tell him—not yet. Not over the
phone. Besides, I need to wrap my head around all of this before
I tell anyone."

"Okay," Isabella said slowly, looking at Morgan warily. "What
are you saying? How long are you going to wait?"

"I'm leaving town," Morgan blurted.

"What?" Isabella bolted out of her chair. "Your ass better not
be doing another disappearing act. Morgan, please. Please don't
do this to that man again. You didn't see him the last time. You
have no idea—"

"Stop," Morgan said and stood. "Let me explain. Drake will
be out of town until Tuesday. I'll be back by then. I just need to
get away for a few days and think, and I'm not going that far. I'll

be at my parents' beach house in Malibu, and I promise I'm coming back."

Isabella moved away from the desk, shaking her head. "I don't like this. I don't like this at all. It feels exactly like what you did back in college."

"It's not, Izzy. I swear, I'm coming back."

"You better, because if your ass ain't here by Monday, I'm coming to get you myself. I will *not* sit back and watch you break that man's heart again."

"That's never going to happen. I'm in love with Drake. I have *never* loved another man the way I love him, and I'm not going to do anything to hurt him ever again."

Except for telling him that I'm pregnant, she thought.

Chapter Thirty-Eight

WHEN DRAKE PULLED INTO THE SMALL PARKING LOT OF OPEN
Arms, it was like déjà vu. Only a couple of months ago, he had
parked in the exact same spot, contemplating a future with Morgan. Now that they were back together, that was all he could
think about.

He had arrived back in Los Angeles a few days earlier than
expected. There was a time he would've gone straight home and
unpacked, or headed to the office for one reason or another.

Not today. Today he planned to surprise his woman.

Drake glanced over at the blueprints in the passenger seat.
Now that he had all the details nailed down, he was ready to
share the plan with Morgan. He also wanted to bring up the subject of marriage. He just wasn't sure how that would play out.
Was it too soon?

As a man who plotted out every detail of his life, he had to remember that everyone didn't operate the same way. That included
Morgan. She was more of a fly-by-the-seat-of-her-pants woman.

It was one of many things Drake loved about her. She balanced him perfectly. She was the fun to his seriousness. The laid-back to his rigidness. And she was everything he wanted in a life partner. Which was why he had already purchased an engagement ring.

Now I just need to figure out when to pop the question.

He sighed and rubbed the back of his neck. Would she be overwhelmed by him planning everything? Then again, she knew him. She knew what he was like. She wouldn't be surprised that he had planned out their whole future . . . would she? Nothing would be finalized without running everything by her.

Damn. I'm doing it again.

They might be in love, but that didn't mean Morgan was ready for something permanent. Hadn't that been the problem the last time? He wanted forever, and she hadn't been ready.

I have to make sure she's ready.

Drake grabbed the lunch that he had picked up from Morgan's favorite burger place, and the coffee and muffins he had gotten for Audrey, the receptionist, and Isabella. He would leave the blueprints in the truck for now.

As he strolled to the door, he started second-guessing the idea of surprising Morgan. When he'd talked with her earlier, she'd made it sound like she would be pretty busy, but surely she'd be able to take a minute for him. Especially since they hadn't seen each other in days.

When he walked into the building, Audrey greeted him with a smile. "Hey, Drake."

"Hey there." He handed her one of the coffees.

"You are a gift from God," she gushed. "This is right on time." She grabbed a napkin and dug through the white paper bag, searching for the blueberry muffin that she loved. "I'm so hungry and we didn't have time to go out to get anything for lunch, so thank you. But I'm surprised you're here, especially since Morgan isn't here."

So much for surprises.

"Where is she?" he asked.

Audrey looked a little confused. "As far as I know, she hasn't been here all day. I haven't seen her since yesterday morning. I'm not sure if she's working from home or at meetings, but Isabella's here. Hold on a second. Let me see if she's available or knows where Morgan is."

He'd had an inkling that something was up when he was outside a moment ago. Now he was having another one. It was her disappearing act all over again, but he hoped he was wrong—she could just be in a meeting and he was worrying over nothing.

While the receptionist was on the phone, memories of looking for Morgan years ago played through his mind. At the time, he hadn't seen her for a few days because one of the twins had been sick, but he had made it a point to talk to her every day.

But Drake had gotten concerned when he hadn't been able to reach her for two days straight. He hadn't wanted to just show up at her parents' house to see if she was there, especially since he hadn't officially met them.

One day he happened to run into Isabella in the hallways at school. The expression on her face when she saw him told Drake that something was wrong. She had sworn that she didn't know where exactly Morgan had gone. All she knew was that she had left the country and was somewhere in Europe. When he asked when she would be back, Isabella told him she didn't know. She wasn't sure if Morgan was ever coming back.

Audrey hung up the phone. "Okay, Drake, Isabella said for you to come to her office."

The smile on the woman's face helped ease some of his tension because if something had happened to Morgan, she wouldn't be smiling.

Still, Drake wouldn't be satisfied until he laid eyes on Morgan. He hurried down the quiet hallway as anxiousness charged through his veins. When he reached Isabella's door, he pounded on it.

"Come in," he heard her say, and when he walked in, she was standing behind her desk.

The expression on her face spoke volumes, and Drake's pulse amped up. Tension filled the room, bouncing off the walls in waves. He almost didn't want to ask the question, but unlike last time, he would do whatever was necessary to find out what was going on with Morgan.

"Where is she?"

His no-nonsense tone was harsher than he'd intended, but worry gnawed at every nerve in Drake's body. Something had happened and he wanted to know what, and he needed to know now.

"She's gone," Isabella said. "She left town, but I'll tell you exactly where to find her."

Chapter Thirty-Nine

MORGAN SAT OUT ON THE FRONT PORCH, WRAPPED IN A THICK blanket as she rocked back and forth in the swing that faced the water. The beach house was one of her favorite places in the world to think. The waves crashing against the shore, the smell of salt water floating through the air, and even the crisp breeze kissing her cheek would normally lull her into total relaxation.

But today she was everything but relaxed. She couldn't shut her mind off.

She missed Drake.

Five days was too long for them to be apart. Instead of her driving to Malibu yesterday, she should've flown to Phoenix to talk to him. But nope, here she was looking out over the ocean, mentally kicking herself for some of her poor choices.

Isabella's words about Morgan leaving Drake again had stung. Her friend knew how hard it had been for Morgan to leave him years ago. How could Izzy think she could do that to him again? But by leaving L.A. without letting Drake know, it seemed she was indeed repeating history.

I shouldn't have left.

Even if he would never know that she left town for the weekend and she had every intention of returning in a couple days, she still felt a little guilty. How could she claim to love him and not tell him that he was going to be a father? Instead, when she'd spoken to him earlier, she'd made it seem like all was well and that she was busy at the office. When in reality, she had indeed run away to Malibu.

What is wrong with me?

The rumble of a large vehicle caught Morgan's attention, and she glanced to the right where her BMW was parked in the driveway. The sound grew closer, and Morgan's breath caught when Drake's truck pulled in behind her car.

Because of the dark-tinted windows, she couldn't actually see the driver, but she knew it was him.

But how was he there? How had he known where . . .

Morgan didn't have to finish the thought. There was only one way he could've known where to find her.

Isabella.

Izzy had been angry about Morgan leaving in the first place. Had she called him? Told him where to find her?

No. She wouldn't have done that, but she would tell him if he'd asked. She would've sung like a canary and would've drawn him a map to get to Morgan.

Another question that rattled around in Morgan's mind. What was Drake doing in California? He wasn't expected back until Tuesday.

Drake climbed out of his huge truck holding what looked to be a rolled-up blueprint. Morgan's heart beat a little faster with each step he took toward her. She was happy to see him, but also concerned.

Did he know about the baby?

Had Isabella told him?

His blank expression gave nothing away, but as Morgan studied his handsome face, she didn't miss the wariness. *No*, she thought as he got closer. It was more than him just being tired, he was . . .

Worried.

The guilt from moments ago returned with a punch to her gut. He'd probably been worried for a number of reasons. Mainly because he feared that she was doing a repeat of what she'd done years ago—left him without a word. Her stupid disappearing act would forever be one of her biggest regrets.

Now that he was only a few feet away, she needed to say something, but *sorry you had to come all the way out here to see me* didn't seem to be enough. She also didn't know how much Isabella had told him.

When Drake reached the porch steps, tears filled Morgan's eyes and her bottom lip trembled. God, she had missed him so much and all she wanted to do was run and jump into his strong arms.

But she couldn't.

He needed an explanation for all of this first.

"Hi," she said, not meaning for it to come out sounding like a sob. But she couldn't help it. She had so much that she needed to say to him. Stuff that could ruin everything between them.

Drake didn't respond. He climbed the three steps, set the blueprint on the porch, and dropped down on the swing next to her. Instead of speaking, he put his arm around her, pulling her against him, and used his foot to push the swing.

Minutes ticked by with no words being spoken as they swung back and forth. Normally, it would've felt peaceful, and Morgan would've snuggled even closer to him immediately, but her guilty conscience wouldn't allow her to enjoy the moment.

"Are you running from me again?" he finally asked. Hurt resonated in his voice, and it made the guilt already clawing inside of her twist around in her gut like a serrated knife.

"No. I'm not running from you, and I never will. I came here to think for just a day or two, but I realized too late that this wasn't where I was supposed to be. I should've come to you. I should've gone to Arizona."

"I see," he said after a slight hesitation. "Tell me what's on your mind. Why'd you have to leave L.A. to think? Why here?"

"It's where I always come to think. It's quiet. Peaceful. And no one usually knows when I'm here. It feels like a secret hiding place."

"What are you hiding from, Angel?" he asked.

Too bad it wasn't an easy question to answer. Morgan hadn't thought of this as hiding, but maybe that was exactly what she was doing. She wasn't ready to face her new reality because it was scary as hell, and it was easier to just hide from everything.

Drake twisted slightly in the swing and pulled her even closer to his body. She leaned against him and suddenly felt the same type of calm that she usually experienced when staring out at the ocean.

"Talk to me," he said close to her ear. "Tell me what's wrong."

Morgan pulled back slightly and turned to better look at him. Her heart flipped inside her chest at the love brimming in his eyes. What she saw in him matched what she was feeling deep in her soul, and once again she mentally kicked herself for running away, even for a day.

"I love you," she said. "I love you so much, it scares me sometimes."

He pushed one of her long braids away from her face and tucked it behind her ear. His silence was a little unnerving, but she continued speaking.

"I'm glad you're here," she said. "I'm sorry you drove all the way out here, and before you arrived, I had just convinced myself to call you. I was going to ask if I could see you in Arizona."

He didn't respond. All he did was keep pushing the swing.

It was up to her to explain everything, but she didn't know where to start. How could she tell him that they were having a baby even though it wasn't planned? That it would throw a wrench in his future plans for them? How could she explain to him that she was terrified of becoming a mom?

"Were you thinking of flying to Phoenix to break things off with me?"

"Of course not!" Morgan leaped off the swing, not bothering to pick the blanket up from the porch. His words shocked her like a bucket full of ice cubes. "You mean everything to me, and I want to spend the rest of my life with you! How could you even think that I want to break up with you?" she said.

"Oh, I don't know. Maybe because you left L.A. without telling me, and you were thinking about flying to Arizona to talk to me. What am I supposed to think?"

It angered her that his calm tone never wavered.

"You're supposed to think that I'm pregnant and I don't know how to tell you because you don't want kids since you've already raised two and now you want to travel and I'm ruining that for you because we're having a baby!"

Her chest heaved as tears blurred her vision while she stood there struggling not to cry but failing miserably.

"Wh-what?" Drake whispered as he stood, moving close to her. "What did you say?"

Morgan swiped at her tears and wrapped her arms around her middle to warm herself. The words had tumbled out of her mouth so fast, she wasn't sure what she'd even said, but she was pretty sure that only one part of it was important.

"I'm pregnant."

She stared down at his feet as he stood perfectly still. When seconds ticked by without him speaking, Morgan finally chanced a glance at him. His eyes were wide, and his lips were slightly parted. And he just stood there.

"Drake, say something, please."

"I-I don't know what to say. I wanted to know what was going on but . . . but that never crossed my mind." He still didn't move, but his gaze dropped to her stomach before meeting her eyes again. "Are you sure?"

She nodded. "Positive. I'm three weeks along. We're having a baby in about eight months or so. I'm so sorry. I swear I didn't mean for this to happen." She brushed away more tears that were falling faster. "I know you have your future planned and I messed it up . . . again."

"Hey, stop," he said and picked up the blanket. He wrapped it around her, then pulled her against his body, warming her even more as he held her in his strong arms. "How can you think you've ruined anything? I'm the one who must've slipped up at some point. I'm the one who's sorry for not protecting you. But Morgan, you have to know, I'm not sorry that you're pregnant. I'm . . . I'm thrilled . . . and shocked."

She leaned back slightly and looked up at him. "You're not upset? Disappointed?"

"Of course not, baby." He lowered his head and kissed her sweetly. "I love you. There's nothing in this world that I want more than to have you in my life, as my wife, and for us to raise this baby together. As a matter of fact, this sort of plays into my . . . *our* future plans."

"It does?"

Drake flashed her a smile and for the first time in the last couple of days, Morgan felt hopeful.

He pulled away and picked up the blueprint that he'd brought with him. "Let's go inside and I can show you part of my plans for us."

WHEN DRAKE WOKE UP IN THE HOTEL THAT MORNING, HE'D only had one thing on his mind—get home and see Morgan. Never in a million years would he have imagined his day turning out like this. One moment, at Open Arms, he thought Morgan had abandoned him again, and then he found out he was going to be a father.

Mind. Blown.

As Morgan warmed up leftovers in the microwave, Drake stared at her from across the kitchen counter. It felt as if he hadn't seen her in weeks instead of days . . . and she was pregnant.

That explained her exhaustion. As he thought back, he recalled other moments that could've been signs that she was pregnant. Thinking back also freaked him out, knowing that she and the baby could've gotten seriously hurt doing the obstacle course.

"I assume you and the baby are doing okay," he said, walking up behind her and wrapping his arm around her waist. He rested his hand on her stomach, marveling at the fact that in a few months, he'd be able to feel their baby moving inside of her.

"We're fine, but I have to make some changes. Take supplements, cut out alcohol, and the hardest one, give up coffee." She shivered, and he chuckled, knowing that wasn't going to be easy.

"While you eat, I want to show you what I've been working on." Drake went over to the large dining table and cleared it. He unrolled the blueprint and stretched it out.

Morgan strolled over and stood next to him with a bowl of chili in her hands. "What's all this?"

"It's the new plans for the Hollywood property. Shortly before the Titan Games, I started thinking about our future as a couple."

"Of course you did." She laughed and fed him a spoonful of chili.

"Mmm, that's good. Did you make it?"

She popped him on the arm. "Are you trying to be funny?"

Drake laughed and looped his arm around her shoulder. He'd been pretty sure she hadn't made it, but he figured he'd ask.

"Anyway, back to the blueprint," he said. "Instead of my company purchasing the building, I'm buying it myself from Jeffrey. Actually, I was thinking that you and I can buy this together."

Morgan glanced up at him. "What . . . what are you saying exactly?"

"I'm saying that if you agree to it, you and I will own this building jointly. I've incorporated both our ideas. If you look here," he flipped to the second sheet, "the top two floors have one-bedroom and two-bedroom apartments that will be rented to Open Arms clients.

"Unfortunately, there won't be room for offices for you and Izzy. I'm thinking that we'll remodel your current building and set it up as an administrative building for the nonprofit."

Morgan set the bowl down and moved closer to the blueprint, taking in the details. "Oh, my goodness, Drake. I can't believe you did all of this."

"Even before knowing about the baby, I knew that I wanted you in my life forever. I know I get carried away with planning everything, but Morgan, I had these plans drawn up to show you how serious I am about having you in my life.

"Jeffrey's love story with his wife started with the Hollywood property, and that's the same for us . . . sort of. If it wasn't for his unusual way of selling the property, you and I might not have ever found our way back to each other. How do you feel about partnering with me on this project after we're married?"

On the ride to Malibu, Drake had assumed that she was breaking up with him. That she was doing a repeat of what she'd done ten years ago. He had planned to do whatever it took to talk her into not leaving him, because his heart wouldn't have been able to take it.

Now it felt as if his heart was going to burst with love for this woman.

She placed her hands on her hips and narrowed her eyes at him. "Drake Faulkner, are you asking me to marry you?"

He folded his arms. "Depends. Would you say yes?"

She twisted her bottom lip between her teeth as if she was thinking, but she wasn't fooling anyone. She was bursting with excitement inside.

As she started to speak, he held up his hands. "Hold that thought," he said and dashed outside to his truck. When he returned, he approached her and then dropped down on one knee.

"I kind of planned for this too," he said and opened the black velvet box.

Morgan laughed and dabbed her eyes with the heel of her hands. "Of course you did, but oh, my goodness, Drake . . ." she whispered as she took in the three-carat oval diamond. "It's so beautiful."

"Angel, you are my heart and I love you beyond words. Will you marry me and be my partner for life?"

Tears rolled down her beautiful face and she nodded before saying, "Yes, baby. Yes, I'll marry you."

Drake slipped the ring onto her finger, then kissed her. He kissed her with everything within him, wanting her to know just how much he adored her. If anyone had told him that he'd get a second chance with the love of his life, he wouldn't have believed them. But now he believed anything was possible.

Epilogue

MORGAN STARED UP AT THE CEILING IN HER AND DRAKE'S BED-room, wondering how much longer she'd be able to lounge in bed before the babies started crying.

Ten months ago, when she learned that she was having a baby, it never dawned on her that she could be pregnant with twins. It should've crossed her mind since twins ran in both of their families.

She had fainted when she'd found out she was having two babies. That memory brought a smile to her face. The last few months had been a whirlwind of activity. Construction had started on the Hollywood property, and it was going to be more impressive than Morgan could've imagined. It helped that her husband was a brilliant real estate developer.

Morgan glanced at Drake and her heart did a little giddyup. There were days she still couldn't believe she was married with kids. Shortly after they had gotten engaged, they'd flown to Hawaii for a little R & R. While there, they decided to elope.

The small, intimate ceremony had been beautiful, and romantic, and one of the most amazing days of Morgan's life. One that she would never forget.

But to say her mother had been livid when they returned married was an understatement. Kalena Redford had threatened to disown Morgan. She claimed that her daughter had deprived her of throwing her a fairytale wedding, which was unforgivable in Kalena's eyes.

Morgan hated taking that pleasure away from her, but she knew her mother. The two of them could barely agree on where to have lunch. Planning a wedding would've crushed their already unstable relationship, but to appease her mother, Morgan agreed to a reception.

Morgan shook her head at the memory of the lavish event that brought out the who's who of Hollywood's elite. No expense had been spared, and anybody who was anyone was in attendance. That only made Kalena hungrier to plan legendary weddings in the future—for Addison and the youngest granddaughters—identical twins—Kahli and Kacey.

Drake moaned in his sleep, then did what he usually did first thing in the morning. He reached for Morgan, pulled her to his side, and kissed her on the top of her head before promptly falling back to sleep.

Morgan grinned. She had the perfect husband, the perfect kids, and the perfect life. After they were married, she had sold her condo and moved in with Drake and the twins. Now that their family was growing, and Nana had moved in, they were in the process of building a home with almost twice the square footage.

It was amazing how everything fell into place. Aiden had been the one to finally talk Nana into moving in and being their nanny. The boy was too charming for his own good. It also helped that Nana had found out that Morgan was having twins and insisted that she would need her help. She was thrilled to have four kids to spoil.

The baby monitor crackled, and Morgan heard Kacey starting to fuss. The girls were identical, but they already had some notable differences. Kacey usually woke up first, and her cries started out fussy, but then she could get loud enough to blow the roof off the house. Kahli didn't cry often. She was more fussy than anything.

"I guess it's my turn to go and get them, huh?" Drake said. His sleep-filled voice was deep and sexy, and made Morgan turn to mush every time he used it.

"So far, I only hear Kacey. Maybe we'll get lucky, and she'll go back to sleep."

Drake snorted. "Yeah, like that's going to happen." Just then, Kacey let out another little cry. "She's getting ready to turn it up. You sure you don't want me to get her before she wakes Kahli?"

"Shhh . . . be quiet before you wake everyone up," they heard Aiden say through the baby monitor. "You should've just called your funcle if you wanted some company. You don't have to cry."

Morgan and Drake chuckled. Neither of them had ever heard the term *funcle* until Aiden introduced it. According to him it meant "fun uncle." He and Addison were amazing with "the baby twins," which was how they referred to them since "the twins" was already taken.

"Alright, KK, how about we sit in the rocking chair until your mommy and daddy get their lazy selves up," Aiden said, and Morgan burst out laughing.

"We need to keep him away from the girls. He's a bad influence," Drake muttered.

On the weekends, Aiden and Addison usually hung out in the nursery first thing in the morning. Addison claimed it was their bonding time with their nieces.

Morgan and Drake would usually listen in when they were awake, and it was always entertaining to hear the conversations. Aiden and Addison knew they had an audience and took every opportunity to say things that would get a rise out of her and Drake.

"You know, I was hoping one of you would be a boy, that way I'd have someone to play basketball with. I guess I'm going to have to teach you. I just hope you're more athletic than your mother," Aiden said. Normally, he talked to Kacey the most since she was usually the first one awake. "When I'm done teaching you all of the sports, you're going to be kicking ass and taking names."

Drake growled. "Remind me to knock the boy upside the head when I see him."

"You're an idiot." Addison's soft voice came through the baby monitor. "Don't be using curse words around them. They're going to be talking soon, and you know kids are like sponges. They soak up everything you say. Oh, hey, Kahli Boo. You're awake too. Come to TT."

Morgan snuggled closer to her husband and soaked up his warmth. She felt so blessed and loved. Their families had meshed seamlessly. Even her mother had shown a side of herself that Morgan had never seen.

A month before the babies were due, she and her mother had gone shopping. It was something they both enjoyed, but usually not together. That day would be forever engrained in Morgan's mind, though. During the shopping trip, she had gone into labor. She had never been so scared in all her life, especially since the babies were coming early.

Her mother was the epitome of calm. It was a side of her that Morgan had never witnessed. She had her driver take them to the hospital, and then she made the calls to Morgan's doctor and Drake.

As long as Drake was there, Morgan hadn't cared about anything else, but he couldn't get to her as fast as he normally would've. It worked out, though. Her mother was there for her every step of the way, keeping her calm and as comfortable as possible. What shocked Morgan was how kind her mother was to the hospital staff. Normally, Kalena Redford was a force to be reckoned with, but that day, she showed a sweet and softer side. She and Drake were in the delivery room with Morgan, and she had been grateful for both of them.

"Your mommy can't cook. So if you think she's going to make cupcakes for your kindergarten class, you can forget it," Morgan heard Addison say. "Don't worry, though, me and Nana will keep working with her. Soon she'll be able to boil water without burning it."

Drake chuckled.

"Remind me to knock her upside the head when I see her," Morgan said, repeating Drake's words from earlier.

It sounded like both babies were awake, and it was only a matter of time before the twins brought them to Morgan for a feeding.

"Don't worry if your mommy can't cook and your dad sucks at basketball. Me and your TT Addy will always be here for you," Aiden said, and Morgan's heart squeezed.

"Yeah, we're going to take good care of you, just like your daddy took care of me and your funcle when we were little," Addison added.

"I know I give your folks a hard time," Aiden continued, "but you two are the luckiest kids on the planet. They are the best, and your life is going to be amazing."

Morgan's hand went to her heart. "Oh, my goodness, they're going to make me cry. That was so sweet."

"They want something. Don't fall for all of those sugary words. It's a trap," Drake insisted. "You'll see. You're going to have to be strong. Whatever they're trying to soften us up for, be ready to say no because I'm telling you, they're coming for us."

Morgan laughed, knowing he was probably right, but still, she loved those kids. With them, Drake, and the babies, her life was complete.

She rolled on top of Drake. "I'm glad you're the type of man who plans everything, because there's no way I could've planned this life for myself. Thank you for giving me another chance with you."

He pulled her up higher on top of him. "I didn't give you another chance. I gave *us* another chance, and I'm so glad I did. You and those kids in there are the best things that have ever happened to me. I love you, baby."

Morgan laid her head on his chest. "And I love you."

She was starting to doze off when she heard Aiden yell, "Urgh! She pooped all over me!" Morgan and Drake burst out laughing.

Morgan kissed her husband. "I love our life."

ACKNOWLEDGMENTS

I'm grateful to God for allowing me a career that lets me do something I enjoy—pen stories. To my amazing husband—my real-life hero—Al, thank you for ALWAYS supporting my ventures and staying up with me when I have to pull all-nighters to meet a deadline! I love you more than I could ever express in words.

Special thanks to Brenda S. and Claire F. You ladies are awesome! Thanks for going on this writing voyage with me and keeping me encouraged. You make the journey so much fun!

Huge shout out to all of the readers and "super fans" who have supported me and my work. Thank you! Thank you! It's because of you that I keep writing!

Photo by Albert Cooper

USA Today bestselling author **Sharon C. Cooper** loves anything involving romance with a happily-ever-after, whether in books, movies, or real life. She writes contemporary romance, as well as romantic suspense, and enjoys rainy days, carpet picnics, and peanut butter and jelly sandwiches. Her stories have won numerous awards over the years, and when Sharon isn't writing, she's hanging out with her amazing husband, doing volunteer work, or reading a good book (a romance, of course).

CONNECT ONLINE

SharonCooper.net

🐦 Sharon_Cooper1

👤 AuthorSharonCCooper21

📷 AuthorSharonCCooper

Ready to find
your next great read?

Let us help.

Visit prh.com/nextread

Penguin
Random
House